EVASION

EVASION

Geoffrey Bowditch

HB

HALDON
BOOKS

Published in 2019 by Haldon Books

haldonbooks@hotmail.com

Copyright © 2019

ISBN 978-1-5272-3498-7

Printed in Great Britain by imprintdigital.com

*For my wife Julia and daughter Emma
with my thanks for their help
and encouragement.*

I

Hemport was the thriving commercial centre of an area covering a hundred square miles of East Devon. Just a short distance from the border with Dorset, less than a mile away to the south were tall cliffs and fossil-strewn beaches beneath. With a gradually increasing population, the demand for services was growing. Banks, professional practices and retail outlets thrived. Along with this was the need for an administrative structure. The government offices in the High Street were kept busy.

The industrial and political turmoil of the mid nineteen-eighties had failed to reach this part of the country. It was market day and the traders' stalls lined the wide pavements much as they had always done, their tarpaulins providing scant resistance to the keen November breeze.

Low grey clouds scudded across the sky carrying the threat of rain. How different it was from the summer months when the weather was clement and the population swollen by trippers and tourists. Today it was the regular shoppers who went about gathering their requirements from the local producers and farmers.

On a stool behind a trestle table bearing neat piles of knitted articles, an elderly lady in a woollen hat clicked busily with her needles, occasionally raising her eyes in the hope that someone might stop and take a closer look at her creations.

The wife of a local farmer worked through the night each

week to bake bread and pastries to fill her table the next day. These were snapped up eagerly by the locals as were the honey, jam and eggs she brought from home.

At the fishmonger's stand, line-caught pollock were arranged alongside crab from nearby Lyme Bay. Leeks, onions and potatoes from the greengrocer's stall would supplement many a hotpot come the evening.

The High Street ran downhill through the centre of the town from east to west. Straight as an arrow, it had been laid by the Romans on the route from London to Exeter and beyond. At the highest point were the remains of the sandstone gatehouse.

The road was bordered by two parallel rows of terraced buildings, most occupied on the ground floor by retail premises. There were still glimpses of the facades of the eighteenth century although much had been demolished and rebuilt following either dilapidation or in order to make way for the functional architectural styles of the 1960s.

Prominent on the south side of the main street was the Plough Hotel. High at the front of the building under its steeply angled eaves was a plaque confirming its date of construction as 1797. Hotel conglomerates had shown interest in adding this hostelry to their portfolios but their advances had been repelled and it had remained in the ownership of the same family for over one hundred years. The accommodation was of a high standard as was its noted restaurant.

On the same side of the road was Margaret's Coffee House, another well-regarded establishment. The sole proprietor after whom the business was named had the reputation for meticulous attention to cleanliness and detail. It was hard to resist being drawn in by the drifting aroma of the freshly ground coffee.

Near the top of the High Street was a large Victorian building which housed various government offices. Wide concrete steps led to an imposing door alongside which was a brass plate listing the departments within. At the top of the list was the Board of Inland Revenue. This was, in common parlance, "The Tax Office", where the affairs of the taxpayers in the region were monitored. The Office for Agriculture, Fisheries and Food was next followed by the Departments of Employment and Social Security. Whereas most of these departments were identified as sources of advice and guidance, the popular conception was that the first-mentioned was best avoided unless absolutely necessary.

Two men descended the steps from the offices each dressed in a dark suit and sober tie, the unmistakable uniform of the office professional. Both carried brown leather briefcases. They were from the top floor – tax inspectors.

They could not have been more different in appearance. James Stedman stood a little over six feet tall, his slim frame topped by short-cropped fair hair. He moved with a litheness that suggested athletic ability. His shorter and younger companion was Brian Day, dark and squat with rimless spectacles.

Day had been a graduate entrant to the Inland Revenue just two years previously and completed his training in London with some distinction. Fifteen years his senior, James was an established and well regarded member of the tax inspectorate.

They turned right at the foot of the steps and made their way towards the car park at the bottom of the High Street, Day hurrying to keep up with his long-striding companion.

The men were of recent acquaintance. James had relocated to his post in the Inland Revenue office at Hemport two years previously. It had been only three weeks since Day had been transferred from Head Office in London.

They made their way past the market stalls sidestepping the shoppers and gatherings of people in conversation.

'Well, Brian,' said James, 'although we've met at one or two office meetings, we haven't had the chance to speak informally and perhaps we can find time today. It was only a little while ago that you arrived here and I'd be interested to know how you've been getting on.'

'Yes,' responded Day, 'I know there's a job to do first but I look forward to having a more general chat when time permits.'

The transfer of Brian Day from London had been the subject of some conjecture among the staff. News travelled slowly through the official channels and the reason for his posting to Hemport was not known. It was of particular interest that he was not a direct replacement to fill a gap for someone who had left.

It had already become clear to James and his colleagues that Day was an ambitious young man. He seemed absorbed in his work and carried with him at all times a copy of the Income Tax Acts, the compendium of the enactments and amendments to Inland Revenue Law over the years. It was Day's bible and he had an uncanny ability to quote passages and references at will. For most, this dry and uninteresting tome was only opened when it could not be avoided.

How his technical knowledge would manifest itself in the practical application of his work remained to be seen. He had not yet been handed his own portfolio of cases to deal with but, once off the leash, his methods would soon become evident.

As with most government departments or, indeed, commercial operations, much of the day-to-day work at the offices of the Inland Revenue is of a routine nature. An effective and organised administrative function is essential to the smooth operation of the whole. The activities at the higher levels must be founded on a solid base.

Files are kept in the office recording the financial histories of the taxpaying individuals in the area. These are reviewed regularly to ensure that annual tax returns are submitted on time and that all the legal requirements are up to date. The unending flow of correspondence passing through the hands of Inland Revenue staff every day needs to be processed, dealt with and filed away.

The investigating inspector is at the sharp end of the function. While the main body of the department works to ensure that the taxpayer complies with the law, this division of the inspectorate is charged with probing for evasion.

It has been said that those who try hardest to avoid paying the right amount of tax are often those most able to afford it. This lends weight to the theory that there may be a correlation between the desire to make money and the dislike of parting with it.

James did not feel a particular sense of inquisitiveness about the reasons for Day's arrival at Hemport. His long experience and generally philosophical outlook had led him to the conclusion that, being the Civil Service, it was best to watch and wait rather than go looking.

Day had been transferred from Somerset House, the London hub of Inland Revenue operations. Many, particularly the younger element, relished the challenge and excitement of working in the capital city. But with the higher living costs and the probable need to engage in the drudgery of time-absorbing commuting, most would find working in the country more appealing.

'As you know,' said Day, 'this is the third occasion I've worked with other inspectors on investigation cases since I arrived. As the District Inspector explained, he wanted me to get a feel for the approach adopted down here before letting me loose on my own, as it were.'

They reached the artisan baker's stall whose produce was always in steady demand. Most of his stock had been snapped up and James stopped to pick up a sourdough loaf. He could be sure there would be none remaining when he returned later in the day.

It was mid-morning and the doors of the Plough Hotel were opening. Some shoppers were already carrying their shopping bags towards the entrance, ready for sustenance.

The two inspectors entered the car park and boarded James's waiting Ford Escort. Day settled and placed his briefcase and a copy of the Taxes Acts between his feet.

James considered his passenger as he wrapped his seat belt around his not inconsiderable girth. Everything about him was scrubbed-up and tidy. His pale, almost white, complexion suggested a shortage of air and exercise.

'What do you think of Hemport so far?' enquired James as he pointed the car towards the exit.

'It's early days and, to tell you the truth, it was a complete surprise to find myself being transferred down here. The personnel department was not exactly forthcoming with the reasons for the posting and I'd fully expected to stay in London for the foreseeable future. That's where you find the bigger and more challenging cases and I'm eager to continue with my career development.

'However, now I'm becoming used to the idea, I can see some benefits. I know nobody in this area but perhaps that's not such a bad thing. I have lived all my life with my parents in Ruislip and I expect it's time I flew the nest.

'Who knows? Perhaps it may be just a short spell and then back to civilisation. I say that with no disrespect to the locals, of course – just a manner of speaking.

'I've managed to rent a bungalow on the southern edge of town, a pleasant position with views back to the cliffs. I am looking forward to doing some walking along the South West coast path, east towards Lulworth and west to Axmouth.'

'I'm sure you'll find the exercise beneficial,' replied James who was now driving west out of town towards the Vale of Marshfield, just three miles distant.

'There are two routes into Deepdene Farm, our destination,' explained James. 'One enters from the north side via the main road. The other comes in from the south and today we'll use this lower route. This means taking the next left just beyond the outskirts of the town. As we approach the turning, you'll see that a sign indicates that the road is unsuitable for large vehicles. This is something of an understatement as I understand it to be single track for most of the way.'

'If the other road is more easily negotiated, why have you chosen to go this way?' enquired Day who was drawing a file from his briefcase.

'Although I've studied this narrow road on the Ordnance

Survey map, I've never driven along it,' replied James. 'I'd like to take the opportunity to see what it's like but when we leave we'll certainly travel back by what appears to be the wider road on the north side. I am interested to see the terrain and the views from the way we'll approach today. Besides, there may be points of interest as we enter the property from this direction.'

'I've never seen this file before so know nothing about the person we're going to see,' said Day. 'I'm trying to find out what kind of activities are carried on at the premises known as Deepdene Farm.' Flicking quickly through the pages of the file, he continued. 'I see that the taxpayer's name is Mortimer and, by the looks of it, he must have been in business for a good many years.'

'I'll tell you all I know,' replied James. 'Yes, the man's name is Mortimer – Albert Reginald Mortimer, as I recall. He's quite elderly, certainly well into his seventies. Our files go back only so far but he's lived and worked there for as long as anyone can remember.

'It's my guess that he was born and bred at Deepdene and that the tenancy passed to him from his late parents. He seems to be perfectly qualified to call himself a true local. Our records show that he isn't married. At least, he hasn't been claiming tax relief for a wife. He could be divorced or a widower but we'll discover more as we go along.'

'I wonder what sort of farming he engages in,' mused Day as he continued to sift through the file for relevant information. 'As you can imagine, I did not gain a lot of experience of agricultural businesses in north London but I suppose it must be either arable or livestock – or both, perhaps.'

'Given the name of the place, you can be forgiven for

thinking that we are going to see a working farm,' replied James. 'However, and although the property is described as such, what's carried on there has nothing to do with farming. For all the years covered by our file he has submitted annual accounts to us in relation to his activities as a dealer in scrap metal. What that means precisely I don't know but I have heard Deepdene Farm mentioned as the final resting place for expired motor vehicles. The full picture should emerge as we take a look and discuss matters with Mortimer and his accountant.'

Day continued to turn the pages of the file. 'Yes, I see here that he is described as a scrap dealer. The last year's accounts submitted to us showed a trading loss which followed a number of years of uninterrupted profit, albeit in small amounts. The declared trading loss was £1,241 so there's no tax to pay on the face of it.'

'I have looked at those accounts,' responded James. 'They were sent in by his accountants Birch and Company who are based in the High Street in Hemport. We passed their first floor offices when we walked down this morning. The sole proprietor is a man named John Birch who is well known to us at the office as he acts for many local businesses. His work is regarded as pretty reliable and I'm not aware that we've had any particular problems with him.

'The fact that the last accounts showed a loss is, of course, of interest to us particularly as it follows a pattern of consistent profit. However, we should bear in mind that there was a fire at the premises during the period. It seems highly likely that this would have had a significant bearing on turnover and profitability. I think there's a press cutting in the file.'

'Yes, the piece from the newspaper is stuck inside the front cover,' said Day. 'There's a picture which shows black smoke rising from what seems to be two large piles of smouldering and blackened material. The group of buildings in the background doesn't seem to have been affected.'

'There was a piece about this on the local TV news but I can't recall the details apart from the fact that nobody was hurt,' replied James.

'The name Mortimer is mentioned in this newspaper report but it says that he was unavailable to comment on what had happened,' continued Day. 'This must mean that he was reluctant to talk to the press about it. I wonder why?'

'He wouldn't be the first one not to want his comments splashed over the local paper,' said James. 'At the time, he must have been deeply troubled by what happened. I suspect he's a somewhat private, if not reclusive, person.

'There is another aspect I should mention,' continued James as he turned into the narrow lane. 'You will be well aware that we are required to follow up letters received from informants and such a communication has been received in this case.'

Day knew perfectly well that the majority of Inland Revenue investigations were commenced on the basis of information relayed by the public, usually anonymously. Many of these communications would turn out to be frivolous or down to sheer mischief but, even allowing for the time-wasters and the malicious, it was undeniable that a significant amount of back tax was gathered as a result of tip-offs.

A catalogue of statistics was maintained based on investigations commenced in this way. As compared to the selection of people for closer examination using other criteria, the "informer" case came out way ahead in terms of tax yielded. At a time when there was a growing emphasis upon the maximisation of returns from manpower within the department, the directive from the top was that such cases should be pursued with vigour.

It was vital that informers should not be discouraged from coming forward and feel confident that their anonymity would be preserved. A special dispensation ensured that no other government department or any court of law would be allowed access to information provided to the Inland Revenue in this manner.

'After completing my basic training,' responded Day, 'I was put straight on to investigation work. My suitability was obviously recognised early on and I was entrusted with a number of tricky cases at Head Office before coming down here.

'And, yes, in the course of this work I became aware of the significance of the informer. We all know what a valuable lever this is in the conduct of an investigation. Even a veiled reference to the existence of such information can cause a suspect to break cover.'

'In this district, we don't have the benefit of seeing this type of letter,' said James, 'but that hardly matters provided we are aware of the substance of what has been reported. In this case, the District Inspector, Mr Greenfield, informs me that there was a short letter, seemingly untidily written on a scrap of paper, stating that it would be to our advantage to look closely at the tax affairs of our Mr Mortimer. All such letters are kept under lock and key in Greenfield's office and, as far as I know, that's been the practice here for a very long time.'

'That's interesting,' said Day. 'In London we were simply handed the communication and told to take it from there. I wonder why things are dealt with differently here.'

'The identity of a person who been informed upon was once accidentally leaked from our office,' replied James. 'This caused huge problems and ever since there has been great sensitivity about the possibility of it happening again. Since then, the letters have been kept out of sight of everyone but the District Inspector. I suppose that the situation might change in time but for the moment that's the way it is.

'The demographic of the locality plays an important part,' continued James. 'Within the vast population of a city it is possible to be almost anonymous. It's difficult to hide in a smaller community.'

'Makes some sense, I suppose,' said Day, not appearing to be entirely convinced.

James eased the car slowly along the winding and narrow lane which rose steeply before them. No effort appeared to have been made to repair the gouged and rutted surface. Rainwater ran down channels on both sides casting loose material across the way.

The car dipped heavily on the passenger side tipping Day to his left. James was now questioning his own wisdom in choosing this hazardous route.

'We must be at about three hundred feet,' said James, noticing the sea mist drifting over the top of the dense hedgerows. Turning around and going back was not an option. He pressed on hoping that conditions would improve.

The land in the Marshfield Vale had been farmed for over

2,000 years. The difficulties in working the clay soil and the undulating nature of the land had discouraged intensive farming. Agriculture had moved forward at a slow pace with the more traditional methods of cultivation often still the most effective. Plough horses were kept until the mid twentieth century around which time the luxuries of mains water and electricity arrived. The small fields were remnants of the enclosures of the Iron Age, marked by ancient hedgerows. These boundaries teemed with life, providing food and safe haven for a wide range of insects, birds and small mammals. Traversing the several square miles of the vale was a network of narrow lanes, interrupted only occasionally by a farm worker's cottage or a small hamlet.

The land rose south towards the cliffs on the edge of the 200-million year old Jurassic Coast. The northern boundary was formed by an escarpment providing distant views to Dartmoor.

Day leaned forward and gazed ahead with some concern. He was not enjoying the treacherous journey in conditions which were far removed from the smooth carriageways of Ruislip.

'What on earth can car insurance premiums be like around here?' exclaimed Day. 'On this kind of road the risk factor must be incredibly high. Anything could come around one of these bends.'

At that very moment, James observed above the winding hedge in front of them the tall chimney of a tractor, pumping black diesel fumes into the still air. He slowed and directed the car into one of the passing places worn into the red earth of the verge. With a crunching of gears, the tractor decelerated and growled slowly past the stationary vehicle, spraying a fine mist of mud as it went. The drivers acknowledged the respective care taken with a wave of the hand.

'Coming this way has turned out not to be the best idea,' said James, 'but at least I'll know not to come this way again!'

After several more minutes of slow progress, James let out a sigh of relief at the sight of what appeared to be the summit of the lane. 'Looks like the worst is over,' he said to his passenger.

James was reflecting on how passive his companion remained when Day suddenly sprang to life. 'What was that?' he asked. 'Not the rabbit – I can recognise that – the thing chasing after it. Now they're appearing again!' he added as the animals darted across the lane in the opposite direction and into a tangle of brambles.

'Stoats catch rabbits, even ones much bigger than themselves,' explained James. 'They're a staple of their diet along with other small mammals and birds.' As he spoke, the rabbit darted across their path once more with the stoat at its heels. 'Rabbits can move very quickly over open ground but when its routes of escape are limited the stoat has the advantage.

'They are relentless in their pursuit and kill with a single bite to the neck. For their prey it's a matter of escape or die.

'What is remarkable is the ability of the stoat to mesmerise their quarry by performing a whirling dance in front of them. Once their victim is entranced, it's easy for them to strike.'

'That's hard to believe,' said Day.

'Strange but true, as they say,' replied James.

Having reached the peak of their journey, the vehicle pulled to a halt and the two men sat back and surveyed the panorama stretched before them. The Vale of Marshfield was a tapestry of every shade of green. Nestling in the hollow below was the curtilage of Deepdene Farm.

II

Central to the view ahead of them was a motley collection of wooden structures of different shapes and sizes, some topped with rusted sheets of corrugated iron, others with bare rafters exposed to the elements. A trodden earthen path seemed to wind between them. Above and beyond, a smoking chimney on top of a thatched roof was just visible.

To the right of the buildings was a large fenced compound enclosing a heap of motor cars, most balanced precariously on top of others.

'Time to go,' said James, releasing his seat belt.

'Aren't you going to drive nearer to the property?' enquired Day.

'Not likely - I'm not going to risk this little car down that bumpy track. I'd prefer to keep my axles intact for another day.'

Day looked first at his shiny shoes and then at the rough ground ahead before following James tentatively down the uneven surface, dodging molehills as he went.

A goat was tethered close to smaller heaps of rusting metal just visible through the weeds and bramble by which they had been overtaken. 'Not a pretty sight,' commented Day. 'It's not exactly your manicured garden. How on earth could planning permission be obtained for this kind of activity in such a lovely piece of countryside?'

'Of course,' replied James as they moved on, 'it could never happen today. What you see before you is likely to be the result of a slow transformation of the use of this land over a very long period of time. I suppose that years ago planning regulations were slack or even non-existent and the gradual change of use might have been almost imperceptible.

'I have never seen Mortimer before but he will be accompanied by his accountant, Mr Birch. Technically, as we know, his accountant is his legally appointed agent and will represent him in relation to all communication with the Inland Revenue. As such, and in theory, Birch could answer all our questions. You and I are aware that this would be very unlikely to happen – not in its entirety, anyway. A total silence on the part of the taxpayer would arouse curiosity and risk intensifying the questioning.

'You have had experience, Brian, in conducting interviews of this kind but I think the idea today is that I lead the discussion with you feeling free to intervene if you wish. Your role today is mainly as an observer but this should not prevent you from raising any salient points that come to mind. Is there anything else you would like to say before we go in?'

'Have you met Mr. Birch before?' asked Day.

'I've met him on several occasions,' replied James, 'usually at meetings like this. I have always thought of him as the personification of what the Americans call the "bean counter".

'His technical knowledge of the taxation system may be a little patchy but his integrity has never been questioned, as far as I know. I wouldn't describe him as the easiest person to get to know and I have no knowledge of his personal life and interests. Oh, and humour is not his strong suit!'

They reached the earthen path which seemed to be the most likely route between the tumbledown buildings to the house beyond. Below a flight of whirling herring gulls, carrion crows on a rooftop were arguing with a group of jackdaws over territorial entitlement.

They continued between the structures, dodging the drips from a cracked black drainpipe. As they stepped into the farmyard, a group of chickens appeared, squawked and flapped away.

Their view was lit by a shaft of light descending from a break in the clouds. On the far side of the yard stood a thatched house outside which a sagging washing line hung between rustic poles. Day, used to ordered suburbia, marvelled that people could actually exist in such a broken-down place.

He turned to his colleague who, to his surprise, seemed to be enjoying the view. James had taken an interest in the local architecture since his arrival in the county and was absorbing the antiquity of what was around him.

'This is typical of Devon farmsteads of the eighteenth and nineteenth centuries,' said James. 'In the same way that there is uniformity in today's housing, so there was a tried and trusted pattern for the construction of the farm dwellings of that period.'

Day looked and listened without sharing James's enthusiasm for what he saw as a derelict muddle.

The wind chased crisp brown leaves over the sparse cobbles at their feet. 'These stones, or what is left of them, would be the originals as laid down when the property was built,' observed James. 'It's simply fascinating to imagine what has taken place here over the last two hundred years or so.

'What you see around you are the utilitarian structures common to the period. Over there is the shippon for the house cow with the calf shed attached. That open-fronted linhay was for the horse and cart with the familiar trap door to the hay loft above.

'For obvious reasons, the pig sty is at the point furthest from the house. This was the essential recycling function for the rural dweller, converting unwanted vegetable matter into meat for the table. The overall state of neglect is sad but does lend a sense of atmosphere and authenticity.'

Complementing the carpet of algae over the yard, the thatched roof of the farmhouse wore a bright green garment of moss, brought on by decades of seepage and damp. The floors and walls of the utility buildings would once have been lime washed to eliminate bacteria and prevent disease. Now, the untended structures were streaked black and grey.

'Well,' commented Day, 'I understand your interest in old places like this but I'd rather live in something a bit more up to date.'

'An understanding of the past is essential to our comprehension of the world we live in,' said James. 'You may come to take an interest in the subject in time, but enough of this history lesson. I can see the front door on the other side of the yard.'

Much of the dark green paint had peeled from the door revealing the colours of several previous applications. Askew on the wall to the right of the entrance was a rusting metal bracket from which a bell would have hung.

They moved slowly across the slippery cobbles, Day recoiling when a group of rats scurried by, paying no heed to the humans crossing their beaten path.

Passing through an opening in a low stone wall that would once have supported a gate, the two men climbed the steps towards the door. Before they were within reach of it, the door shook as if someone inside was trying to force it open.

They stood in anticipation of what might be revealed. The efforts to release the door continued for a few more seconds and then stopped.

'Somebody has seen us coming,' said James, as he put down his briefcase and went forward to investigate. 'I'd better try and give a hand.' Day stayed put and watched.

'Leave it to me for a moment,' James called through. He took hold of the outside handle, lifted and heaved against the door with his shoulder.

With a judder, the door sprang inwards and he was carried by his own momentum into the narrow dark passageway within.

James came to a halt just in time to avoid colliding with the person inside. He blinked as he adjusted his eyes to the dim light and saw before him a lady who was clearly startled by the suddenness of his entry.

Their eyes met and no words passed between them for a few moments.

The petite lady was shorter than he by about six inches. Under a white pinafore tied tightly at the waist was a dark green dress buttoned at the collar. Her hands and clothes were dusted with what appeared to be flour.

'I am sorry,' said James as he considered her fine features and shoulder-length brown hair. 'I hope I didn't shock you.'

'No, it was kind of you to help,' she said nervously. 'I doubt it would ever have opened without you pushing it the way you did. This door is not used that often as most visitors know to go around the back. Nevertheless, it really is too much that it hasn't been put right and now it seems to have become even worse in this damp weather. I am afraid I have no influence over maintenance here or, should I say, lack of it.'

Her clearly enunciated words were spoken without trace of a regional accent. Despite the season, James detected the aroma of summer.

A bare light bulb above them illuminated the passageway furnished with peeling wallpaper of a dark blue and green floral pattern. 'Surely, she could not live here,' he thought to himself, already wanting to know more of the lady and her circumstances.

She must have been well over thirty years younger than the age they knew Mortimer to be. It was not impossible that he had attracted a younger woman but that seemed unlikely.

A more credible explanation was that she came in to help with housework but, if that were the case, there must be more agreeable surroundings in which she could have found employment.

'I am sorry that we seem to have caught you at a busy time,' said James. 'You are obviously otherwise occupied.'

'Just the daily routine,' she replied timidly, still a little shocked.

Day stepped forward and James introduced him as his colleague.

'We have an appointment with Mr Mortimer at 11.30. I don't know whether you were expecting us.'

'Yes, I have been asked to show you to where Mr Mortimer is working at the moment. He said that Mr Birch, his accountant, would also be arriving. If you would like to follow me I'll show you the way.'

She led them through to the kitchen where several baskets of dough were proving on a pine table prior to being finished off in the oven.

'What a wonderful smell of baking,' remarked James, at which the lady turned and smiled in acknowledgement. Day noted that the loaves lacked the uniformity of the sliced supermarket variety to which he was accustomed.

The kitchen was tidy, clean and organised, belying the exterior of the house. The working surfaces were uncluttered and the crockery arranged neatly on a Welsh Dresser.

She led them from the kitchen and across a flagstone floor to a passage leading to the rear of the house. Outside the back door, they descended a flight of several worn stone steps before crossing a patch of weeds and couch grass. She halted and pointed to a large corrugated iron shed fifty yards away. 'Continue across here, through the large double doors ahead of you and into the workshop. Mr Mortimer is there.'

As the lady turned and made her way back to the house, James's eyes followed her until she had climbed the steps and closed the door behind her. He was intrigued by this well-groomed lady and the part she played in this scene of disorder and confusion.

On their way to the entrance to the workshop, they made their way around piles of worn tyres, old batteries and pools of oil. Barking threateningly as it scampered towards them, a wild-eyed black and white dog circled the visitors before retreating. From within the building came a grinding metallic din.

One of the tall doors to the building was ajar and they

stepped inside to be met by the stench of diesel oil. In the centre of the cavernous space was a workbench where sparks plumed from the activities of a man in blue overalls. His task completed, he switched off, wiped his brow and laid the tool on the bench in front of him. The room fell shockingly silent as a column of blue smoke continued to rise towards a fluorescent light suspended above.

The dog began circling Day who withdrew his leg quickly as the animal sniffed around his shoes. 'Go away, beast,' he muttered under his breath.

The animal ran towards Mortimer and sat alongside him. His master had not yet spotted the visitors and began rummaging in a rusting tool box alongside his bench. James continued to watch and Day looked at his colleague as if to suggest it was time to make their introduction.

James saw that Mortimer was about five feet nine inches tall and stooped. His movements were laboured and he winced as he bent and lifted something on to his work surface. It was clear that this kind of work was beyond the comfortable reach of a man in his condition. It appeared to James unlikely that he could continue this kind of labour for much longer. Perhaps the next accounts submitted to the Inland Revenue would be the last before he retired.

James called out 'Mr Mortimer?' but there was no response.

'He doesn't seem to be wearing any noise protectors,' said a surprised Day.

'His hearing is not what it was,' came a voice from behind them. It was Birch, looking businesslike in his grey mackintosh and trilby. The accountant was dark-featured and almost as tall as James, probably younger than his staid appearance suggested.

As both Inspectors turned to face Birch, the man they now knew to be Mortimer began a coughing fit, still without noticing he had company.

James advanced towards Birch, shook his hand and introduced him to Day. With the accountant leading the way, all three walked towards Mortimer who then became aware of their presence.

Mortimer did not come forward to extend a greeting to the men but leaned on his bench and turned an ear towards Birch.

The accountant faced his client and spoke loudly to ensure he would hear what he had to say.

'You know why these people are here, Albert, don't you?' he asked, pointing to the visitors.

His client nodded without speaking.

Turning to the two inspectors, Birch said, 'I have told Mr Mortimer you were coming and that you would be wishing to ask him some questions about his business. He is a practical man with little knowledge of financial matters and I know you will take this into account. If I consider that I am best placed to deal with a particular question, I shall do so.'

Mortimer seemed to have understood what had been said and his eyes darted nervously between the two inspectors who he identified as adversaries. A short silence followed after which Birch spoke again.

'I suggest we go to the office in the far corner,' he said, pointing towards a space where an arrangement of old office partitioning provided some detachment from the open workshop area. In the centre of the makeshift room sat a large old wooden desk behind which was a revolving office chair. Other similar chairs were scattered around the room together with some randomly-placed filing cabinets. Two metal tables were heaped with a disarray of finger-marked papers kept in place by small, grimy metal objects.

Birch moved behind the desk and cleared an area among a muddle of papers. After placing his satchel before him, he directed the inspectors to the chairs opposite him and told Mortimer to sit to his right.

'I think this is close enough for us all to hear and understand one another,' said Birch, settling into position.

James watched Mortimer as he moved to take his place alongside Birch. At close quarters, his infirmity was more obvious.

No doubt his discomfort was aggravated by the anticipation of the ordeal to come and, once seated, he glanced at Birch as if to seek reassurance that his long-time accountant would guide him through.

James could conduct a tough interrogation if he had to – he had done so many times before. The intensity of the questioning was dependent on the nature of the person under examination and proportionate to the degree of co-operation that was forthcoming. It had already become clear to him that this wasn't the time for a rigorous approach. The frail individual before him would need delicate handling if the interview were to be productive.

The inspectors took their places after checking that there was no undesirable material on the seats of their chairs. Each withdrew a file and a pad of paper from their briefcases.

Mortimer did not remove his overalls before sitting. One of the arms of his chair was missing and so soiled was the upholstery that it was impossible to discern what the original colour might have been. In a large plastic pot behind him, a wilted palm leaned precariously in its inconsonant surroundings.

Birch had placed two thick files on the surface of the desk. Having switched to his reading spectacles, he looked up and met the gazes of the other three as they waited for him to speak.

Looking at James and Day, he began. Although his speech was slow and clear, it was delivered in a monotone that was less than captivating.

'I think it would be useful to provide a brief background to my client and his business,' he commenced.

'Tell us when you started in business here, Albert,' he requested.

Mortimer leaned forward and placed both elbows on the desk. At the same time, he craned towards his accountant.

Birch realised Mortimer had not heard him and repeated the question more loudly. His client replied in a deep and hesitant voice interrupted occasionally by a clearing of his throat.

'I was thinking about this recently. I'd worked here for Dad until he passed away during the war. He'd been sent back from the trenches with bad breathing problems. They put him in hospital but he wanted to come back here when he realised he didn't have long to go. He joined up in 1942 so I suppose you could say that's when I took over. He never did another day's work.'

'So you've been doing this for 40 years?' asked Birch.

'Well, over 40 by now. I don't know how much longer I'll go on.'

Birch turned to the inspectors.

'Mr Mortimer does not own these premises and neither

did his father. The whole property is held on a lease from the local landowner. Under a succession clause, it was transferred to my client after his father died. Sadly, Mrs Mortimer passed away some years ago. Because there are no children, the lease will expire on his death and the freehold will revert to the landlord who will then become absolutely entitled to the property.'

'Does the lease also extend to the residential part of the property?' enquired Day.

'It does,' replied Birch. 'No part of this land or the property situated on it belongs to him and the lease has no value since it cannot be transferred. In a sense it's academic. What's mattered to him is that he's had security during his lifetime.

'The same trade has been conducted by my client as a sole proprietor over all these years. I took over responsibility for the case about 15 years ago from the previous accountant who had retired. I don't know the full history before then but as far as I know no Inland Revenue investigation has previously taken place.

'You'll know as well as I do the profit pattern over the years,' he continued. 'My client has made a living but not much more. Equipment has been patched up rather than replaced and a look around you will make this obvious. There has been no investment in the infrastructure, just essential maintenance carried out by Albert himself. It's a classic case of the tenant not wanting to spend on what doesn't belong to him and the landlord failing to meet his responsibility to keep up a property.

'His earning capacity diminishes with each passing year but his personal outgoings are modest.'

James took the opportunity to speak and turned to Mortimer as he did so.

'Mr Mortimer,' said James, remembering the need to articulate loudly and clearly. 'First, I would like to thank you for allowing us to visit you to discuss your tax affairs.'

Mortimer had turned an ear in his direction and nodded his understanding of what had been said.

'Our duty as tax inspectors is to ensure that the people of this area comply with their tax obligations. Most people pay the right amount of tax. It would be very unfair to them if others were allowed to get away with not paying their fair share.

'We are guardians of the public purse but also see our role as protecting the interests of the community as a whole.'

Mortimer responded. 'If I understand correctly what you're saying, I'm glad to know you chase those who don't pay what they should. I've come across quite a few in my time who manage to stay well clear of paying any tax. And they're probably the same ones who squeeze as much as they can out of the Social Security system.'

'I understand your feelings, Mr Mortimer,' said James.

'One of the things we do is to look a little more closely at how a business works and what books of account are kept. Our hope is that we'll find everything in order. Sometimes we may discover that this is not the case. Then we try to put matters right by discussion and giving guidance for the future.

'But there is a difference between the avoidance of tax by accident or misunderstanding and the evasion of tax by deliberate means. In the case of innocent error, any tax found to be lost to the Exchequer would still need to be made good. The Taxes Acts provide for evasion to be dealt with more severely and there can be heavy penalties for the worst offenders.

'We asked to see you today to have an open discussion about how your business operates. We have no preconceived ideas and I am pleased that Mr Birch is here. His comments will be valued and taken into account.'

Mortimer's face was highly coloured which may have been caused by his recent exertions with his machinery but, thought James, might indicate a deeper malaise.

'I'm no numbers man,' said Mortimer, 'and Mr Birch advises me as to procedures. He sees my books every year so everything should be in order. I pay him enough,' he said, aiming a nervous chuckle in the direction of Birch.

'Of course, Mr Mortimer,' replied James. 'We quite understand that accountancy is not your speciality and that's why we'll listen carefully to what Mr Birch has to say about the accounts he prepares for you.

'Your work, as I understand it, involves the receiving of scrap metal and processing it for sale to others who then recycle it for alternative use. Is that a fair summary of what you do?'

'That's about it,' replied Mortimer, leaning back in his chair and wiping his brow with a rag drawn from the top pocket of his overalls.

'Written-off cars are brought up that drive on recovery vehicles and I usually buy them. Some parts are stripped out and sold on. What's left is taken for crushing.

'Some smaller items like cookers and fridges come in from local people. I accept stuff like this to help them out more than anything.'

Day made his first intervention. 'Mr Mortimer, what you

do must involve a lot of heavy work. I suppose you can't manage it all on your own.'

'I couldn't do it all even though I take on a lot less than I used to. John Irvine from the village comes in to help. He drives the truck when we need it as well as doing other things.'

'Would you call Mr Irvine an employee?' posed Day.

'Not in the way I think of an employee, not on the cards, sick pay and that kind of thing. He comes in when I need him and I pay him at the end of the month for what he's done.'

'Does he work the same number of hours each week?'

'He knows I can't guarantee him the work but he does come in a fair bit. He usually gives me a list of the time he puts in. I'd need to try to find the sheets to tell you what it all adds up to.'

'Does he come in every week?'

'When I think about it, I suppose he must have come in most weeks, but I can't really remember without looking at what I've written down.'

'And where are these sheets?'

'I can't remember now – I'll have to take a look around.'

'Do you pay him by cheque?'

'Sometimes, but more often it's cash. If I've got a little bit on hand it's a way of getting rid of it rather than having the bother of taking it to the bank.'

'We'd like to see the sheets,' said Day turning to Birch who nodded and made a note of the requirement to find them.

'When we came to the door today we met a lady,' said Day. 'Does she do any work for your business?'

'Not really, but I suppose you could say that if Ruth didn't deal with the housekeeping I wouldn't have the time to come out here and do my work.'

'Does she live here?'

Mortimer explained that she did. Ruth had lived with him since she was forced to leave her family home a few years earlier.

'She's known better times but hasn't had much luck in life. That's why she's ended up here. She's a lovely girl and nobody would be happier than me if she found somewhere better to go. I'd manage somehow.'

'And is she paid for what she does?'

'I do give her cash every week but that's mainly for food and housekeeping. She gets her keep and pays me no rent.'

After a few moments during which he made more notes, Day continued.

'Could you give me an example of a typical business transaction? If, for example, a lorry comes here and takes away a load of scrap for the crushing plant, what documentation would be involved? How would you be paid and where would the money end up?'

'I've known all the lorry drivers for years so we don't worry too much about paperwork when they take stuff away. I can remember what's been taken and when. After about four weeks, a cheque arrives and I get Ruth to take it to the bank when she's next in town.'

'Do you have just one bank account?' asked Day.

'Yes, I've only ever used the same bank. It was the Western and Provincial when I first started. Now it's called Westbank, or something like that.'

'So you don't send a bill to the people you've sold to?'

'No – there's no need – a piece of paper always comes with the cheque. This shows what they've paid me. Ruth knows where to file it away.'

James detected that Mortimer was starting to become weary of Day's questioning and decided to take the pressure off by switching attention to Birch.

'I can see a duplicate receipt book on the windowsill over there,' said James to the accountant. 'I think it's the sort you can buy at W H Smith with carbon paper in between the pages. Can you tell me, Mr Birch, what use you make of this when you prepare the accounts for the business?'

Birch shifted and thought for a few seconds. 'People come here to look for a spare part for their car and payment is usually made in cash. A lot of the customers don't have a bank account so there's no option. My client used to accept cheques but was caught out more than once when the bank refused to honour the payment. After that, he decided it would be simpler to accept cash only.'

'So you are saying that he makes out a receipt and gives the top copy to the customer,' interrupted Day.

'In an ideal world that's what would happen,' answered Birch. 'In reality, there's no such thing as a watertight system when cash changes hands. Most of the buyers don't want any paperwork and just go on their way.

'A larger concern would probably employ a qualified bookkeeper or even have an accounts department but it's different at this level.'

'What you are saying is that, in the absence of complete records, you don't know how much cash is received,' said Day, staring directly at Birch.

'I act for any number of small businesses and sometimes

it's necessary to use estimates when full checks and balances can't be carried out. Some accountants can't sleep at night if everything doesn't add up but I'm experienced enough to know that you have to be pragmatic at times.

'This is something we discuss every year when the annual accounts are prepared. With Albert's assistance, I work out an estimate of the amounts that may not have found their way into the book. There's no other fair way of doing it.'

'So the total income shown for the year is guesswork,' stated Day.

Birch was irritated by this suggestion and responded with some force.

'There's a major difference between what you describe as guesswork and an informed estimate. I'm surprised you seem unable to understand this. It's commonplace and all professional advisers have to take a view on such situations in order to try to reach a reasonable conclusion.'

Day then fired a question at Mortimer. 'What happens to the cash you take from customers? You said you gave some to Mr Irvine. Do you take the rest to the bank?'

'First I put it in my tin,' he responded, pointing to a red cash box on the desk and lifting the unlocked lid. If it reaches a certain amount I take it to the bank but that doesn't happen very often. I meet my expenses out of it and my needs are not great.'

'And you keep a note of what you take out of the box?'

'If I remember, I write down the amounts I take as Mr Birch has told me to. There's been a lot less in there since the fire last year. Business has been quiet – it's taking me a long time to build up my stock.'

'I think that Mr Birch may be reminding you that it's not good enough to keep written records only when you remember to do so, as you put it,' responded Day. 'Accuracy is all important.

'Has a petty cash account been drawn up, Mr Birch?' asked Day. 'What I mean by this is a detailed list of all the amounts put in the box and all the cash taken out.'

'I know what a petty cash account is, Mr Day,' said Birch, his voice rising. 'I am an experienced accountant. This account is drawn up at the end of each year at which time any necessary adjustments and estimates are incorporated in the accounts.'

'Turning to the cars that you buy in, Mr Mortimer,' continued Day, becoming more tenacious, 'how do you pay for them?'

'If I have to pay for a car, I would usually take cash from the tin if there's enough in there. A lot of what comes in I get for free. If a car is clapped out and not driveable, it's cheaper for people to drop it off here than pay someone to take it away. I would usually only pay for something if it's more modern. Then the parts are worth a bit more.'

James introduced himself into the conversation.

'I was sorry to learn that there was a fire here last year. That must have been an awful experience for you. How did it affect the business?'

'It was a disaster and I had to virtually start from scratch. Luckily, the car compound is not near the other buildings so it didn't spread.'

'No insurance proceeds then?'

'No chance of that,' said Mortimer with a resigned look. 'Insurance companies won't touch this kind of business, what with gas bottles for the cutting equipment, petrol left in tanks and so on.

'We managed to find a landfill site for what was left.'

'At what time of the year did this unfortunate incident take place?' enquired Day.

'I remember it was June and it hadn't rained for weeks. Everything was parched so it went up like tinder.'

'Your annual accounts run for the year to the 31st December,' continued Day, 'so it was about half way through the period. Did you manage to dispose of the fire-damaged remains using your own transport? You mentioned that Mr Irvine drove a truck for you.'

'As far as I remember we did.'

'My final question is whether you were charged by the local council for tipping the remains into the landfill.'

'We must have been but I don't remember the details now. Ruth writes out the cheques for me so if they'd sent us a bill we'd have paid it.'

Birch cut in. 'There is a purchase invoice file so any documentation relating to payments made would be in there.' He agreed to search for the council invoices and supply copies.

'I don't want this initial discussion to take longer than necessary,' said James, 'and I feel that we have taken up enough of your time for one day. Would you like to ask any questions?'

'Yes, I would,' said Mortimer. 'I understand you have a job to do but what I'd like to know is why you've picked on me after all these years. It's never happened before and it never happened to my father. Did my number just come up?'

'It's certainly not a question of everybody taking their

turn,' said James. 'Many factors influence how we decide to proceed. All I can say is that we shall be very happy to close our enquiry once we are satisfied that all is in order.'

'How long will all this take?' asked Mortimer. 'I don't like the idea of this kind of thing hanging over me for years on end, particularly at my time of life.'

'I understand your concern and hope it will not take too long,' said James. 'Your co-operation in replying quickly to any further queries will help us to close everything as quickly as we can.'

The meeting concluded and James and his colleague walked along the rising track to where their car had been left. 'We've given them plenty to think about,' said James. 'There's nothing further we can do until we have the responses from Birch.'

III

'As mentioned earlier, I think we'll return by a different route,' announced James. 'It will be quicker and more direct, probably only three or four minutes to the main road.'

'Thank goodness for that,' said Day. 'I look forward to a less bumpy ride!'

From their parking place they circled the farmstead along an unmade track. Soon they joined a lane surfaced with tarmac leading to the junction with a busy road.

'We'll turn left here and drive towards Hemport. The Pot Inn is on the left less than a mile ahead. I thought we might call in there for some refreshment. When we leave there we'll just carry on in the same direction to get back to town.'

'Do you think it's wise for us to go to a licensed premises while we are on duty?' enquired Day, casting a questioning look at the driver. 'This is something that would be frowned upon in London.'

James was impressed and slightly amused by his companion's fastidious regard for the rules.

'It's lunch time and I consider that we're off duty. We're due to take a break and I thought we might have a change of scene. Anyway, I have a thirst and wouldn't mind a bite to eat if there's anything on offer.

'Whatever the pub may be like,' continued James, 'I remember they have a proper coffee machine. It will be an opportunity for us to talk over what we found at Deepdene Farm.'

Soon they arrived at a large tiled property standing alone at the side of the road. "The Pot Inn" was written in large white letters across the blue-painted side wall and a wisp of smoke rose from a tall brick chimney. There were only three vehicles in the large concrete parking area including a red MG sports car.

'I know that car,' said Day. 'It belongs to a neighbour of mine named Miles Kemp. He lives a little further down the lane from me and has stopped to chat on several occasions on his way to the coastal path. He's always been alone but for his Jack Russell.

'I don't know much about him but he's said he runs an Estate Agency in the town. I haven't yet seen his premises so must take a look one day.'

'I also recognise that car,' said James. 'I met Miles soon after coming to work here. He was the first estate agent I contacted with my requirement to purchase a property in the area. As it turned out, he came up with the house I eventually bought. His offices are down the High Street, not far from where we work – he's quite a character and well known around the town. I bump into him occasionally but couldn't say I know him well.'

They disembarked and entered the pub, ducking as they passed through the low porch. Their arrival was signalled by a bell which tinkled as they pushed open the narrow door.

Through a blue haze of wood smoke they saw a man clutching a brass hand pump, perhaps trying to anticipate the likely choices of the two men.

The walls were covered with the familiar trappings of the

country pub; horse brasses, old farm implements and hunting prints. The worn floral carpet and fading flock wallpaper suggested there had been little investment in the décor for some time.

Two elderly men sat either side of a fireplace within which the dying embers of a log fire smouldered in an iron cradle. One gazed absently into the hearth while the other studied the back page of a newspaper. Between them were two pint glasses of cloudy cider.

Elsewhere, a couple of retirement age in matching hiking apparel chatted enthusiastically while studying an Ordnance Survey map. They looked up and smiled towards the new arrivals.

James and his colleague studied what was on offer while the man at the bar awaited their orders. Their silent host, probably the landlord, looked about sixty years of age, his portly frame clad in a sleeveless red woollen cardigan showing signs of a visit by the moth.

The coffee machine was immediately behind him but showed no signs of life. Neither was there any suggestion of food but for a few crumbs under a plastic dome on the bar.

'Can you make a coffee?' asked James.

'We haven't sold any this morning so it'll take a while to get the machine heated up.'

'Are you serving food?'

'Afraid not – not the call for it, only on Sunday when the wife cooks a roast. Well, there were a few rolls but they've gone.'

'We'll just have two coffees then, please,' requested James. 'How much would you like?'

'Let's see, twice fifteen pence is thirty pence in total, please.' Although the conversion to decimal coinage had occurred over ten years previously, James noted that there was still a fading decimal conversion chart on the wall behind the till for the benefit of those who, even at this late stage, needed to think back to "old" money to work out the real cost of anything.

A man seated on a bar stool raised his eyes from his newspaper and turned towards the newcomers. 'I thought I recognised your voice, James. Oh, and it's Brian, my new neighbour.' Miles slipped his not inconsiderable frame off the stool and, smiling widely, shook hands with both men. Noticing they were dressed for the office, he asked whether they worked together.

'Yes,' replied James, 'Brian was transferred here recently from another branch.'

'Brian told me a bit about that when we had one of our chats while I was out walking the dog,' said Miles, settling back on his stool.

'I come out here occasionally to have a break from the office,' he continued, 'and catch up with the financial pages.' He waved the pink newspaper in his hand. 'Can't seem to do this at the office with the telephone ringing all the time.'

Kemp seemed a little unsteady, possibly stiff as a result of being perched in the same position on the stool for some time. In front of him on the polished oak bar was a half-empty pint glass.

With his Harris Tweed suit and matching waistcoat he was the epitome of the country Estate Agent. Even-featured, dark and ruggedly handsome, there was, nevertheless, a sense that his engaging presence concealed a layer of vulnerability.

News travels quickly within the professional circles of a

small town and the word was that Miles's business was not doing well. Rumours abounded as to the reasons for this, one being that he could be spending a little too much time in places like the one in which he had just been discovered by James and Day. But he was a likeable character who, whatever his foibles, presented no problems to anyone other than himself.

Kemp and Company were the local estate agents. Miles's father had died five years previously at which time his only son inherited the sole proprietorship of the business. Having learned his trade as his father's assistant over many years, the transition had been seamless.

Miles was steeped in the long-established procedures at the office and had made little effort to change the tried and trusted methods which had brought a measure of success over the years. Times were changing, however, and he had for some time been conscious of being left behind by outmoded working practices.

'I read the other day that house prices are still rising fairly sharply,' said Day. 'It must be the case – everything else being equal – that Estate Agents' turnover goes up in direct proportion to the increase in property values. Double the price means twice the commission, doesn't it?'

Day's mathematical assessment was probably on the button but not of much encouragement to Miles.

'All very well in theory, Brian, but you have to sell the same number of houses to make that work.' After glancing from side to side, he leant forward and spoke quietly. 'The fact is that we are not selling as many as I would like.'

The local property market had changed in recent years. Many employers had relocated their businesses to the town attracted by government incentives and the desirable surroundings. Employees were generally happy to move to a pleasant rural location. Communications were good and the rail connections facilitated travel in all directions. Hemport had escaped the Beeching cuts of the nineteen-sixties and kept its station on the Waterloo line.

There were excellent leisure facilities in and around the town as well as the attraction of the sea and coastline nearby. Along with the easing of planning regulations, residential development was on the move and the buyers were flocking in.

Retirement money from up country poured down as the area began to feature on the map as a desirable place to live. The national chains of Estate Agents were not slow to recognise the potential and opened offices in the town. Now there were three major firms with national connections competing for the local business. This presented a major challenge to the previously cosy existence of Kemp and Company.

'There are a lot more sale transactions than there were ten years ago,' continued Miles. 'The housing stock in Hemport has increased by fifteen per-cent over that period and, generally speaking, sales rise at the same rate. The difficulty lies in maintaining your share.

'The big firms are serious opposition. Their people are well trained, ambitious and driven by generous financial incentives, plus the backing of slick marketing and national coverage. I'm the first to admit that it's extremely difficult for a one-man band to keep up with them.'

Miles emptied his pint glass and continued. 'When Dad died, I inherited two old retainers. The ladies are getting on a bit now and are not exactly high fliers. They're not really paying their way but Dad wouldn't have heard of them being made redundant so I'm honouring what would have been his wishes. If I could cut out the expense of just one of them, the cost saving would help to balance the books. So it's a struggle and I'm forever trying to think of ways to stretch the limited budget and generate new ideas.

'One step I've taken is to establish an agency with a major insurance Company so that I can offer clients a full range of investment-linked products, particularly Life Assurance to cover mortgage loans in connection with property purchase. I can hold clients' funds for investment in Personal Equity Plans, stocks and shares and the like.

'It's early days but I am hoping the commission I earn will make a worthwhile contribution to the business.

'Between you and me, if I didn't have the freehold of the premises we would be really struggling. Having to pay rent for a High Street premises, even in Hemport, would be a real drain. The trouble is a growing chunk of the property is in the hands of the bank as collateral against the advancement of working capital. Oh dear, I have revealed all!' he said, grinning awkwardly.

James had heard more than he wanted to and thought how unwise it was for Miles to speak so openly about his financial affairs. Confidentiality came naturally to the Inland Revenue men but there were plenty of people out there who might try to gain advantage from the knowledge that he was in difficulty. But Miles was no more than an acquaintance and James did not see it as his place to try to offer advice.

The two cups of coffee were finally delivered and James pulled up a stool alongside Miles while his colleague stood rather stiffly to one side. James offered the estate agent a drink.

'I shouldn't, but go on then – a pint of the Old Sheep Dip. It's brewed down the road and you wouldn't find a better real ale around here. Have one, yourself, James. I recall you saying that you liked a glass of the good stuff.'

A notice on the beer pump handle advertised the relatively high alcohol content of the brew and James declined. 'Were it the evening I'd like nothing better than to try one, but not now as there's work to do this afternoon. It would probably send me to sleep but I'll keep it in mind and sample it next time I get the chance.'

Miles started on what was probably the third of his drinks for the session and enquired whether James was still happy with the house he'd bought through his agency.

'I'm quite happy with where I live,' replied James. 'It suited me that there was nothing much to do in the way of repairs and decoration so I was able to just give it a bit of a clean and move in.'

Coming so soon after the loss of his wife, James had little motivation to become involved in domestic projects and just wanted to try to settle into his new location with the minimum of effort.

'There you are,' said Miles, thumping James firmly on the shoulder, 'another satisfied customer of Kemp and Company!

'But back to what I was saying,' he continued. 'I have a theory that things go in full circle. For the moment, we may be battling to hold our own against the onslaught from the outsiders but things can change quickly. I hope that people will come to realise they can place their trust in a local firm with long experience in the area.

'Have you heard about the new housing development planned for the edge of the town?' asked Miles. Both men shook their heads.

'I'm not surprised as it hasn't been made public yet.

'You would have heard of Barford Construction, the national house builders. They've just signed a contract to acquire land from the local council with existing permission to build new homes.

'I'd like to be appointed the selling agent for those. New housing developments sell quickly and without a great deal of effort.

'But no use dreaming about that as I've no doubt they'll choose one of the big agencies.

'I am fortunate to have the management contract with a company called Nelson Properties which at least provides steady cash flow. Following a programme of acquisitions over the last few years, they've built up a portfolio of seven blocks of flats around the town, mainly for retired people. As well as rent collection, I carry out a number of other duties including arranging for any necessary repairs and maintenance and dealing with any queries from tenants. If a tenant leaves, it's my job to find a replacement. The two directors have made their money and reached the point where they can well afford to delegate this kind of thing. Luckily, the work came my way.

'But I have to get it right. They are serious businessmen who want value for money and there's a no-notice clause in the contract. I am under no illusion that they would replace me without ceremony if it suited them.'

'The main thing is that you're still in there battling,' commented James, 'and I'm sure it will come together in time. I always recommend you if anyone asks me for the name of a local firm.'

Miles and Brian Day entered into conversation about life in their part of the town while James wandered to the bay window overlooking the road outside and watched the passing traffic.

There was potential for Kemp and Company but was it too late? The debt ratio and overheads seemed high and, although the proprietor did have some ideas, was he sufficiently grounded to carry them through?

James reminded himself that it was not his affair and returned to his companions.

'Will you be at the stables on Saturday morning, James?' asked Miles.

'Brian doesn't know about this so I'll explain for his benefit,' said James. 'Miles is referring to the racing stables of Charles Edgcumbe at Lower Barton, just two miles away from here. He's a trainer of National Hunt racehorses, that is to say horses that race over fences rather than on the flat.

'By coincidence, both Miles and I are members of a syndicate which owns a horse known as Southern Pride.

'I don't know whether you have any interest in racing, Brian,' said James, 'but it may come as a surprise to you to think that I, a modestly paid Civil Servant, am involved in the so-called "Sport of Kings" with its connotations of wealth and position. It's only because of the affordable option of being a member of a syndicate that I can be part of it. For a modest monthly payment, most of the benefits of ownership can be enjoyed.

'I've been keenly interested in the sport since my father first took me to the races at Salisbury when I was just thirteen. I've followed racing closely ever since and being an owner had always been a dream of mine.'

'I'll be frank with you,' interjected Miles, 'the syndicate fees are something I could well do without but it's a way of networking and having social contact. I couldn't afford the cost of corporate hospitality myself and it's a good way of getting out and about and meeting potential clients.'

'This Saturday we have the opportunity to visit the stables, talk to the trainer and watch the horses working,' added James.

'That's interesting,' said Day. 'I suppose that, as an owner, you might be aware of the likelihood of the horse winning.'

'We would certainly be aware of the horse's well-being but I have been following the sport for long enough to know that there's no such thing as a certainty. The unexpected can happen in any race and animals do not always perform to their best on the day. They're not machines, after all.'

'That's true and the fact is that we've been disappointed with the horse's performances to date,' said Miles. 'Although he seemed in good heart at home, the promise wasn't fulfilled at the racecourse. On both occasions it ran, it failed to complete the course. It ran out of steam towards the end so the jockey did the wise thing and pulled up.'

'Yes, I'm sure Charles will be working on this and trying to correct whatever the problem may be,' added James. 'We'll find out more on Saturday.'

The two coffees had been little better than tepid when they arrived. The colleagues wasted no time in downing them before they became completely cold.

Miles finished the last of his pint and eased himself from his stool. 'Thanks for the drink – enjoyed seeing you both.' He took a few moments to steady himself then made for the exit, hitching up his trousers as he went.

'In tomorrow?' called the landlord.

'Not sure yet,' replied Miles. He pulled the door inwards and the bell announced his exit.

'Is that machine still on?' enquired James of the landlord. 'The last cup was barely warm.'

'I've turned it off – didn't think you'd want another one.'

Scanning the bottled drinks on display, James asked for a bottle of tonic water with ice and a slice of lemon.

'No lemon until the delivery tomorrow, but I think I can find some ice.'

'That'll be OK,' said James. 'What about you, Brian?'

Brian settled for the same and, after collecting their drinks, they moved to the two seats near the fireplace which had now been vacated.

'I think Miles is basically a decent man with his heart in the right place,' said James, 'but it's a bit worrying that his apparent financial problems may be getting to him. Nobody likes living with the sense of insecurity it can bring.'

'I wonder how long the lunchtime drinking has been going on?' mused Day.

'I don't really know him well enough to say,' replied James. 'I don't go into pubs in the daytime as a general rule so would be very unlikely to bump into him as we have today.'

'With his business in such a frail condition he needs to be in control of all his faculties,' said Day.

They sipped at their drinks. 'At least I was expecting this one to be cold!' smiled James, making sure the landlord was out of earshot.

'Have we ever looked into the accounts of Kemp and Company?' asked Day, sensing that this might be a case which could prove to be of interest to the department.

'I have no idea, but now is not the right time to think about it,' replied James. 'We have just engaged in sociable conversation in a public house with a man we both knew previously. What has been said here should be erased from your mind from a professional point of view.

'Let's talk about first thoughts after our meeting with Mortimer and his adviser.'

'Regardless of the informer's letter, I don't think there's any doubt that we need to call in his accounting records and investigate further,' said Day. 'The more we learned about the conduct of the business, the more the questions arose. We need to consider the return to financial viability after the fire and find out how he managed to get back on his feet so quickly.

'He says no insurance proceeds were received for the loss of his stock of vehicles in the fire but, if this was the case, where did the funds come from to get him started again? Money must have been brought in from somewhere to acquire more stock. Was cash borrowed from his bank or was there another source? Did he have reserves of his own and, if so, how did they accumulate and where were they kept? A careful study of the bank statements would be essential. He says there's only one account.'

'I don't doubt there are aspects which might need further explanation,' said James, 'but this has been a very difficult time for him. Age is slowing him down and the fire must have been a huge blow, both financially and to his confidence. His tax returns show no investment income which suggests that he has no savings in an interest-bearing account. He's never claimed tax relief on pension contributions so the chances are he's made no provision for an annuity when he retires. The implication is that whatever profit he's made has been either spent or put back into the business. I can understand that he might wish to continue working so that he has something to occupy himself, but illness or infirmity could bring it all to an end.

'I am interested by the role of the lady we met named Ruth. Without being unkind to Mortimer, she seems to be from a totally different background. The way she presents herself suggests she cannot always have lived in surroundings like this. I wonder how she came to be here. Her role is not exactly central to what we are investigating but her story may form a relevant part of the overall picture.'

'Nothing to do with the fact that she is an attractive lady?' enquired Brian, with a mischievous grin. James offered no reply.

'Given that Mortimer doesn't own the property, his personal asset value must be negligible unless, of course, there is something we don't know,' said James.

'Unless there's an ingenious concealment, everything about his way of life suggests a straitened existence. There's evidence everywhere of a lack of essential maintenance.'

'I understand what you're saying, James,' responded Day, 'but this could be the classic situation where an individual simply does not spend on anything but the bare necessities of life and takes pleasure from hoarding what he gathers in the course of his trade. In its most acute form it can amount to just not wanting anyone else to benefit from the money accumulated, including the Inland Revenue.

'The circumstances demand that a close investigation should be carried out.'

'I respect your view,' said James, 'but I would not wish to be too hard on a man who is in poor health. Look, let's allow it all to sink in and decide upon the next move another time.'

The walkers got up and left, calling a cheery goodbye as they went. The man behind the bar looked first at the clock behind him and then at James and Day, who were now the only two remaining customers.

'As you well know, we are judged by the amount of tax we collect based on our success in investigation cases,' replied Day. 'We get little credit if the return on our efforts is relatively small. A decision needs to be made early on as to whether the estimated yield would be worthwhile in terms of the time it takes to bring matters to a conclusion.'

It was becoming clear to James that the new man would be uncompromising in his approach towards those who might not be paying their full share of tax.

'How are you settling in at the office?' asked James, ready for a change of topic.

'When I was informed that I was being transferred to the South West, I wasn't given any particular reason. Nor was there an indication of how long the posting would last. I decided not to ask too many questions and just keep my head down and wait to see how it would unfold.

'However, I continue to speculate about why this has happened. To the best of my knowledge, I have not blotted my copybook, so it would not just be a case of putting me out to graze, as it were.

'I can only conclude that it must be down to a requirement to adjust the balance at your office. As far as I know, I am not a straight replacement for someone who has moved on so it could just represent a planned increase in the complement of investigation staff.

'I was called in by the Head of Personnel following my

last annual appraisal interview a couple of months ago. Without blowing my own trumpet, I received a high rating for my work over the previous twelve months. During that period, I had been engaged in investigation work of the kind we've been working on today.

'I don't need to tell you that we are rated under a long-established points system. Our scores are based on additional tax found as a result of our efforts.

'There were six investigation Inspectors in the office where I was employed and I was rated top. Reading between the lines, I got the impression that if I continue in the same way there could be another move up the ladder. So I am puzzled why coming here is regarded as a positive career step.'

'I can understand that you're bemused,' replied James, 'and I also find it difficult to understand the philosophy of a system which considers it a good idea to keep people in the dark. It may change in time but for the present we need to accept it and make the best of it.

'I think it's pretty clear that something is considered to be lacking in the Hemport office and that you have been identified as someone who can redress the balance. You should take that as a compliment and it's an opportunity for you to grow your experience in an environment very different to what you have been used to.'

The man behind the bar had left his post and was moving towards the exit with a set of keys in his hand. He shook them so that the remaining two customers would be aware of his intentions.

James and Brian day left quietly leaving the door bell tinkling behind them.

IV

It was Saturday and the day of the planned visit to the Lower Barton racing stables of Charles Edgcumbe.

The Southern Pride syndicate had been invited to inspect the facilities at the stables and watch their horse at work. For James, it was the first time he had visited a racing establishment and he looked forward keenly to the experience. He could never have imagined he would become an owner, albeit of just a small share, but dividing the costs with others had made it possible.

The early experiences had been a little disappointing. Charles had assembled the ownership syndicate and bought their horse at the Doncaster Sales. It had run in some flat races for a previous trainer but the conformation and breeding of the horse suggested to Charles that it had the scope to jump obstacles and make a steeplechaser.

The syndicate followed their trainer's advice and the horse was registered in their name. The process of serious training commenced and the early signs were promising. When the time seemed right, Southern Pride was entered to run in a novice hurdle race over three miles at Newbury. The horse ran well enough in a field of ten horses but weakened in the home straight. It was pulled up by the jockey who had judged there was no prospect of winning or being placed in the first three. It was reassuring, however, that the horse had shown an aptitude for jumping, the essential requirement for National Hunt racing.

They hoped that the experience might benefit Southern Pride and that he would fare better in his next race. However, the pattern of the second race was remarkably similar to the first. After running well for a long way, the horse tired towards the end and, as before, was pulled up well before the finish.

Today, the owners would be keen to find out whether Charles may have got to the bottom of whatever was causing the horse to flag in the latter stages of its races.

James turned his car into the long straight drive leading to Lower Barton. The approach to the property was lined with young silver birch trees and flanked on either side by white post and rail fencing. Mares with foals grazed contentedly in the bordering paddocks. To his left and in the distance was a wide swathe of mown turf rising towards the highest point in view. This three furlong stretch was where the horses would work every day to build their strength and fitness.

The carriage drive terminated in a turning circle outside the entrance porch to an imposing farmhouse. James noted that it had been constructed from the prized pale stone from nearby Beer quarries.

Several vehicles were lined up in a neat row and James parked alongside them. To the right of the house, the stable block with its tall clock tower was in sight.

Charles Edgcumbe would be considered a minor trainer on account of the relatively small number of horses in his charge and the unspectacular success in his career to date. There are two codes of racing. One is dedicated to racing "on the flat" with no obstacles to jump. The other category is

National Hunt racing when horses are required to clear either fences or smaller obstacles known as hurdles. Charles trained only jumping horses for that was his real interest.

The origins of the sport are rooted in the hunting field. The centuries-old country pursuit led to the breeding of horses which can gallop, jump and cope with the challenge of the obstacles which present themselves in the course of the chase. It was a natural progression that hunting folk would match their steeds in cross-country races which became known as steeplechases. Racing from one church steeple to another was a convenient way to mark the beginning and end of a race.

The sport evolved into point-to-point racing, an annual fund-raising jamboree conducted by the supporters of the hunt. This amateur sport became well organised and popular, giving people from all walks of life the opportunity to enjoy a sporting day out in rural surroundings.

It would be more correct to refer to the trainer as The Honourable Charles Edgcumbe for his late father was Sir Edward Edgcumbe, Baronet, who had died three years previously. Charles avoided using his formal title considering it to be outdated and pretentious.

Sir Edward had been a man of his time, disinclined to modify his ways to adapt to the changing world. He was a countryman first and foremost. An agreeable and thoughtful lord of the manor, he behaved dutifully towards the tenants resident on his estate. He recognised his duty to his staff and refused to be overly influenced by commercial pressures. As the output of the ageing workforce and their dated equipment diminished, so did the productivity of the agricultural enterprises conducted on the estate, but this did not persuade their patron to change his approach. What mattered was loyalty and continuity.

The level of maintenance of the house, the cottages and the agricultural buildings fell in line with decreasing profits and the depletion of the cash reserves. Sir Edward sailed on like a mariner in a leaking boat but always with the confidence that the rocks would be avoided.

Sir Edward's main asset had been the 200-acre estate comprising the Manor House with its sweeping parkland, tenanted cottages, and including Lower Barton Farm with its 80 acres. The Capital Transfer Tax payable on his death came to far more than could be met out of what cash was left in the bank. The only way to fund payment of this liability was to dispose of assets so there was no alternative but to break up the estate. The main house and most of the acreage had to be sold.

The disposals were painful given that the property had been in the family for generations but it was the only way. When tenants retired, they had been allowed to remain in their cottages as reward for their loyalty and dedication, a right that would continue for their lifetimes.

Having cleared the death duties out of the sales of property, both Charles and his sister had been left with something to shore up their futures. Lower Barton Farm remained intact and passed to Charles. His sister Gloria received a legacy of equal value out of what remained.

For Charles, this meant the opportunity to start up his training operation and he felt happy enough that the business had, to date, broken even. Recruiting enough paying owners to establish financial viability is a difficult process and it was an achievement to have got this far. Given the slice of luck that all risk-takers need, he was hopeful that he would become established over the coming years.

Both Charles and Gloria had been immersed in country sports since they could walk. Dad had loved field sports and participated with rare skill. It was a natural progression for his children to follow in his footsteps. Gloria became an accomplished horsewoman and, riding side-saddle, was a graceful sight in the hunting field. She had achieved considerable success in pony club events before progressing to three-day eventing.

Charles was a horseman first and foremost and gained a reputation as a fearless rider over all types of country. As an amateur rider, he had won numerous steeplechases including prestigious events at leading meetings such as Cheltenham and Sandown. Jumping large obstacles at speed requires bravery on the part of both horse and rider as well as a large measure of mutual trust. Charles would never drive his mount too hard and would ask for no more if he felt the horse had become exhausted – one fence too many could be the downfall of one or both of them. Should a horse suffer an injury, ample time would always be allowed for its full recovery.

Charles's approach to the welfare of the horse was, sadly, not reflected throughout the racing industry. Some horses were pushed harder than they should have been as owners became impatient for returns on their investment.

His ambitions were rooted in the National Hunt game. Now that his riding days were behind him, it was a natural progression of his lifetime interest that he should become a trainer of racehorses. It was the inheritance of the farm that created the opportunity for him to practise his chosen profession. He knew only too well that his nascent training operation would be unable to bear the cost of renting a ready-made establishment.

Though like his father in many ways, he had grown aware of the need to make decisions based on sound commercial principles. His previous salary as Estate Manager ended with his father's death and his only future source of income would be whatever profit could be made from training. What made the future challenging, and perhaps more exciting, was that the clock was ticking and there was only so much time to make a success of it. Cash reserves were limited and the bank account needed to remain firmly in the black.

James had pulled on the handbrake and removed his seat belt when another car drew alongside him. It was Miles in his red car.

Both emerged and Miles was his usual cheerful self. 'Here we are then,' he chirped. 'Looking forward to this. Anyone else here?'

'Let's go and see,' said James, and they walked together through tall open gates into a rectangular cobbled yard surrounded by rows of individual stables. Lads and lasses wearing their full riding gear and protective helmets were busy preparing their steeds for exercise. The horses looked magnificent in their shining coats, a reminder of just how much effort went into their preparation.

The stable staff chorused an enthusiastic welcome to the two arrivals. They knew only too well that owners were the lifeblood of the racing stable and that their wages were dependent on the training fees they paid.

As the pair surveyed the scene, Charles arrived alongside

them. 'Good morning and welcome. Glad you could come and I hope you'll find it interesting. I did invite all the syndicate members but you seem to be the only ones who could make it. We can arrange something for another day with the others.'

Charles called across the yard. 'First six to the bottom of the gallop, please – you know the order.' The staff responded with immediacy – clearly Charles commanded their respect. He exuded an infectious energy which transmitted not only to his employees in the yard but to all who shared his company.

Turning to his owners, Charles explained that they would go to the top of the gallops in his four-wheel drive vehicle and watch the horses come up. 'They'll work in pairs as that allows useful comparisons as to relative performance and progress. I know that neither of you has witnessed this before so we can watch the first couple to see how it works and then follow up with your horse in the second pair.'

The group disembarked at the top of the ridge and gathered together. Two hundred feet up, it was cold and windy and overcoats were buttoned up. Miles soon realised that he was ill-prepared for the weather conditions in just his suit and waistcoat.

Charles drew his binoculars from their case and focused keenly on the starting point below where six horses were wheeling in a wide circle.

'The first pair you will see are what we call selling platers,' said Charles. 'This means that they run in the lowest grade of race. We have concluded that they are not capable of winning anything of a higher standard and there is no point in running them in races in which they would be out of their depth. Placing the horse at an appropriate level is vital if there is to be any chance of success. You won't see these animals at the Cheltenham Festival but for most owners it is the prospect of having a winner that provides the excitement, however lowly the contest.'

Charles raised his arm to signal the first two to come up. Already aware of the order in which they would set off, two riders peeled away from the rest and turned towards the beginning of the gallop, first at the walk and then into a trot. Soon the horses' heads were bobbing as they broke into a canter and for the first stretch they moved side-by-side under the restraint of their riders.

Charles had directed that at half way both horses would be urged to accelerate so that their respective abilities might be compared. At this point, the jockeys became animated and pushed their mounts forward.

'Based on previous performances, there is not much between this pair. The grey horse is four years old, two years younger than the chestnut alongside him. Of the two, I think the grey should have more scope for improvement.'

Having been asked to quicken, the horses bumped together briefly then straightened their paths as the riders asked for more effort.

'How interesting,' commented Charles. 'This is not quite what I had expected. The chestnut horse has moved steadily ahead leaving the grey behind.'

Then, suddenly, and with a shake of the reins from its rider, the grey found a burst of speed the other could not match and went several lengths ahead, a lead that was maintained until the finish.

After looking at his stopwatch, Charles commented. 'The

time was slightly better than average and the margin between them shows that both have improved. The grey horse did rather better but there is greater scope at his age. You see, you need to be a mathematician as well in this game!

'I expect you chaps are feeling the cold so we shall watch yours next and then go down into the warm for a chat.

'I needn't say too much about Southern Pride as you are well aware of what happened in his two previous races but, just to remind you, we've been working on improving the apparent lack of staying power shown in the final furlong or two of his races. With this is mind, we have given him extra road work and today should show whether it has had the required effect.

'My sister, Gloria, is here for the weekend and I have asked her to ride him today. As you know, she has vast experience and I value her judgement.

'We are matching yours with Regal Lord, an experienced handicapper who has had some success of late including a win at Newton Abbot a couple of months ago. I have asked Gloria to tuck your horse in behind Regal Lord and see what he finds when asked to overtake.'

Charles raised his arm once more and the two horses moved towards the start. The riders exchanged words as they set off. Reaching a steady canter, Gloria positioned herself behind the leading horse as planned.

'Now we shall see,' called Charles to James and Miles who were watching with keen anticipation.

The owners had seen the way in which Southern Pride had succumbed tamely in his races and waited to see whether there were indications that the tendency might have been reversed.

The outcome was better than they could have hoped for. At the three-quarter stage, Gloria pulled out her mount and urged the horse to quicken. Southern Pride passed Regal Lord with ease and was several lengths clear at the end.

'That looked pretty good,' said Miles, aiming a broad grin first at the trainer, then towards James.

'Without wanting to appear over-optimistic, it looks as if he's heading in the right direction,' said Charles.

'All trainers would love to be able to guarantee that work on the gallops will be reproduced on the track. We try to get the best from these animals but, like the rest of us, they can have off days. But what we have seen today has been encouraging.'

At that point Gloria arrived, having brought Southern Pride to a halt at the top of the gallop and walked the horse back to join the group of men.

'What did you think?' asked Charles.

'I rode this horse at work once before,' she replied. 'As you can see, he is not blowing too hard and is not at all overheated.

'I think he's a lot fitter than the last time I rode him. I'd say he isn't far off his peak.'

'Thanks Gloria,' said Charles, 'we'll let you get back to the stables.'

Gloria trotted down slowly and Charles and the others watched the way the horse moved.

'He seems relaxed and did that piece of work well,' said Charles. 'We should now reflect on this and come to a decision as to his next run. There's a two mile novice steeplechase at Wincanton in the near future which might be suitable.

'Let's jump into the car and go back down.'

They bumped their way down over the rough grass alongside the gallop. 'Ready for a hot drink?' asked Charles.

'I've nothing else on today and that would be very welcome,' replied James.

'Same here,' said Miles, who was shivering and looking forward to being indoors.

They entered the large and welcoming kitchen of Lower Barton. In the centre was a long pine table surrounded by eight chairs. For James, this was a striking contrast to his own galley-style kitchen with its fitted electric appliances and no room for a table.

Copper pots and pans hung over a wide brick fireplace inside which a large cooking range radiated warmth that filled the room. What seemed to be the complete equine history of the family covered the walls and shelves around the room; silver-framed photographs, medals, rosettes, certificates and trophies.

'Sit wherever you like chaps. The kettle's already boiled so it won't take long to brew up. Do you take milk and sugar with your coffee?'

James took it white and without sugar. Miles's preference was for milk plus "enough sugar to make the spoon stand up".

Moving across to the tall sash window looking over the yard outside, James viewed the bustling activity. Grooms were leading horses which had completed their morning's work back to their stables while others were being readied for their turn on the gallops. Some of the lads and lasses were heading for breakfast in the stable canteen in the far corner of the yard, always served after the first lot had been exercised.

'I'm glad to have the chance to chat,' said Charles, as he reached the coffee jar from a shelf.

'In a syndicate,' he continued, 'there can be people from all walks of life from shop-floor workers to factory owners, but all share a common interest and can enjoy being part of a dream. Most are totally philosophical about the idea of financial gain and know that only a very few make a return on the investment. As long as the cost of their participation is limited to their subscription, most people are happy to enjoy the involvement and a day at the races. I always spell out the risks and pitfalls at the beginning. However, our aim is success and the excitement it generates if we can bring in a bit of prize money.

'I am pleased that you, Miles, are part of the group given the long association between Dad and your late father. They got on very well and Dad always consulted him about anything to do with finance and property. They often took a glass or two in this very kitchen while discussing politics, the countryside and pretty well everything else under the sun.'

'I'm proud of what Dad achieved. He's a hard act to follow but I'm doing my best,' said Miles. 'It's a long time ago but I can just remember sitting with Dad in this kitchen and listening to the chatter. I had no idea what it all meant but it sounded very important!'

'I've known Miles for over two years,' said James. 'He helped me to find somewhere to live when I relocated to Hemport from another office. It's a world apart from this wonderful house but I don't need much space.'

'Are you married?' enquired Charles.

'No,' said James, hesitatingly. 'I was… but… I'm afraid that I lost her. It was a sudden and short illness.'

'I see… I am sorry,' said Charles turning to the stove and pouring the steaming water from the kettle into the coffee press.

Charles brought the pot to the table with three cups and saucers.

'Wonderful aroma,' said James, lifting the reviving concoction to his lips.

'Ethiopian Sidamo,' said Charles. 'We are fortunate around here in having a number of artisan suppliers and one of them blends and roasts coffee. This delights me as I am a bit of a connoisseur and this is as fine as it gets.'

'By the way, Charles,' said Miles, 'I'll take the opportunity to mention that my business is now able to offer investment advice as well as the usual house buying and selling services. This is something which, to the best of my knowledge, has not previously been available in Hemport so if it's of any interest to you or your acquaintances I'll be glad to help. Perhaps I could drop in a few of my brochures when they're ready.'

'Yes, that's fine,' responded Charles. 'I'll certainly bear it in mind.'

'You mentioned a race at Wincanton,' said James.

Gloria entered, still wearing her riding gear and carrying her protective helmet. An elastic band held her long fair hair in a pony tail.

'I smelt the coffee from the other side of the yard,' she said, with a chuckle. 'I'm free for a bit until my next one comes up and I know your brew will be a cut above that instant stuff they dish out in the canteen.'

Gloria puffed out her cheeks, dropped herself into a chair and wriggled out of her padded jacket, her round and even features glowing with the freshness of the morning air. Her frame was amply covered but not overweight. She flicked her bright brown eyes between the two visitors.

Charles brought another cup from the dresser and filled it.

Gloria's life had taken a very different course from his. She was artistic and developed her skills in the fashion quarter of London's West End where she benefited from the tutelage of some of the leading exponents of her art. Rising rapidly, she soon gained a reputation in the design world. Her fresh and uncluttered ideas were a revelation and her standing grew to the point where her services were in strong demand. The inheritance from her late father had enabled her to break free and establish her own studio. She grew and thrived under her new-found independent status.

Her collaborator in this enterprise was Gary with whom she had worked since she first entered the industry. Her late father Sir Edward was uneasy with those of a Bohemian persuasion and would be unlikely to have approved of this unconventional young man.

As time went by, Gloria allowed Gary to share her flat in Bloomsbury. Their co-habitation was a matter of convenience and most months Gary would come up with his half of the rent. Despite his unreliable ways she had something of a soft spot for him.

'As you might expect, Gloria, we have been talking about Southern Pride and maybe you could tell us how you found him today,' said Charles as he filled her cup. 'You're not given to exaggeration but I think you were quite pleased with that performance.'

Gloria looked at James who was waiting interestedly for her comments. For a few moments they held one another's gaze and a faint smile crossed her lips. James returned the smile shyly before reaching for his coffee.

'It was pretty good,' said Gloria, stretching for the biscuit barrel in the centre of the table. 'It comes down to whether this improvement can be maintained, but I do have a couple of comments to make.

'First, the ground today is not as soft as when I rode the horse previously and I think that this accounts, at least in part, for its better performance. He could be even better on a sounder surface.

'The second thing to say is that a strong rider is necessary if we are to see the best of him. I have already mentioned this to you, Charles.'

'I was about to raise this with James and Miles,' replied Charles. 'In its first two races, the horse was ridden by our amateur rider, Sam Fitzherbert. Sam is a good horseman but, as he would admit himself, he's a bit short on racing experience. I suggest that we consider recruiting the services of Jeff Cameron for the next outing.'

'The owners probably know already that Jeff has a chequered history,' said Gloria. 'Some sections of the press seem to enjoy making him a scapegoat.

'I remember the newspaper headlines following that day at Plumpton when he came off at the last fence a little too easily for the liking of the stewards. Matters were not helped by the fact that the horse that won had been heavily gambled on just before the off.'

'It is true that the circumstances were persuasive,' said Charles. 'But it was all too easy for the various vested interests to arrive at the conclusion they did without giving sufficient consideration to whether there might have been a reasonable explanation. When he was interviewed by the stewards afterwards, Jeff told them his saddle had slipped and that this caused him to slide off. The fact that the eventual winner had been heavily supported in the betting market could have been just a coincidence. His explanation was not accepted but how much were the stewards influenced by his perceived reputation and the possible outcry from the betting pubic had they found otherwise?

'I would prefer to speak as I've found,' continued Charles. 'Although Jeff has not ridden for us on many occasions, he has never failed to do what was asked of him. I recall that when Dad had the odd horse in training he would often turn to Jeff when a forceful ride was needed.'

Cameron was a man who never used two words when one would do and came across to some as gruff and irritable. Since a rash of uncomplimentary newspaper articles a few years previously, he wouldn't speak to the press. His numerous brushes with the racing authorities only increased his distrust of the people in charge.

He had been suspended on several occasions for failing to ride out a horse to the best of its ability. The racecourse stewards were quick to react to any suggestion of non-trying in order to protect themselves from the ire of punters who may have felt they had not had a fair run for their money. Jeff had disputed all such charges but had been branded as one to be watched.

Strong rider he was, but it was not his way to drive a horse when experience told him that the pounding heart beneath him had no more to give. Better to wait for another day than to risk souring the animal such that its appetite for racing would be lost for ever. He knew this and so did other true horsemen, but the establishment needed to justify its existence.

Cameron had been retained by a leading Lambourn

stable in his youth and achieved notable success. The trainer by whom he was employed was as economical with conversation as he was but there was a strong mutual respect that did not need to be expressed in words. Their prolific partnership spoke for itself.

The end of his career would not now be far ahead as age and the catalogue of injuries sustained over the years took its toll. At his peak, he owned a large house with land near the Berkshire Downs which he shared with his wife. Amid tales of excesses and misbehaviour, that way of life dissolved and now he lived alone in a rented cottage near Swindon.

Yet his reputation as a fearless rider had never diminished and he enjoyed the respect and admiration of his fellow professionals as a man who rode with style and determination. His courage was not in question and he would never admit to the pain he lived through each day. The need to maintain a low riding weight meant a strict diet and created unnatural demands on his body.

Knowing that the career of a jump jockey was of limited length, most tried to make provision for life after riding. Some would move on to training but the irascible Jeff might fall short in the public relations department when it came to keeping demanding owners happy. Whatever ideas he had in mind were kept to himself but he would need an income from somewhere. He was unlikely to have made prudent provision for his retirement out of the periods when he earned well.

'It seems to me that the real point is that we, as owners – albeit minor ones – must trust the judgement of the trainer,' said James. 'Without that confidence there is no basis for the relationship. Your advice and expertise is what we pay for and I say that if you believe that Cameron is the right man then that's what we should do. I am sure the others would say the same.'

'I am all for giving someone the benefit of the doubt,' said Miles. 'He sounds the right man for us.'

'I'll ask Jeff to come down and ride out for us,' continued Charles. 'I haven't seen him for some time and it would be an opportunity to renew our acquaintance. I would value his opinion on two or three of our horses, but mainly Southern Pride. I doubt he's as busy as he once was and would probably appreciate a day's work. After that, a decision can be made as to whether he should ride your horse in its next race.'

The door handle turned and Gary entered. Gloria's associate had travelled down with her from London for the outing.

'Morning all – hope this isn't a bad time!' he said brightly, glancing at those assembled around the table. 'Don't think I know you two,' he continued, glancing from Miles to James.

He was slimmer and shorter than Gloria and wore a boldly checked shirt outside worn and faded jeans. His shoes were splattered with paint of various colours.

'It's just I was wondering if it might be time to think about heading back to cityville,' he continued. 'This country air has been cool but maybe it's time to refill with some smog.' He issued a deep cough as if to reinforce his point.

Not wishing to disconcert his sister, Charles veiled his disapproval of Gary. His father might have been more direct and he could hear him saying, 'Layabout – wouldn't put anything past him!' Charles kept his thoughts to himself if only to keep the peace but would have had more to say if he felt that Gloria was being taken advantage of.

Gloria had explained to Charles that her relationship with Gary was entirely Platonic. Through their long time spent together, both at their workplace and the place of residence they shared, a bond of convenience had been shaped. This had developed into a way of life that was easier to maintain than deconstruct.

Gloria put up with Gary's failings and accepted that his contribution to the domestic arrangements, practical or financial, could not be relied upon. What money came his way seemed to quickly disappear on what he considered to be the essentials of life which, in his case, was inexpensive wine from the corner off-licence and the funding for his regular trips to the betting office.

Friends expressed concern to Gloria that this arrangement with Gary was not in her long-term interests. She would reply that she was "not exactly being chased up and down the King's Road by ardent admirers".

'What have you been doing Gary?' enquired Gloria.

'I've just had a wander around the yard and they allowed me into the stable canteen for a hot drink and a wonderful bacon sandwich. Your staff are very friendly, Charles, but I wish they'd be a bit more forthcoming with the tips. I'm fed up with funding my local bookie's pension scheme. I could do with a nice winner!

'I heard that you were thinking of giving a ride to that bent jockey Cameron,' Gary went on.

Charles took a few moments to withhold the annoyance that rose within him and managed to quell the urge to respond with the most frank disapproval of Gary's thoughtless remarks.

'The staff must have taken to you,' said Charles, remaining composed, 'otherwise they would never have let you into their canteen. Perhaps they found you interesting.'

'I think they did and they liked hearing about what I do which is in complete contrast to their work,' replied Gary.

'They loved the idea of flexible hours and a lot less of them.'

'I don't think getting up earlier would do you any harm,' said Gloria.

'Let me remind you that my people are here because they want to be,' added Charles, 'and they enjoy what they do.

'This is a labour intensive operation, as a glance outside will tell you.

The work they carry out is vital to the industry. Most trainers would like to be able to pay their staff more but the rate of pay is linked directly to the amount of money that filters down to this level of the training operation. We can only hope this will improve in time but, for the moment, all we can do is concentrate on providing them with a thorough training and a good grounding for their futures. A number will move on to become professional jockeys and some may branch into other areas of the equestrian world. We do the best we can and never underestimate what a valuable job they do.

'I won't ask the number of hours that you work each week but what is the nature of your gainful employment at the moment?' enquired Charles, fearing that this man may have been spreading his questionable and disruptive philosophy among his employees.

By now, Gary had picked up a mug from the draining board next to the sink and was helping himself to coffee from the press on the table. 'Any milk anywhere?' he asked. The enquiry drew no response and he went to the fridge to find some.

'Sorry, Charles, you asked me about my work,' said Gary with his back turned to the large window.

'A lot of what I do is investment for the future. If, for example, I knock up a piece of pottery, it's quite likely that it won't sell just like that,' snapping his fingers. 'But what I make is an advertisement for my skills so buyers can see the quality of what I do. It's the same if I paint a picture. OK, nobody wants it at the moment but I smack it on the wall and wait to see what happens. Someone may see it and want some more the same.

'Think of any kind of industry,' he continued. 'Before the money can start coming in there has to be investment in whatever it is – materials, marketing, advertising and so on. After that, you need to wait for the returns – basic economics.'

'I suppose you would consider yourself to be in the research and development phase,' said a doubtful Charles, trying to avoid becoming too searching with his enquiries.

'Let's just say that at the moment I am giving away more than I sell,' replied Gary. 'Most of what comes in gets ploughed back into stock.'

Gloria interrupted. 'Gary's sort of doing his best to get things off the ground but it takes time. I suppose we all need a slice of luck in life – it's just that he seems to need it more than most.'

Gary picked up a newspaper from the table and sat in an armchair near the hearth.

'Do you have an interest in art, James?' asked Gloria.

'I can't claim any kind of expertise but I do like the work of the Art Deco period. The style appeals to my nature, possibly related to my interest in architecture and my liking for the balanced and symmetrical. I may be missing out on something but I find it a bit difficult to come to terms with the abstract. In painting, I love the wonderful precision of still life, particularly the work of Paul Cézanne.'

'Do you know, Gary,' said Charles, with a smile, 'it is no secret that some of the great creative people of the past have only managed to project their work with the aid of a mentor or benefactor who can provide financial or moral support. Perhaps you could find someone like that.'

'Did you hear that, Gary?' said Gloria, turning to him. 'You could do with an injection of capital, couldn't you? It's all very well trying to be creative but there has to be a practical side if you are going to make it work. It's no good bashing away unless you are targeting a particular market. The bills have to be paid.'

Gary was sensitive to criticism and buried himself behind his newspaper to shelter from the mounting wave of scepticism.

'Does your work ever take you to London, James,' enquired Gloria after silence had prevailed for a minute or two.

James replied that he had not been to London for over two years and then it was to watch a cricket match at Lords for the day. The unfortunate loss of his wife had sent him into periods of contemplation and adjustment from which he had yet to fully emerge. His challenging work as a tax inspector had helped to relieve the tendency to dwell on what had been a distressing period but it was taking time.

'I need to go to London for a training lecture in the not too distant future and I'm hoping there might be a little spare time to look around,' replied James.

'You may find it amusing to visit the arty quarter where I live. Actually, there's a local man of French origin who makes furniture in the style of the period that interests you. I agree with you that there is great appeal and simplicity in the Art Deco genre.'

Gloria could not help liking James. His methodical ways and clear thinking were a contrast to the wayward behaviour of some of the types she came up against in her profession. She saw herself as somewhere in between and, although revelling in the untrammelled life of the artist, the discipline of her upbringing and schooling had not left her and she was uncomfortable with the disorganised.

'Thank you,' said James, 'I'd like that. Perhaps I could let you know when the opportunity arises.

'It's time I got on my way,' said James. 'It was really informative to see everything at first hand and very many thanks for your hospitality.'

Miles rose and said that it was also time for him to leave and check things out at the office. 'Thanks for an interesting time – look forward to seeing you at the races.'

'Glad you both enjoyed it,' said Charles, 'and I'll be in touch shortly about future plans.'

James drove off turning over in his mind the events of the morning and the future prospects for Southern Pride.

V

James had arrived at his desk to make ready for the day's work.

He looked at the pile of files awaiting his attention and wondered where to start. All were bulging with correspondence and calculations.

Finding the motivation to get started difficult, he leaned back in his chair and looked around his office. The walls of the small room were unadorned but for the calendar of the Civil Service Benevolent Society on the wall opposite him. There was nothing much else but for his desk and chair, a grey filing cabinet and green carpet tiles. The bright ochre paint on the walls was presumably chosen with the objective of brightening the dimly-lit room and lifting the spirit of the occupant. Set high to his right was a small window through which a small triangular patch of sky was visible above the red brick wall of the building next door.

There was a tap on his door and a head appeared wearing a floral turban. 'Coffee or tea, Mr Stedman?' enquired the tea lady. 'Nothing today, thank you, Beryl.'

Only if he were desperate could he manage to drink the powdered coffee mixed with hot water from the urn perched on the top of Beryl's trolley. The tea could be more palatable but only if taken towards the beginning of her round and before it had become stewed and tepid in the large aluminium pot. The time of her arrival told him that he was one of the last in line today.

Gathering his thoughts, he loosened his tie and pulled down a file from the top of the pile in front of him. He had begun leafing through the papers to remind himself of the history of the case when the telephone rang. It was Arthur Greenfield, the District Inspector.

In the hierarchy of the Tax Office, the District Inspector was at the top of the tree. Greenfield was usually referred to by the staff as "the boss" or the "DI".

'I don't know how busy you are, James, but when would be a good time for you to come to see me today?'

'Early afternoon would be best for me,' replied James, thinking that he would need time to get himself into gear after his slow start. 'What about two o'clock?'

That agreed, James considered how to pass the intervening hours. His concentration was lacking and an infusion of caffeine was the answer. Nothing suitable having been available from the trolley, he decided to go to Margaret's coffee shop in the High Street where a proper cup would be guaranteed.

He looked out to see a herring gull wheeling in the clear blue sky. It would be cold but not wet. He donned his overcoat and left his room.

As he passed through the main office on the way to the swinging exit door, he called to a colleague that he would be away from his desk for an hour or so if anyone was looking for him.

He went down the narrow steps and into the domed entrance hall. Arched over the large circular space was an ornately decorated plaster ceiling, the aesthetics of which had not been continued into other areas of the building. To one side was a long desk manned by two uniformed ladies.

In front of this were three rows of tubular metal chairs for those waiting to be called to their appointment.

One of these rows was reserved for the specific use of "State Benefit Claimants". In winter, the unemployment levels in Hemport rose significantly as the seasonal work in leisure and agriculture dried up.

James tucked his scarf inside his overcoat and hurried through the hall towards the exit. Turning right outside, he made his way downhill into the face of a stiff westerly breeze.

Finding a gap in the traffic, he crossed the busy road towards Margaret's Coffee House. Miles Kemp was just ahead of him and making for the revolving doors into The Plough. He did not trouble to call to his acquaintance who was no doubt hurrying to meet someone to discuss business matters.

Outside the café, he peered through the steamed and dimpled glass windows. It was busier than he would have liked but his cup of coffee beckoned and today he would share a table if he had to.

Once inside, he joined a short queue in front of a wooden pedestal attached to which was a notice requesting customers to "Wait here to be seated". Looking about, there was not one vacant table. A few were occupied by just a single person. He was not really in the mood to strike up polite conversation with a stranger but his need was great and he waited regardless.

When his turn arrived, an elderly waitress in a black uniform with starched white cuffs and collar came forward and asked him to follow her towards a table in a bay window overlooking the High Street.

'Would you like to sit here, sir?' said the waitress, a direction more than a question. She pointed to a chair at a table occupied by one other person who was hidden behind a wide open copy of the Daily Telegraph. Having no choice he nodded his agreement.

Within seconds of taking his seat, the waitress handed him a small menu card and left. As he was examining the list of what was on offer, the newspaper dropped to reveal its reader who James recognised immediately as the lady known as Ruth who had admitted him and Brian Day at Deepdene Farm. Her clothing was different from the everyday apparel she wore then but it was the same face he had pictured many times since. Today, her soft brown hair was tied back revealing small pearl earrings.

The lady looked at James and smiled politely before returning to her reading matter.

'I hope you don't mind my sitting here,' said James, nervously, 'but I'm afraid there was no choice but to share a table. I suppose the waitress might have asked you whether you were agreeable to my joining you rather than just asking me the question, but I expect that's the way they do it. Perhaps there's a sign somewhere saying that sitting somewhere does not give exclusive rights to all the chairs at the table! In some places, people are not expected to have to share a table with someone they don't know but it's a busy time of day and they want to cater for as many as possible, I suppose.'

Thrown off balance by this remarkable coincidence, he was beginning to ramble and he knew it. He had thought about this lady many times since that first brief meeting and could hardly believe that she was here, sitting opposite him.

He knew her name which had been mentioned at the meeting at Deepene but he wanted to know more – her past, her thoughts… her life.

'That's quite all right,' said the lady, smiling. 'I know the way it works here and it's just something that one accepts. Anyway, I've had some interesting conversations as a result of getting pitched in with someone I'd never met before!'

The waitress returned and he requested a small pot of coffee with some warm milk.

On the table in front of his unexpected companion was a china teapot with a matching rose-patterned china cup and saucer.

She placed her folded newspaper on top of her gloves which rested beside her on the white tablecloth. There were no rings on her slim fingers.

James gathered himself and spoke. 'My immediate thought was that I had seen you somewhere before and now it has come to me,' he said, not being quite truthful. 'I came with a colleague to the house of a Mr Mortimer at Deepdene Farm a short time ago and I'm sure it was you who opened the door to us.'

She listened with her head tilted slightly and then looked about for a few moments in an effort to recall the meeting James was referring to.

'I hope this doesn't seem rude,' said the lady, 'but I'm afraid I can't bring it to mind. I do live at Deepdene but people are always coming and going and I'm usually the one who answers the door. It often happens when I'm busy with something else so I often find myself hurrying visitors along to where they need to go – usually Mr Mortimer's workshop – so that I can get back to whatever I'm doing.'

'I wonder if it might help you to remember if I mention that the front door was stuck. You were unable to open it and I had to give it a shove to free it. You were just inside when I burst in and almost knocked you over!' James smiled and waited, hopeful that this might spark her recollection.

'I'm afraid it doesn't,' said the lady. 'I can't count the number of occasions I've been almost squashed behind that door. I have mentioned it to Mr Mortimer but nothing ever happens. If it goes on much longer I shall probably put up a sign asking people not to use it at all. Someone could get hurt if they trip over while trying to push their way in.'

James felt some disappointment that he had not made sufficient of an impression on the lady for her to remember him but, at the same time, felt some relief that he would not need to engage in a discussion about the specific reason for his call.

James was by no means shy of revealing the nature of his occupation but did not make a point of it in social conversation. Reasonable people took the view that his work was an essential and valuable function in ensuring that individuals paid the amount of tax they should, but there would always be the misguided element who saw the Inland Revenue as the enemy.

The waitress returned and placed on the table a small silver coffee pot with a cup and saucer and a jug of milk.

'No, please don't apologise,' said James. 'I wouldn't have expected you to remember me. It's just that the memory of that day is still quite clear in my mind. There was flour on your hands and a wonderful smell of fresh baked bread as we followed you through the kitchen.'

'Baking bread is a bit hit or miss but I must have

managed to put together a reasonable mix on that day.'

James observed that she was coming near to finishing her tea and hoped she would not leave immediately. He poured some coffee and searched for words to maintain the conversation.

'Do you come to town regularly?' he asked.

'I don't have a car,' the lady replied, 'not that I particularly need one as there's a pretty reliable bus service into town from where I live. The buses stop running at about seven so it's more difficult if I want to come in after that, but there's a good local taxi firm that helps me out in the evening or if I need to get to the railway station.'

When other railway lines were lost two decades earlier, Hemport had retained its station on the Exeter to Waterloo line, a further attraction to those considering relocation to the area.

'And you work here in town?' enquired the lady. 'Yes,' said James. 'I work at the government offices at the top of the town. It doesn't sound very exciting does it? – but it has its moments!'

'I am sure that a lot of important work goes on there,' she replied with a smile. 'I need to go there occasionally and have always found the staff helpful and friendly.'

She looked at her watch and turned to recover her jacket from the back of her chair. James sprang to assist and helped guide her arms into the sleeves. There was the smell of summer he had first caught at Deepdene.

'Thank you – goodbye,' she said cheerfully as she moved towards the till near the door.

James murmured that he hoped they might meet again but thought that she had probably not heard. Returning to his seat, he watched as she turned right outside and made her way along the pavement.

After refilling his cup, he noticed that the lady had left her newspaper on the table. No point in trying to chase after her. She might not want it and could be anywhere by now.

He picked up the newspaper to look at the headlines and saw a pair of black leather gloves underneath. He held them for a while before folding them and placing them in his overcoat pocket.

As he drank the last of his coffee, he reflected on the chance meeting, so soon after their first encounter. He wished there had been time to introduce himself properly.

It was time for him to return to the office. He hadn't really got started with his work that morning and later there would be the meeting with the DI.

James returned to the government building and saw that the queue for the State Benefits desk was no shorter than when he had left. The majority of those waiting were young people, perhaps not long out of school. The rapid development in the area had created the need for more training schemes for those leaving education and the local authority had been slow to react.

Along the narrow corridor leading towards his office, James met Brian Day coming in the opposite direction.

'Ah, James, could we have a word?' he asked.

'I don't have too much time but I can spare a few minutes. Your place or mine?' asked James.

'My office is just here,' said Day, motioning towards the door alongside him.

His office was identical to the one in which James had been billeted, the only difference being the colour of the walls. That in itself was unusual as there were economies of scale to be gained from the use of the same paint throughout. James guessed that a previous occupant had, perhaps on the grounds of an allergy to bright yellow, appealed successfully for magnolia.

His mind was elsewhere but he took a chair in the corner of Day's office and waited for him to speak. From where he sat he could see that the view from the window in this room differed from his own only in that there were drainpipes on the facing brick wall outside.

'I needn't keep you long, James,' commenced Day, 'but I wanted to tell you about a conversation I've had this morning with the DI. He called me in to talk about the plans for my immediate future and said I should now be sufficiently acquainted with procedures here to manage my own portfolio. He asked me to take over a number of cases including Mortimer, the scrap merchant you and I went to see. Obviously, this was a case you started off and we were going to have another chat about it before taking the next step.'

'It's your case now so there's no need for me to be involved any further,' replied James, 'but I'm happy to talk about it if you wish. After the meeting we both attended, you know as much about it as I do, so the timing of the changeover is ideal. You're qualified to take it on from here so the decisions are down to you.

'I think we would probably handle it differently, but we're individuals and that's only to be expected. You have a record of success where you worked before and I'm sure you'll be bringing that experience to what you do here.

'What I will say,' continued James, 'is that my actions would have been influenced by the personal circumstances of the individual. We both know that he is ageing and in poor health. As far as we can tell, he does not have any reserves of cash. He is well past normal retirement age and will probably have to see out his days where he lives. That's not much of a prospect given the state it's in. I expect it will just continue to fall into further disrepair around him.

'What I admire about Mortimer is that he seems to have worked hard throughout his life. My guess is that his formal education was limited and his life experiences may never have extended much further than the bounds of the property where he lives. It's sad in a way, but not everyone has great ambitions and I expect it's been fulfilling for him. What's important is that he has kept his business going and is unlikely to have been a problem to anybody.

'I am not discounting that there may be more than meets the eye, but I would tread carefully in the absence of anything concrete to go on. It would not be right for this vulnerable man to be hounded for the sake of relatively minor misdemeanours. Realistically, this is the kind of business where some cash will inevitably slip through the fingers but it's a matter of scale.

'When an investigation is started following receipt of an informer's letter, we are required to follow it through to its conclusion. But for that, I might well have been recommending the termination of the enquiry into Mortimer's financial affairs. We can draw a line under any investigation if we think there are valid reasons.'

'There are bound to be fundamental differences in our general approach to cases,' replied Day, 'but, as you have already said, there is nothing surprising about that given our different backgrounds.

'It's our duty to serve the taxpaying public at large who, in the main, pay what is due. I accept that the tactics employed to regain lost tax will depend on the inspector handling the case but, in my book, evasion is evasion and should be dealt with accordingly.'

'I understand your point of view, Brian,' said James, 'but I repeat that we should be careful how we handle this man. We must be wary of intimidation.'

Although unsettled by Day's unmitigated determination, James had been around long enough to avoid becoming involved in matters which no longer concerned him.

James returned to his office and worked steadily at his desk, dictating a number of letters and memoranda into his recording machine. This resulted in about half of the files on his desk being cleared by the time he needed to think about going to the DI's office. He called Greenfield's secretary to make sure that the meeting was still on and said he would be there in ten to fifteen minutes.

The conversation would probably be about the shuffle of work connected with the creation of a portfolio for Day. It was likely that a selection of cases was being drawn from all the existing Inspectors so the DI would no doubt be briefing each one about what was to be handed over to the new man.

The DI's imposing oak door faced down the long corridor leading through the main office. James knocked and waited to be beckoned.

He entered and the DI looked at him from behind his desk which was larger than the standard issue elsewhere in the office. On the green leather surface was a large purple glass ashtray in which lay a briar pipe not yet completely extinguished. Light wisps of smoke rose to join the blue cloud suspended over the desk.

Greenfield was a large man in his early sixties, about six feet tall and somewhat overweight. Despite his ample girth, he had not lost his straight-backed military bearing.

Tucked into his navy blue waistcoat was a black and white striped tie, one of a number of different ones he wore, all no doubt having a connection with a particular regiment or association.

He had served with distinction in the Second World War, rising to the rank of brigadier, but was disinclined to discuss his wartime experiences. To his mind, it was all over and there was nothing to be gained from reviving memories of the terrible conflict. He was respected by the staff for his quiet authority, only intervening when it could not be avoided. As he would put it, "Most ailments resolve themselves – others need a little surgery".

'Thanks for coming – take a seat,' said the DI, tapping the final embers from his pipe into the ashtray. 'Just give me a moment.' He placed the empty pipe to his lips and sucked it a couple of times before putting it to one side. Drawing his chair closer to the desk, he leaned forward to look at some documents contained in a folder in front of him.

While he waited, James looked over the surface of the desk. In addition to the folder there was a filing tray, some framed photographs, the subjects of which he could not see, and a dictating machine with its tiny green light illuminated.

'You would have heard what's happening with the new man Day,' announced the DI. 'Now he's completed his induction period, I need to see that he has his own allocation of work to get on with. I expect he's mentioned that I've asked him to take over the Mortimer case. It seems a suitable one as he's already attended an interview with you and knows the history. This is the only one I'm drawing from your portfolio. The others will be gathered from the other investigating inspectors in the office to make up the required number.'

'Yes, he's already told me he was taking over the Mortimer file,' said James. 'He's studied the papers and met the taxpayer and his agent, Mr Birch, so he's well placed to carry on. I've given him my ideas but from now on it's up to him. He knows I'm happy to help if he needs any further comment.'

'How do you think he's settling in?'

'I've known him for only a short time so there's not much I can say,' replied James. 'He seems decent enough and certainly very keen to make his mark. I think he'll probably benefit from broadening his horizons and discovering what life is like outside London.'

'In due course, I shall need to make an assessment of this man and that will include his interaction with colleagues,' said the DI. 'Perhaps we can talk about this again in the future.

'Do you feel he'll handle the Mortimer case in the same way you would have done?'

'That's highly unlikely as we can all come up with a different solution to the same problem. But that does not make anyone right or wrong. It's a matter of interpretation.'

James was puzzled that the DI seemed to be taking such a close interest in the new recruit. It was necessary for him to monitor Day's progress but his degree of inquisitiveness was unusual. The DI was known for his fairly relaxed approach towards staff training. His normal practice was to allow an individual to develop gradually and with the minimum of interference. In this case, he appeared to want to know much more about this man and earlier than usual.

'It's my job to keep in touch with how he's getting on,' said Greenfield. 'I'll need to complete an appraisal report on him in due course as I do for all of you. I suppose I'm a little more enquiring on account of the circumstances of his arrival. It interests me that he came here without any explanation. We haven't lost a member of staff recently so he's not a direct replacement.

'It might not be a coincidence that I've just been contacted by the Efficiency Unit at Head Office. A man named Nicholson telephoned me to say that he'd been asked to look into performance at this office and produce an internal report for his department. He said he'd be turning up to discuss the matter with me but wouldn't say when.

'He didn't say why they want to look at us or what has driven their interest. I suppose they think that by not telling us their precise reasons we'll be prompted to scrutinise all our systems and procedures before they appear.'

'I know something of this Unit,' said James. 'They like to swoop in at short notice and leave no stone unturned in finding ways to cut costs and improve efficiency. On the positive side, I suppose we can all benefit from an external view – it's possible to be too close to things to spot the obvious.'

'Perhaps I'm becoming too imaginative,' continued Greenfield, 'but I wouldn't like to think that Day has been put here in an undercover capacity so that he can report back to the Efficiency Unit on what he's found. He seems to be a bit of a high-flyer so perhaps he's the type to be entrusted with that kind of role. What do you think?'

'I wouldn't like to speculate but Day has also said to me that he doesn't know the exact reason for his transfer to this office,' said James.

Greenfield continued to ponder the reasons behind the interest of the Efficiency Unit.

'As we all know, investigating inspectors are judged on their success in recovering evaded tax. Put in its simplest terms, this means a point for every pound gained following completed investigations. I can only imagine that the statistics show that we're not at the required level as compared to the national average. Of course, we don't have the overview to judge this.'

Analysing the subtleties and innuendo of the atmospheric world of those who looked down from above was something in which James had no interest and had no wish to be inveigled in. He confined himself to the defined duties of his job and looked no further than trying to perform to the required standard.

'I am beginning to understand the problem,' said James, 'but I don't know what practical advice I can give. I can't see any point in trying to second-guess these people. We'll find out their motives soon enough. The visit of the Efficiency Unit may be totally unconnected to Day's transfer here but surely that will also become apparent in time.'

'As you know, James,' continued the DI, 'I have less than two years left in harness in this job. I have been in charge at this office for a good number of years and we have largely been left alone to run things as we see fit. We have reaped the returns from evaders and must have been feeding enough revenue back to central funds to keep them happy.

'But I can accept that times change with ever-increasing efforts to generate more funds to service the growing National Debt. I want to leave here with a legacy that can stand up to examination, not just for my own satisfaction but for all those who have helped towards keeping a tidy ship.

'I think we need to review how we do things before the Efficiency Unit boys turn up. I need to give more thought to what changes we might need to implement and I'd be grateful if you were to do the same.

'I'm pretty sure they will think we're too soft here – not tough enough on the dodgers. But there are two sides to this and hitting people too hard can just drive them underground. This can compound the problem in the long run. It's not about striking fear into the general public. I have always believed in trying to build a respectful relationship with the public and a climate of reasonableness and co-operation.

'I have been thinking about your investigation into the affairs of that local taxi driver who was let off without being asked to pay any additional tax. This might be the type of case where they would expect us to have been tougher. Just remind me how it went.'

James remembered it well and it was, indeed, typical of his style in dealing with what might be regarded as a relatively "small" case in monetary terms. He began to recite his recollection of events.

'The taxi driver's name was Watson. He ran a small day-time operation mainly taking people to transport links – airports, ferries and railway stations. His profits showed a steady decline over a period of two or three years and I asked to see his records. They were supplied promptly and amounted to bank statements, a series of handwritten sheets, a diary and a pile of receipts – records typical of a small enterprise without a professional book-keeper. It took me a disproportionate amount of time to sift through it all but there was a particular point that caught my attention and I called him in for interview.

'After covering various general points including reference to how he might improve his record keeping, I asked him to explain why there was no income banked for a particular week in September, the last month of his accounting year. I showed him the blank page in his diary and he responded immediately by saying he had been to visit his daughter in Germany during that week and that this explained why there were no takings.

'I knew this was a fabrication and studied his expression for any sign of shiftiness. There was none so I concluded that he may have been practised in concealing the truth.

'Within his records was a thick pile of petrol receipts. He always bought his fuel at the same local garage. For the week he claimed to be abroad there was the usual pattern of daily purchases from the filling station with all the receipts showing his vehicle registration number. It was clear that he had decided to have a tax-free week by not entering his takings in his book. He had overlooked that filling his petrol tank regularly at the same place was a sure sign that he was working as normal.

'I put it to him that the purchase of petrol during the week showed that he must have been taking fares. This was met with the sheepish silence common when an individual has been caught with no excuse to offer.

'I did not prolong his agony and sent him away with the

strongest warning that he must never try that on again. He assured me that he wouldn't repeat his misdemeanour.'

Greenfield reflected for a few seconds before replying. 'We discussed the closure of this case at the time and I endorsed your recommendation to drop it with just a warning. I mention it because it is an example of the type of situation that we might need to deal with differently in future given the likely need to tighten our procedures.'

'That particular case could have gone either way,' said James. 'It was in the balance but it's worth remembering that my decision was influenced by the number of investigations I was working on at the time. I was trying to net some bigger fish and it was a question of making optimum use of my limited time and resources.

'Now this might seem unfair, and arguably it is,' continued James. 'On another day I would have proceeded to seek a financial settlement from the taxi driver. It would not have been too difficult to present him with calculations using estimates of what he had failed to disclose over the years. With interest and penalties, it would have yielded a reasonable sum but less than the potential yield from the other cases I was pursuing. This led to my conclusion that my time should be concentrated on what were likely to be more profitable lines of enquiry. This meant letting off the taxi man with a warning.'

'Yes, I remember that you were handling a larger workload than most at the time,' said the DI. 'Your capacity has been greater than certain others I could mention. More than one of your colleagues is in sight of the Civil Service pension and treading water. They can't be swapped for someone from another office. Without being unkind, nobody would want to take them in exchange for a more efficient officer – that would just amount to transferring the problem from one place to another.

'This has been something that we've had to shoulder and that's fine as long as it is accepted that our performance level may be lower than an office manned by thrusting and ambitious graduates. The Efficiency Unit probably won't accept this and expect everyone to work at the same rate.'

The DI reached for his pipe with thoughts of refilling it from the tobacco pouch which he drew from his jacket pocket. He decided to rest both alongside the ashtray for the time being.

'I'm sure we'll be having further conversations on this subject as time goes by but, for the moment, I'd like to turn to another matter,' said Greenfield, reaching for a sheet of paper resting at the top of his filing tray.

'Information Services at Somerset House have sent me this,' said the DI. 'Now and again they send a questionnaire listing companies with registered office addresses in our area. The first thing I do is hand the list to one of the clerical staff to make sure we have a file for all of them. There are not usually that many and they often turn out to be dormant companies which are not trading.

'This time there is one entry which draws my attention. The name of the company is Nelson Properties and I have established that there's no file in the office for them. Ordinarily, I would assume it to be another instance of a long dormant company and, therefore, of no particular interest to us. But in this case there are two reasons for wanting to know more. The first is that it did not appear on any previous list but that could be because the company was formed only recently.

'More importantly, we have received an informer's letter about this company. Briefly, it says that it would be in our interests to look into how it conducts its financial affairs. We are obliged to take all such letters seriously although many are not worth the paper they're written on.

'As you are well aware, the current policy in this office requires that communications from informers are kept in my personal possession. For reasons of confidentiality and security, it is considered best that they do not circulate within the office. As is the case with all such letters, it will be kept under lock and key in there,' he stressed, pointing over his left shoulder to a metal filing cabinet in a corner.

'The list sent here by Information Services shows the registered office address which appears to be a private residence in this locality. This need not, of course, be the same as the trading address, if indeed there is one. Someone named Skinner is shown as the company secretary.

'Here are the details,' said the DI, handing James a slip of paper. 'Please look into it and let me know what you find out.'

VI

James returned to his office and examined the details written down by Greenfield. Deciding to deal with it while it was fresh in his mind, he filled in a standard enquiry form requesting details of the company's trading activities and copies of trading accounts prepared to date. He addressed it to Mr Skinner, the company secretary of Nelson Properties, at 17 Rosemount Drive, Hemport and placed it in his out-tray for collection by the post clerk later.

There seemed to be something familiar about the address. Then he recalled it was a road he passed every day on his way to the office. Many times he had glanced down the cul-de-sac with its two parallel rows of modern detached houses. Curious to know what number 17 looked like, he decided to take a closer look the following morning.

Leaving a little earlier than usual the next day, he stopped his car opposite the sign on the corner of Rosemount Drive. A smaller notice below it indicated that the odd numbers were on the left and even numbers on the right. Looking down, he could see that there were about a dozen houses on either side so number 17 would be about two-thirds of the way down.

In the half light, he turned into the residential road and drove slowly past the identical dwellings. The unkempt front garden of number 17 stood out among the manicured plots behind the low picket fences of the other houses.

Pulling up outside the house, James noticed there was post protruding from the letterbox. Eager to know more, he left his car and walked up the drive towards the front door. A flickering security light in the entrance porch caused him to stop and look around before continuing.

He reached the door and drew out the letters which could now be examined under the light above him. Several letters addressed to Skinner were accompanied by a number of circulars.

Suddenly, the road was illuminated by the headlights of a car. He quickly re-inserted the mail into its former position and retreated the way he had come. As he did so, he was caught in the powerful beams of the vehicle as it swept into the drive of number 15, next door.

His throat dried and he began to wish he had never embarked on this venture, now fearing that he would be thought of as an intruder. He continued to walk quickly down the path towards his car when the driver of the vehicle which had parked next door emerged. 'Can I help you?' called a deep male voice.

James turned and walked back towards the person who was now standing alongside the low hedge separating the two properties.

James called "hello" and moved closer to the figure. He was relieved to find that the round-faced middle-aged man before him wore a smile and seemed to be of a kind disposition.

'I came in connection with a letter I sent here. As I was passing, I thought I would try to make sure that the person is still living at the property.' He knew from the other letters lodged in the letterbox that he was not the only one writing to Skinner at the same address.

'Do you live here?' enquired James.

The man from number 15 explained that he and his wife had only lived there for a couple of months. He had been transferred to the area in connection with his new employment with a firm of structural engineers in the town.

'I've never seen anyone in the house but apparently a gardener turns up now and again to keep it tidy – not for a while by the looks of it! The people at number 13 say that somebody calls to collect post from behind the front door occasionally so, if you've written, I expect it will reach whoever it is eventually. Someone said that the property is rented out but we've never seen any comings or goings. It's a bit of a mystery but not really anything to do with us.'

After thanking the person for his help, James hurried away not wishing to allow the conversation to develop into questions about the reason for his interest.

Having driven back to the entrance to the cul-de-sac, James saw a postman emptying the postbox on the corner. He stopped the car and spoke to him through his open car window.

'Excuse me,' called James, 'but do you deliver here as well as collect?'

'I do deliver to Rosemount Drive most days.' replied the postman as he continued to empty letters out of the box into a large mailbag.

'What do you know about number 17?' asked James. 'Does anyone live there? It seems a bit deserted'

'My job is to deliver letters to the addresses specified on

the envelopes,' said the postman, not happy with being questioned about the conduct of his work.

James decided to try one more question before the postman's patience ran out. 'No mail redirection?' The postman made no comment, heaved the sack over his shoulder and walked towards his waiting van.

As he drove off, James considered what he had found out. Nobody seemed to be in residence at the house which was the nominated registered office address of Nelson Properties. It was not uncommon for a private house to be used as the official address of a company, particularly in the case of a small enterprise. He had been told that the mail was being collected regularly but by whom? Was it Skinner, the company secretary, or someone else who owned or had lived in the property? It remained a mystery and he would try to establish more through checks with the Land Registry and Community Charge records.

On his return to the government buildings, he went directly to the Community Charge Office situated on the lower ground floor to see what he could find out about the ownership of number 17 Rosemount Drive.

The word "Enquiries" was etched on the frosted glass. He tapped and entered. 'Good morning Graham,' he said to the man seated at the first desk inside the office.

'What can I do for you James?' responded the long-time servant at the department, looking bored and uninterested.

'I'd like to see the page for Rosemount Drive, please. Is it handy?'

'Yes, the book you want is on top of that reading table. Someone asked for it yesterday and it hasn't been put away yet.'

James studied the index and turned to the page he wanted. He ran his finger down the list and stopped at the relevant entry.

'There's no name against number 17,' said James. 'Why would that be? Someone must own it.'

'It's not the function of this department to establish ownership. Our job is to identify who occupies a property so that the appropriate community charge can be levied on that person. If there's no entry for a particular property, it means that, as far as we know, there's nobody living there at the moment.

'The Land Registry deals with the title to land but they're based in London and you would need to send a written application. Oh, and there's a charge so you'd need to enclose a cheque. They're not quick in replying – it can take three to four weeks.'

James thanked the clerk and left.

Back at his desk, James opened his drawer and took out a list of departmental telephone numbers. Among these was a direct line to an Inland Revenue man at Companies House who was on hand to deal specifically with enquiries from investigating officers.

He dialled the number and the answer was almost immediate. 'Hello John, we seem to be speaking quite a lot lately. Do you have a few minutes?'

'OK James, fire away.'

'Nelson Properties Limited – give me a run down on recent activity, please.'

'Wait while I get up the microfiche.

'The records show that the company has been in existence for about five years. Dormant accounts have been filed every year. This means, of course, that a statement has been made to the effect that the company has not traded or engaged in any business transactions. There's no indication of who prepared the accounts and sent them in but the annual return forms have been signed by the company secretary whose name seems to be Skinner. Of course, it's not uncommon for a company to be registered in anticipation of trading without business activities ever actually commencing.'

'What address is shown for the company secretary?'

'17 Rosemount Drive, Hemport.'

'Are the directors listed?'

'It's not very clear but their surnames appear to be Shaw and Greene.'

'Addresses?'

'No – that's something which should have been picked up on at the time. Director's addresses should be entered on annual returns. Too late now.'

'Any other statutory declarations?' asked James.

'Doesn't look like it. Oh, wait a moment. A couple of things have been filed very recently. I can see that a form was submitted stating that the name and address of the company secretary has changed and is no longer Skinner, the person in Devon.'

'And who is the new company secretary?' asked James.

'It's a company secretarial agency in – wait for it – Grand Petra. Isn't that an island in the Caribbean? How unusual.

'A few days after that,' continued the man at Companies House, 'we received a communication from the agency stating that the company was no longer active.

It requested that it should be struck off the register of companies. I can see from a note on the file that the process to delete it from the records at Companies House is already under way.'

'It's interesting that a statement that the company is not trading is accepted without asking for evidence of some kind,' said James.

'I take your point, James, but the function of this department is to process the forms that come in without making further enquiries. I suppose a spot check is made from time to time but I don't know who does that.'

James pondered what he had learned and decided to call Greenfield.

'James here - sorry to trouble you but I would appreciate a quick word about the company which you asked me to look into following the informer's letter – Nelson Properties, if you recall.

'I've made some progress but what I have discovered raises more questions than answers. I wondered whether there was anything else in the informer's letter that might help?'

'I don't have the letter to hand at the moment, but I recall that what it amounted to was a single sentence of typescript suggesting that we should take a closer look at the activities of the business. It was delivered by hand and there was obviously no suggestion of where it came from or who sent it. Nothing to add, I'm afraid. You'll need to work with what you have.'

James thought and came to the conclusion that the way forward might be found in the Plough Hotel. He arrived there at 5.30, pretty sure that a man would be there who might be able to help.

Having taken up a seat at the long bar, James ordered a glass of the local pale ale. The early evening drinkers were starting to arrive.

At 5.31, Miles Kemp entered and went to the bar to place his order. The Plough was his first port of call each day after locking up his office.

Miles beamed and called, 'James – a surprise to see you here. I keep meeting you in hostelries these days!'

'What are you having?' asked James, reaching to his inside pocket. 'Had a good day?'

I've viewed a couple of properties which will be coming up for sale but whether I'll get the instructions I don't know. Mine's a pint of the best bitter – thank you.

'I've stuck with Dad's philosophy that properties should be valued realistically and at a price at which they will sell. There is no point in doing otherwise. Some agents quote an inflated value in order to persuade vendors to instruct them to sell. When nobody wants to pay the asking price, it ends up being reduced to what it should have been in the first place.

Miles settled on the stool alongside James and quaffed from his pint glass. 'That's better,' he said, wiping the excess foam from his upper lip.

'I mentioned to you before about the new estate agents in the area being ultra-competitive in order to bring in business. Now there's a virtual commission war with some firms offering as low as one per-cent.

'I grew up with rates of two per-cent across the board, with all agents charging the same.'

'What's the letting market like?' asked James.

'Pretty buoyant. A lot of people are moving down to this part of the country and some prefer to rent before they buy so they can get a feel for the area first.'

It was an outside chance but James had hoped that Miles might know something about the property in Rosemount Drive. Even if he had not been the letting agent perhaps he might know who was.

'I wonder whether you might be able to help me,' said James. 'It concerns 17 Rosemount Drive which I believe has been let recently. I've sent a letter there addressed to a man named Skinner and I'd like to be sure that he still lives there. If I knew who the letting agent was I might be able to find out more – any ideas?'

Miles took another draw from his ale and paused while considering his reply.

'I was the agent for the letting of that property but the arrangement was unconventional to say the least.

'There are rules of confidentiality so my normal response to a question like yours would be to say that I can't discuss it at all. However, and knowing you as I do, I think I can make an exception, particularly as the circumstances were unusual.

'Anyway, even if I told you everything I know it would not amount to the disclosure of anything confidential about the tenant. Nevertheless, what I shall say is conditional upon you keeping it to yourself.'

'You can be sure of that,' said James, sensing that he might be about to get somewhere.

'A while ago, a man entered my office and said he wanted to rent a furnished property for six months only. The house you mention had been on my books for a long time and nobody seemed to want it. I don't know why as it's a clean and tidy house. It was nicely decorated and up to date.

'The property belongs to the executors of a deceased estate and the administration period had been going on for so long they decided to try to get some rent for it.

'The man, who called himself Skinner, said that he would only rent the property if he was allowed to pay for the whole six months in advance, and in cash. This seemed a bit odd but I wasn't going to turn it down. I banked the cash, kept my slice of commission and sent a cheque for the balance to the executors.

'I gave him my number and asked him to contact me if there were any problems. I've heard nothing since.'

'How long is left on the tenancy?' asked James.

'That's a good question and something I need to check. I think it's probably less than a month.'

'What about when he leaves?' asked James. 'I suppose you'd need to make arrangements to check everything out and get the key back.'

'He said that the key would be returned to me before the end of the six months and that the property would be left exactly as he found it. You meet all sorts in the letting game but I reckoned he was a man of his word. In the worst case, I would have to change the lock. It wouldn't be the first time.

'But I'm guessing you may have a professional interest,' said Miles.

'It's true, but that's only because of the letter I mentioned and the fact that I'd like to know whether it will reach the person it's intended for.

'If there's nobody living here, I suppose that any post for Skinner would be sent on to him. If I knew the redirection address, I would be able to send my next letter there.'

'Can't help you, I'm afraid,' replied Miles who finished his pint and readied himself for another. 'One for the road?'

'Not for me, – in a bit of hurry, but thanks for the offer.'

On his way home, James concluded that he had exhausted all the possibilities in his search for Nelson Properties. The company had moved offshore and successfully covered its tracks. The question was whether unquantified tax liabilities had been left behind them.

VII

The sun would not rise for another two hours but the alarm clock sent a clanging reminder to Jeff Cameron that it was 5.30 in the morning and time to get up. He reached to turn it off and made another promise to himself to change it for one that heralded the day with a gentle flow of music.

Wearily, he switched on the bedside lamp, alongside which was a crumpled copy of the previous day's *Sporting Life*.

Cameron lived in a cottage in Berkshire which was once the lodge to a large country estate. The opportunity to rent the property came through his long acquaintance with the landowner whose horses he had ridden in the past. It was small but he had lived alone for five years and its location near the village of Lambourn and a number of leading racing stables was convenient.

The undulating chalk downs of the county of Berkshire provided ideal conditions for training thoroughbred racehorses and a number of the country's top National Hunt trainers were based here. His usual early morning routine would be to ride horses at exercise at one or other of the nearby training establishments which used his services.

Jeff rolled out of bed, gathered his thoughts and shuffled down the corridor to the bathroom. On the way he passed the second of the two bedrooms. There was no bed in this room, just a dark brown single wardrobe and pile of cardboard boxes.

He went downstairs after pulling on his working clothes of sweater, jodhpurs and soft brown leather boots. Before entering the kitchen, he unlatched the door at the foot of the stairs and put his head outside. It was cold but not freezing with no sign of impending rain.

Breakfast would amount to one slice of toast with a little jam, no butter, followed by a vitamin tablet washed down with a cup of strong black coffee. It was hard to imagine that so meagre a repast could generate sufficient energy for one whose work required considerable physical strength, not to mention the high level of concentration needed to control half a ton of horseflesh travelling at speed.

The kitchen was small and narrow. Against one wall was a small table with a chair at either end. The remnants of the meal of the previous evening were on the draining board next to the sink together with an empty tumbler and a quarter-full bottle of single malt whisky.

This had been his home since his wife left with the majority of their possessions. He wouldn't dispute that he had not been the easiest to live with. His wife of twelve years decided enough was enough of his increasingly wayward behaviour.

The change in his domestic circumstances coincided with the end of his heyday. He had started his career as a National Hunt jockey at a leading racing stable and became apprenticed to one of the masters of the art of training. The combination of the expert tutelage and his natural ability led to his swift ascent to number one rider at the yard. Consistent success took him to the highest echelons of the sport. Over a hundred winners a season became the norm, including some of the richest prizes at the likes of Ascot and Cheltenham.

His percentage of prize money brought greater financial rewards than he could ever have dreamt of. Most of his contemporaries in the small Lancashire town where he grew up would follow the family tradition and work in one of the local mills.

When he was eight years old, his father brought home a pony which had become too expensive for a workmate to keep. It was kept in a shed at the bottom of the garden. Jeff's riding skills developed not as a result of formal instruction but by the desire to avoid falling off the animal and the trouble of having to catch it. The common land near his home was the ideal schooling ground and, by jumping obstacles such as gorse and fallen branches, he learned the importance of placing the horse in the right position for take-off.

Progressing to the local gymkhana circuit and riding horses of greater ability, his natural talent developed to the point where he became the rider of choice for many owners. It seemed a natural step to join the ranks of the racing professionals.

Jumping fences at racing speed on an animal of immense power carries high risk. Many riders whose careers have been shortened by heavy falls will attest to this.

A jump jockey will part company with his mount at the rate of around once in every twenty rides. Jeff had assembled the complete catalogue of typical riding injuries, from collar bone and wrist fractures to breakages of arms, legs and vertebrae.

His legacy was a life that was lived with a constant degree of pain and the prospect of related arthritic difficulties in later life. As he would often say, "the positive side is that it's only the worst pain you notice".

In his hometown community, the only required financial expertise was to eke out the wages until the next pay packet arrived a week later. There were perils as well as pleasure in his new-found wealth.

He was one of a number of young jockeys who had risen through the profession and had money in their pockets for the first time. Those whose modest backgrounds had taught them the value of prudence put a bit away for the future. Others took the view that money was for spending at whatever level was required in order to extinguish it by the time the next lot arrived. At that time, Jeff was in the latter category.

He had always enjoyed a glass or two but, fuelled by the euphoria of success and more than adequate funds, the liquid flowed at an unchecked rate.

He had not always felt comfortable around women but his social life blossomed as his fame grew and his features began to figure regularly in the press and on television screens.

Horses are allocated a certain weight to carry in a race. At five feet ten inches, Jeff's natural weight would be in the region of twelve stones but he needed to be able to weigh out at two stones less, including his saddle. This meant fasting and, although the nutritional benefits were questionable, a cigar and alcohol helped to quell the hunger.

Early starts and riding horses at exercise every morning took care of his fitness but word travelled about his excesses and a diminishing number of owners and trainers sought his services. Having lost his retainer to the leading stable to which he had been attached, he became freelance, picking up rides from the owners who had remained faithful to him over the years.

Although nobody doubted that he still possessed the skill, strength and tactical expertise ground out over his career, he did not always meet the requirements for the clean-cut image which had by then become the vogue.

His former drinking and carousing pals had gone their own ways, some into havens of domestic bliss, others entering activities on the fringes of the racing world.

Whatever else, he was a man of routine who could be relied upon to meet his obligations. Perfect timing was a prerequisite whether turning up for morning stables along with everybody else or being at the races well in advance of the announcement of the time for jockeys to mount.

After so many years of working to the clock, punctuality came naturally. The office worker arriving late could make up the time at the end of the day. For the professional sportsman, it was a case of turning up on time or not at all.

Jeff did not have a ride at either of the two National Hunt meetings on the day. This morning, he would ride out two lots at exercise for a local trainer and then his afternoon would be free.

He had been called by Charles Edgcumbe asking him to come down to his stables to ride Southern Pride and give an opinion of the horse's potential. The offer of a day's pay and travel expenses was readily accepted.

There were plenty of talented jockeys about and Jeff knew he was being called on for a particular reason. He had ridden steeplechasers for the Edgcumbe family in the past and they were aware of his strong riding style. The invitation to travel such a long way to ride the horse suggested to Jeff that it might be something special.

It was late morning when he lifted a small suitcase into

the boot of his car and set off on the 100-mile journey to the West Country. Charles had booked accommodation for him at The Plough in Hemport. The following morning he would ride out for the trainer at Lower Barton before setting off to Newbury for a booked ride in the afternoon.

Charles had telephoned Jeff in the morning to say that he would be unable to join him that evening but was looking forward to seeing him at the stables the next day.

'My sister, Gloria, who you know,' Charles had said, 'has a friend named Gary who is hoping to meet you. He can be a bit of a nuisance but he's been given the telephone number of the hotel so that he can call you to try to arrange something. It seems he's a bit of a fan of yours. I'm sorry about this but please feel free to tell him that you are too tired, too busy or whatever.'

Gloria had come down from London to meet with Charles and Jeff to discuss Southern Pride and, as usual, Gary had tagged along.

The idea of socialising with a stranger was as appealing to Jeff as riding a novice steeplechaser over the Liverpool fences for three miles in driving rain. He hoped that he would not have to go through the whole autobiographical thing with someone who might even want to know what he'd had for breakfast. He would have preferred a couple of reflective drinks on his own but decided to go through the motions in the interests of keeping everything sweet. He was hopeful that his trip to East Devon might result in some race rides in future.

The journey was a long haul in his tired Ford Granada which had carried him over 100,000 miles to racecourses all over the country. A busy jockey spends more time behind the wheel than anywhere else.

At least the weather was bright and his journey would take him along good trunk roads ending with the A35 from Honiton to his final destination, arriving at about 5.30.

After driving through the coach arch at the side of the hotel, he parked at the rear and made his way through the drizzle and darkness to the glass doors leading to the reception area.

At the desk, a beaming young lady asked how she could help. 'Are you Mr Cameron?' she enquired. Jeff confirmed and she continued. 'My Dad is a big racing fan and you are one of his favourite jockeys. If you are riding in one of the races on the telly on a Saturday he always puts your horse in his accumulator.'

'That's nice of him,' said Jeff, 'I hope he doesn't lose too much.'

'Oh no, he says you always win.'

Jeff cocked an eyebrow and smiled at this inaccurate conclusion. Winning once out of every five or six rides would be a more than satisfactory percentage for any jockey. Some of the horses he rode had little or no chance and there can only be one winner out of an average of a dozen or more runners in each race.

'Your room number is 124 on the first floor and here's the key. The stairs are just behind you.'

Jeff inspected his room, unpacked and showered. He was preparing to go downstairs when the telephone rang. It was Gary, the man he'd been told about.

'Hi – my name's Gary and I think Charles would have mentioned that I'd very much like to meet you for a drink, if that's OK. If it's not too early, I'm at reception downstairs.'

Gary was looking forward to the prospect of meeting someone famous from the world of racing and seemed to have chosen to forget that he had been uncomplimentary about Jeff in the past. Until now, "J Cameron" had been just a name on the lists of runners and riders on the wall of the betting office.

With some reluctance, Jeff accepted the offer and made his way down. At the foot of the stairs, he looked across to the reception desk and saw an individual who he assumed to be Gary. He was leaning over the desk chatting animatedly to the pretty young receptionist. The long-haired and unkempt man was not his type. 'Better get it over with,' he thought to himself.

Gary turned and recognised Jeff as he came towards him. He straightened and held out his hand. 'I'm really pleased to meet you,' he said, beaming. 'It's great to see you in the flesh, as it were. I don't really go to the races much but I've seen you a lot on TV. Let's go through to the bar and I'll buy you a drink.'

'I'm not drinking in here,' said Jeff, 'not at hotel prices. I saw a pub across the road – I'm going there.'

Jeff headed for the exit picking up a complimentary newspaper from a table as he went. Gary hurried behind.

The bar of the Cutler's Arms was warm and welcoming and the number of jostling customers was an indication of its popularity. Jeff stood at the bar and surveyed the shelves lining the wall behind.

'What's your poison?' asked Gary, 'pint of something?'

'No, can't drink pints – too many carbohydrates. I have to stick with spirits of one kind or another. Gary gulped at the thought that this might be an expensive round. 'Ah, they've got my favourite – mine's a large Lochnagar.' If he was going to have to entertain this young man he might as well make the most of it.

Gary led the way to a copper-topped round table surrounded by four uncomfortable-looking wooden chairs and placed his pint of lager in front of him.

'You're staying with Charles, then,' said Jeff in his familiar direct manner.

'Yes, I came down from London today with his sister, Gloria. We are both artists and share a studio in London. I often tag along when she comes down – it makes a change from the smoke.'

'And what do you do in this studio?'

'I turn my hand to different types of projects – pottery, wood-turning, basketwork or whatever comes to me at the time.'

'I expect you make a tidy sum out of that kind of stuff in London.'

'Gloria is well established and she's built up a good following but I'm still trying to get to that point. I produce as much as I can but at the moment most of it goes out as free samples or on sale or return.

'It's the old story about chucking pebbles in the pond and waiting for the ripples to come back to you,' said Gary, forcing a note of optimism.

'How do you manage to live if you don't sell much?' enquired Jeff, teasing the flavour from another sip of the single malt. 'It's a bit pricey up there, isn't it?'

'I get by,' replied Gary, knowing that his best chance of a windfall rested with picking a string of winners at the betting office.

He began to feel uneasy at the line of questioning and did not want anybody to get the idea that his existence was being subsidised by Gloria. It was time to change the subject.

'I hear it's the plan for you to give an opinion on the prospects of Southern Pride. Gloria's been riding the horse at exercise from time to time and I know Charles wants your view before making a decision about the next step.'

'And what interest do you have in this horse?' asked Jeff.

'I've put no money into it – I couldn't afford to be in the syndicate that owns it but I'm very interested in following how it gets on. I like a bet as much as anybody else so a bit of information wouldn't go amiss, certainly in my present financial position.

'I read a biography about you a few years ago so I know a bit about your background,' said Gary. 'It was a fascinating read – you've certainly led a colourful life,' he said with a smirk.

'Just talking about that book makes me angry,' said Jeff, scowling. 'It was unauthorised and I didn't make a penny out of it. Most of what was in it was just made up. Somebody decided what my image should be and then invented the stories to match.

'What's your interest in racing, anyway – is it just the gambling?'

'No, not at all, I find it very exciting to watch and I have great admiration for the horses and riders who slog around the racecourses in all weathers.

'Do you remember when you first sat on a horse?' enquired Gary.

'Let's just say that I'm not from a privileged background. I was lucky enough to have the opportunity to ride a pony when I was young but that was only because it didn't cost anything. With a bit of luck here and there, I managed to get to ride better animals. What you learn when you're young sticks with you.'

Jeff reached for the newspaper and turned to the sports pages. There had been two race meetings that day and he had not been offered a mount at either. He was becoming worried about the reducing number of rides being offered to him.

He needed to make enough from his profession to cover his living expenses. His rent was reasonable and his food bill was limited by the number of calories he could consume. If he put on the pounds, the number of his rides would decrease proportionately.

The riding fees for a dozen or so mounts a week was just about enough to keep him solvent. Riding a winner meant that his earnings would be lifted to a more comfortable level by his percentage share of the prize money.

He had not invested in a pension scheme and there was no point in starting now. It was too late to build up a fund large enough to provide a decent pension on retirement. He never saw saving as necessary in the days he was earning well, but the money disappeared quickly. There was also the haunting uncertainty of how long he could go on. Injury could strike at any time. These were matters Jeff did not dwell on.

'So what's coming up for you in the immediate future?' asked Gary. 'Any fancied rides?' As usual, Gary was on the trail of inside information.

'If you've read the book you mentioned, you probably know I ride as a freelance. This means, in case you don't know, that I am not attached to any particular trainer and that I'm not under contract with anyone. There are two sides to this. The benefit is that you can pick and choose but if you're out of luck you might not get any rides at all.

'So, to answer your question, I don't know what the future holds, at least no further than the end of the month. It's good for your confidence to be chosen to ride for your own ability rather than just because you happen to be the stable jockey. It's a bit more interesting, but you never know what your income is going to be from one week to the next.'

Gary leaned forward and rested his elbows on the table. Jeff prepared himself for the next question which he hoped would be the last.

'I suppose it's fair to say that you would have a better idea than most of what's likely to win a race,' said Gary, his gaze fixed on the man opposite him. 'I mean, you know the other jockeys and have probably already seen some of the horses running. You may have even ridden some of the horses yourself in the past. I imagine there's a fair amount of chat between the jockeys about what's on form and what isn't.'

Jeff thought this might be coming. This man was a punter first and foremost and his real purpose in wanting to meet him was to see if he could winkle out some information that might, at least for once, give him the advantage over the bookmakers.

The jockey prickled at Gary's remarks but his reaction was tempered by the fact that this was a small-time punter rather than one of the professionals who sometimes come looking for tips. They were prepared to pay for information but Jeff had been wise enough to stay out of their clutches.

'It would be very strange, wouldn't it, if I couldn't work out the likely outcome of a race better than you,' replied Jeff. 'That's because I have been in this game for a long time and can read the signs.

'However much you know, it's unpredictable. Look at the number of winners at big odds which should never have won on the basis of what they'd done before.'

'In that book about you, it was suggested that some jockeys go as far as arranging the outcome of a race between themselves and then make money from betting on the result,' said Gary.

'If I knew that such a practice existed, I certainly wouldn't be telling you about it. I think you probably know that jockeys are not allowed to gamble on their horses.'

'But there must be ways and means,' chuckled Gary. 'Rules are made to be broken and all that.' Jeff offered no response.

Nothing would have pleased Gary more than to be able to boast to his mates at his local betting office that he had inside information from a famous jockey, but it was becoming increasingly obvious that this wasn't going to happen.

Gary downed his pint and Jeff saw this as an opportune moment to end the conversation.

'Time for me to move on,' said Jeff.

'It's been great to meet you and look forward to seeing you tomorrow,' said Gary.

The two men parted outside and Jeff returned to the hotel. It was too early to go to his room so he settled into an armchair with the newspaper.

Jeff had ridden for Charles's father on a number of

occasions. He knew his children, Charles and Gloria, who were often in the paddock when their father's horse was being saddled before a race. Although in touch with them less often now, Jeff valued the association with a family he liked and trusted.

It was not quite light when Jeff Cameron arrived at Lower Barton stables the next morning. The brightening sky was edged with a thin layer of red cloud suggesting that the day would bring inclement weather but for the moment it was cold with just a light breeze. The restless clouds to the north threatened to bring wind and rain later.

Jeff strode towards the gates into the yard with his saddle under his arm and reflected on how many years it had been since he last visited. Since then, Charles had become the master of the stables and was seeking to make his mark as a trainer. Certainly he had the experience and the ability. All he needed was a slice of luck.

Entering the cobbled yard unnoticed, Jeff looked about for faces he knew.

He spotted Charles in conversation with his sister and a small group of men. The yard was bustling and a number of horses were being groomed and tacked up, with some already saddled for their exercise spin.

Charles spotted Jeff and stepped forward to greet him. 'Jeff, thanks so much for coming – as usual you're on the dot!' They shook hands warmly and Charles made the introductions to the others present.

'You remember Gloria, of course, and I know that you met Gary yesterday. The people to my right make up the syndicate which owns Southern Pride.' Charles gestured towards the group who called their greetings to the jockey.

Among the gathering were James Stedman, who had managed to arrange a couple of hours off, and Miles Kemp who was not going to miss this important event in the career of the horse. The future plans for Southern Pride would be likely to be determined after Jeff had ridden him on the gallops a little later.

'Which one is Southern Pride?' asked Jeff, surveying the horses being led around the perimeter of the yard. 'The one on the far side,' said Charles, pointing to the rangy bay gelding. It took no more than a glance for Jeff to assess that the tautly muscled animal was in peak condition.

'He has a good temperament,' added Charles, 'and is not at all quirky. He's very straightforward to handle and train and the staff love his kind nature. We're still trying to work out why he hasn't been finishing his races in the way we would want him to but I hope it's just a matter of time before it comes right. We just need to get him spot on for the racecourse and this is why we've asked you to come along. You know the history of his recent races and we need your opinion on where to go and what to do next.'

'I appreciate your confidence,' said Jeff. 'If looks were everything, I'd say you have a fine animal here but let's see what happens.

'When did you last ride him, Gloria?' asked Jeff.

'I rode a piece of light work on him last week. I think he's probably as close to race fit as we can get him. We wouldn't want to do too much and risk taking him over the top. There's an old adage about races being lost on the gallops.'

'I think we'll say no more and leave it to your judgement, Jeff,' said Charles. 'We'll see what you have to say later. I want you to take Southern Pride up the gallops alongside a young horse which has just come to us and which is showing signs of being pretty quick. On the way, I'd like you to cross two of the practice fences.'

After being legged up, Jeff slid his feet into the irons and waited for the horse's girth strap to be checked for tightness. He circled the yard a couple of times to get a feel for the way Southern Pride moved, then left the yard followed by the apprentice jockey on the horse that was to accompany him.

Charles and the others watched in silence as the two horses wheeled together at the foot of the gallops. Jeff nodded that both were ready and the trainer signalled for them to set off. The pair walked forwards then quickly broke into a canter. The younger horse ran freely and fought for its head while Jeff held Southern Pride in behind on a tight rein.

Ranging alongside one another, the two horses approached the first of the two practice fences. Jeff's mount cleared the fence by a wide margin. The other brushed through the twigs at the top but landed safely on the other side.

At this point, the young horse rushed on despite attempts at restraint by its rider. Jeff kept his mount balanced and followed the leading horse towards the second obstacle which both cleared without difficulty.

With a hundred yards to go, Jeff decided it was time to test the horse's finishing speed and drove on. Southern Pride quickened impressively leaving the other horse in its wake.

Jeff slowed to a halt and turned back at a walk with the younger horse just behind. Southern Pride was showing no signs of fatigue after the sharp burst of exercise.

'That seemed pretty good,' said the trainer after Jeff had

arrived back in the yard. James, Miles and the others closed in to hear the jockey's comments.

'Did you say that the horse was entered at Wincanton shortly?' asked Jeff as he slid down from the saddle.

'Yes, a two-mile steeplechase for novices which I thought might be suitable,' replied Charles.

'Is it a valuable race?'

'It's a good pot and likely to attract some decent types of horse.'

'Is the horse entered in any other races?'

'Well, there is an entry in a lower grade hurdle race at Exeter in a few days but I was rather thinking we would miss that and go straight to Wincanton,' replied Charles. 'We believe the horse will be better suited by the race over steeplechase fences. The Exeter entry was made just in case anything changed.'

'I agree that this is a steeplechaser in the making,' said Jeff, 'but I think he should run in both races. There's a good chance that a clear round in the hurdle race would give him confidence and sharpen him up for the bigger prize at Wincanton where he would tackle fences for the first time. It would also be a chance for me to get to know him a bit better.'

'Will you take the rides?' asked Charles, to which Jeff nodded his agreement.

Turning to the members of the syndicate, Charles summarised. 'We brought Jeff here to give us the benefit of his advice. I think we should take it and make plans for the Exeter race but you are the owners and the ultimate decision lies with you. Does anyone have any thoughts or questions?'

The group cast glances among themselves and an elderly

man spoke. 'I've been following the sport for a very long time and I believe we should listen to Jeff. Taking the advice of a top class jockey goes without saying to me.' None of the others dissented.

'That's good,' said Charles. 'We'll need to get on and make the necessary arrangements. While we are all together, perhaps I could ask you to indicate whether you will be able to attend the meeting at Exeter next Tuesday. All but two or three confirmed their availability and Charles took a note of the number so that he could order the owners' badges that would allow admission to the course.

'There won't be time to have the entry badges sent to you before the day so I'll arrange for them to be left for you to collect at the entrance for owners and trainers at the racecourse. Thank you for coming today and please feel free to have a look around the yard before you leave. Sam Fitzherbert will guide you and I've arranged for an urn of tea to be on the go in the stable canteen.'

The group of syndicate members moved across the yard in animated conversation about the prospect of an exciting day at the races the following week.

Gary remained alone making notes on a scrap of paper while Gloria hurried after James who was behind the main group.

'Good morning', she said, looking up at James with a smile. 'What did you think of all that?'

She was not riding out this morning so was not wearing the clothing in which James last saw her. Today, she looked fetching in a padded green jacket over a checked skirt. Her hair, free of its usual elastic band, hung just below the level of her shoulders.

'It was really interesting,' replied James, 'and as well as hearing Jeff's opinion, it was good to know that everyone had confidence in him.'

'It was the opportunity to watch Jeff in the saddle again that I most enjoyed,' said Gloria. 'It's been a long time but he's lost none of the poise and judgement which took him to the top. At every stage, not only was he in complete control but was also totally aware of what was going on around him. That's very important under race conditions when you have to keep your horse balanced and out of trouble. It's vital to know how the other runners are travelling.'

'Are you going back to London today?' asked James.

'Yes, and probably quite soon' said Gloria. 'I had really only come down this time for Jeff's visit. I did have a few words with him on the 'phone beforehand and, now the decision's been made, I'm no longer needed. So, it's back to London and, hopefully, into creative mode.'

'You once kindly suggested that I might be able to call in to see you when I'm in London,' said James. 'I still don't know exactly when my trip will be, but I hope the offer still stands.'

'Sure, just let me know – Charles can give you my number. That reminds me that there's something I need to talk to Charles about before I go so I'd better get on my way. Bye for now.'

When Gloria entered the kitchen, Charles and Jeff were seated and discussing the Exeter race.

'I think the horse should continue to work quietly before the race, probably no more than walking with the odd trot to keep him supple,' said Jeff.

'As it happens, I have been offered a mount in the first

race at Exeter next Tuesday. I think you said Southern Pride is in the third.'

'Yes, we're entered in the two-thirty, and that reminds me. Gloria, would you have time to call Exeter racecourse to confirm that we'll be running in that race? Also, who will be driving the horsebox? If you'd like to come, perhaps you could drive. Otherwise Sam or I could do it.'

'I am not sure yet whether I'll be able to come but, if I do, I don't mind driving. I'll let you know over the next couple of days.'

Gary and Miles were in conversation in the stable yard discussing what they had seen on the gallops.

'To me,' said Gary, 'it seems certain that Southern Pride will win one of its next two races. The likelihood is that Exeter will be just a warm-up for the run at Wincanton but, who knows, he could win both. I'm in contact with one of the lads at the yard so I'll see what I can find out. I'll be honest with you, backing a winner wouldn't go amiss given that I am a bit short of readies at the moment. From what I hear, you wouldn't turn your nose up at a few quid.'

'I don't know where you got the idea that my financial situation is not what it might be but I suppose we would all like a bit extra given the opportunity,' replied Miles, disturbed by Gary's impertinence.

'Come on, Miles, we're birds of a feather so let's put our heads together on this.' The idea of any form of an association with Gary was unattractive to Miles but he was not in a position to rule anything out.

'The successful gamblers in this world are the ones who have more information than the average punter. It stands to reason that to have any chance of beating the bookie you need to have inside knowledge. Normally, blokes like you and me are at a disadvantage – all we know is what we read in the form guide.

'But now there's the chance to be a step ahead. We know the trainer and we know Gloria's opinion of the horse. Most of all, we know Jeff who is the most important person of all as he's ridden the horse and will be in the saddle on the day.

'Jeff will be leaving soon to get to Newbury for his ride this afternoon. Let's try and have a word with him.'

At that moment, Jeff emerged from the house with his kit under his arm and made for the gates leading to the parking area. Gary hurried to catch up with him and Miles followed with some hesitation.

'Saw you leaving and came to say goodbye,' called Gary. This is Miles. He's one of the syndicate members.

'Good ride at Newbury this afternoon?' enquired Gary to which Jeff delivered his standard reply to enquiries of this kind.

'Hoping for the best.'

Gary realised that time was running out as Jeff neared his Ford Granada.

'I wonder whether Southern Pride might win at Exeter?' enquired Gary, almost at a trot.

'Don't know what the opposition is,' replied Jeff who climbed into his car and drove off.

'No joy there then,' said Gary. 'We'll both be at Exeter so we can listen out for the vibes on the day. I'll be bringing as much cash as I can get together in case it's positive and I need to pile on.'

VIII

It was late afternoon in Hemport High Street and the glow from the bay windows of the premises of Kemp and Company lit the wet pavement outside.

Two ladies carrying shopping bags were peering through the glass at the display of photographs of properties for sale. Most had been crossed with a yellow banner indicating that they had already been sold. The rain began to patter and they hurried away.

Beyond the window display and inside the office, two ladies were busy. One was removing her coat from a rack and preparing to take a large bundle of envelopes to the nearby Post Office. The other was engaged in a telephone conversation. Both the bespectacled ladies were dressed smartly in skirts and jumpers and were probably in their early sixties.

Their desks were arranged to face the entrance to the premises. A light shone through the open door of the back office occupied by Miles Kemp, the proprietor.

It was almost 4.30 and his desk was clear but for a pot containing pens and pencils, a blotting pad and a desk calendar bearing the name of the Sun Alliance Assurance Company. He was passing time until his two visitors arrived and swept his hand across the desk to remove imaginary traces of dust. Normally relaxed and confident with people, he felt the apprehension he always did before meeting the two men who had made an appointment to see him.

His late father had started the business 35 years ago and ran it with moderate success. A temperate man, the reasonable profit he made was enough to provide a living for his family, a state of affairs with which he was content. There were no great ambitions beyond the continuation of a traditional service to the community in which he had lived and worked all his life.

Miles, his son, had not excelled academically and joined the family firm after completing his GCE "A" level examinations. The experience gained over the following years as his father's assistant had prepared him for the day when he took over as head of the firm.

In a corner behind his desk, a number of "For Sale" boards were lodged alongside a narrow window. This was the only source of natural light in his room but the open door gave him a view into the main office and to the High Street beyond. He had learned his profession alongside the two ladies in the outer office who occupied the same chairs and desks they always had.

The bell over the front door rang as one of the ladies set off for the Post Office. As she left, she held the door open for the two men who had arrived at the same time. They thanked her politely and entered.

Hearing his visitors arrive, Kemp rose from his desk and went out to meet them. Having taken their damp overcoats and hung them on a coat rack, he returned to his office and took his place on the high-backed chair behind his desk. The others arranged themselves on the chairs facing him.

Even before the conversation began, Miles was feeling the customary warmth beneath his collar which arose whenever he encountered these people. Past experience told him that small talk would not be on the agenda and that the preliminaries would be kept to a minimum. To these inveterate businessmen time was money.

Periodically, Shaw and Greene would ask for a meeting to be arranged for what they described as an "update". A significant portion of the income of Kemp and Company arose from the management fees paid by these clients, the directors of Nelson Properties.

The niceties were passed over and the conversation commenced. 'All well with the block lettings?' enquired Shaw, who spoke slowly with a broad midlands accent. 'Any problems?'

Shaw was short and stocky and probably in his mid fifties. His moustache matched his sprouting grey hair. Behind his wire-rimmed spectacles were tired eyes showing no sign of emotion.

'Nothing much to report,' replied Miles. 'There have been a couple of plumbing issues at block A, but nothing serious and I've arranged for my usual man to attend to them this afternoon. The tenants are not without water so it isn't desperately urgent. As I've mentioned before, there are two or three tenants running late with payment of their rent but I'm keeping on top of this and will visit them at the end of the week if the money hasn't come in by then. A few apartments are still vacant and I'm doing all I can to get them let. They're on show in the window outside and there'll be an advertisement in the local paper this weekend.'

It was Greene who spoke next, a man of similar age and origin to his fellow director but taller and with hawkish features. Drawing a sheaf of folded papers from the inside pocket of his jacket, he said, 'I have with me your monthly statements for the last twelve months.' There was a familiar questioning tone in his voice which suggested he had found something to complain about.

'Maybe I haven't been studying them carefully enough in the past but it's clear that the level of occupation has been dropping steadily. It's been taking much longer to find new tenants for empty properties than it used to.'

He glanced down at the statements and then again at Miles. 'I wonder how you can account for this given that there seems to be a high demand for rented property in the town. I read in the local paper that landlords and estate agents can't cope with the demand. This would suggest there are potential tenants out there looking for somewhere to live so why aren't they coming to us? A lot of people are relocating to the area.'

Greene set everything down on the desk and waited for the response.

If Miles were to be blunt with these men, he would tell them it was their own policy of underinvestment that was the root of the problem, but that would not be what they wanted to hear.

They had short fuses and would probably become annoyed at the suggestion that they were in any way responsible for the under-occupation. As they saw it, it was the duty of their agent to ensure that the properties were yielding the maximum return regardless of anything else.

Miles knew to tread carefully knowing they could sever the association with his firm without notice if they had a mind to do so.

It was not altruism that influenced the directors'

preference for retired tenants. Experience informed them that the elderly were not as demanding when it came to redecoration and modernisation. They were less likely to make a fuss about it than the younger element.

Urgent problems relating to plumbing or electrical failures would be attended to in order to protect themselves from any accusation of negligence towards their tenants. Otherwise, there was an implicit direction for Miles not to hurry to follow up requests for non-essential work. As the owners saw it, this was the way to save money and increase what ended up in their pockets in the short term.

Miles leaned forward uneasily, fingering his lips. It was pointless to attempt to conceal the truth.

'If I show a prospective tenant around a property and they decide not to proceed then it's my job to find out why. Location will always come into it but, in the main, people refer to the likes of outmoded kitchens and bathrooms. This shouldn't surprise you as it's been mentioned before.'

'We have plenty of tenants who have lived in the same property for many years – they don't seem to complain,' said Shaw curtly. 'It's a formula that's worked in the past.'

'That's true,' responded Miles, 'but times have changed and people's expectations have risen.'

'And where do you think the money is coming from to pay for these improvements?' asked Greene.

'I don't know what your profit and loss account looks like but I would normally expect expenditure of this kind to be coming out of the income from the flats,' replied Miles. 'Isn't it common for rents charged to include a provision for ongoing maintenance?'

'We've been in business together a long time,' said Shaw, glancing at his colleague.

'We know only too well that some things need to be sold rather than bought. The advantages of what's on offer should be stressed instead of dwelling on minor negative points.

'It's no good just leaving people to make their own decisions. The public needs direction – clear advice.

'Neither is it about hard selling, just making sure that the right emphasis is placed. You're a salesman and I'd expect you to be advising people what's best for them. We'd like to see more keenness on your part. Perhaps you could review this and give us a report very shortly on how you consider revising your approach in future.'

'Do you have any thoughts about this?' asked Greene.

Miles had probably been a little more direct than he had intended and reminded himself that these were his paymasters. The income he received from them was vital to his existence.

In truth, he was in difficult financial straits and feared he could not go on much longer unless there was a change in his fortunes. He wasn't selling enough houses and without the management fees from Nelson Properties it would be difficult to stay afloat.

His business had been shored up with loans, all of which were bearing interest at increasing rates. His house had been used as collateral for various advances from his bank so that the value of the remaining equity in his home had diminished to a fraction of what it was.

An impatient creditor who demanded payment could tip the balance between survival and insolvency. Nevertheless,

Miles presented a brave face and a cheery disposition, essential in order to maintain the confidence of the local people. If his financial plight became generally known, the doubts would set in.

He summoned what he hoped might be a convincing response.

'We have worked together for a long time,' said Miles, looking earnestly at his clients.

'Loyalty is all-important and I want to continue to serve you in the same way I have over the years.' The truth was that he would have liked nothing better than seeing the back of these mean-spirited men.

The three had first met in the bar of the Plough Inn several years previously. Miles was not averse to convivial discourse over a glass or two and used it as a way to spread the word about the services he offered.

He had engaged in conversation with Shaw and Greene who had just acquired the letting properties and were looking for someone to help with their management. They took to him and came to an agreement.

'I've always done my best but I accept that it's healthy to review procedures. I'll look at this as a matter of urgency. I'm sure I can come up with some fresh marketing ideas. Leave it with me for a little while.'

'Fair enough,' said Shaw, 'but we need to find the solution quickly.'

To Miles's relief, his clients suddenly appeared a little more relaxed having dealt with what was probably the main item on their agenda. They even went on to talk about their recent holiday in Grand Petra, the Caribbean island. 'The wives love it there,' said Shaw.

Miles couldn't picture either of them wearing Bermuda shorts by a sun-drenched swimming pool.

'There's another matter we want to talk to you about,' said Shaw, 'but it's something that requires the utmost confidence. Given our relationship, I'm sure it won't go any further than this room.'

'Naturally,' replied Miles, relieved now that the worst of the storm might be over. 'You can rely on me.'

'We've spent a lot of time on the island and identified a number of business opportunities. The government is eager to bring in new investment to stimulate the economy. We've become friendly with some of the government officials who have been appointed to promote development – housing, hotels and the ancillary infrastructure. Through our contacts we've been able to take options to acquire some stretches of land all of which have considerable potential.

'One of the consequences of the economic turmoil in the region is that the Caribbean Dollar has weakened significantly against its American counterpart and also in relation to the pound sterling. What this means in simple terms is that if we take up options now out of money held in the United Kingdom, we would acquire the land at less than half the real cost of twelve months ago.

'This is an opportunity that was too good to miss. We've been granted planning permission to start work on the construction of villas and a luxury hotel. All we need to do is press the button and off we go.

'There are one or two other things,' said Shaw, turning to Greene.

Kemp had hoped that matters had been concluded and prepared himself for what might be coming next. He was already looking forward to opening time at the Plough where he could recover from this ordeal while taking his usual refreshment.

'At times, we've provided you with loans to tide you over,' said Greene. 'We've been pleased to be able to help but, looking at our records, I see that no repayments have ever been made. I'd need to produce more detailed calculations to work out the amount of compound interest over the period.'

Miles flushed and considered how to respond to this undeniable statement of fact. It was true that advances had been made to him. No repayments had ever been sought and none made. He disliked the notion that he was beholden to these men but there was no way of escaping the situation, at least not yet.

'Of course,' said Miles, 'and I was grateful for your support at those times.'

'Perhaps there should be a scheme of repayment,' continued Greene, 'so that we all know where we stand.' This was the last thing Miles wanted to hear. He was in their grasp and they knew it.

'Do you remember the amount involved?' asked Shaw. Miles said that he would try to look it up later but had no real intention of doing so. It would be far too depressing. He could feel that the screw was being turned but why? What had changed so that they felt now was the time to put on the pressure?

'I have always tried to be absolutely honest with you,' continued Shaw. 'I sense that you are not in the healthiest financial position and the existence of this debt can't be helping.'

Miles wondered what he was aiming at. How could it possibly be of any help to him if he were asked to repay the loans out of money he did not have?

He was suffering from fierce competition from the new Estate Agents in town. So that his clients and creditors would not sense that he was in difficulty, it was essential to present a positive front but it was becoming harder.

'I'll take a closer look at the figures and perhaps we can discuss the matter further when we next meet,' concluded Shaw.

The visitors rose from their chairs and Miles went to collect their overcoats. He thought about asking them across the road for a drink and a little bonhomie, but decided against it, preferring the thought of his own company. He would be able to think over what had been said and try to work out some marketing ideas to keep them at bay.

IX

James was at his desk reviewing the first file of the day needing his attention. It was the familiar story of cash being extracted from a business without being declared for income tax purposes.

A local shopkeeper had been putting his hand in the till. This was patently obvious as the profits shown by his accounts were simply not enough to cover his regular outgoings including substantial mortgage repayments.

'Mr Sutton,' he had said to the culprit at their last meeting, 'I've shown that you have failed to declare your true profits for a number of years and you are not denying this. We call this evasion or, at the very least, negligence. You will have the right to appeal against my calculations which will show my best estimate of the tax payable in order to correct the matter. I have to remind you that interest will need to be added to the settlement to take into account that the money has been in your bank account rather than ours for a considerable period of time.

'The Taxes Acts allow for the imposition of penalties where a taxpayer has taken deliberate steps to avoid payment of tax. The amount of the penalty is at our discretion and the degree of co-operation by the taxpayer is always taken into account.'

'Since you started questioning me I've hidden nothing

from you,' said Sutton. 'I spent most of my life in employment and always had the dream of running my own business. Finally, I made the break and opened the shop three years ago. I was meeting the overheads and making a living.

'When you're new to something, there are always people who think they know better. No sooner had I started than some of the other local traders started coming in and giving me advice, mostly unwanted. There was always talk about what I should do to pay less tax. Some of what they came up with seemed very questionable, but they carried on as if it was the normal thing to do. I realise now that it was a mistake for me to listen to them and you can be certain it won't happen again.

'From what you've said, you'll be asking me to pay up in the near future. I don't have much cash over and above the bit I'm trying to put together for our retirement so whether I'll be able to carry on at the end of it all I don't know. I suppose it might mean back to employment after all!'

James laid out before him a large sheet of squared analysis paper. Interest would need to be added at the going rate to the tax which should have been paid earlier. He needed to decide the number of years to be covered by his calculations as well as the amount of the estimated understated profits for each of the years under examination.

Although he was capable of coming down hard in extreme cases, James would incline towards leniency where he could, particularly when the taxpayer had put his hands up and confessed to what had taken place.

Sutton was a family man who had managed to make the break from what was to him the drudgery of routine employment. He had no experience of running a business and it was an achievement that he had made it work, albeit at a modest level. James could see that he had been misguided by others around him and persuaded into malpractice. He had a pretty good idea who those individuals might be and entries would be made in his notebook for future reference. There was no doubt that the chattering shopkeepers nearby would soon find out that Sutton had been caught out. This might result in their thinking about amending their own ways.

Sutton had said that his lesson had been learned and that he would not repeat the same mistakes. James was prepared to give him credit for this. This man required correction but not with a heavy hand.

James decided to make the assumption that the understatement had occurred for the last two years only and decided to add the sum of £500 to the profits declared for each of those years. He reckoned this would be the minimum to bring the profits of the business to a reasonable living wage for a man with a mortgage and family. He would ask for the tax on the omitted total profits of £1,000 plus the interest lost to the Exchequer.

James had examined Sutton's bank records and assessed that he would probably have just about sufficient liquid funds to cover the bill. He reasoned that this man would probably pay his dues, go away and behave more responsibly in future.

His calculations completed, James placed them in his tray

to be typed and sent off to the taxpayer for agreement.

He was ready for a break from the columns of figures and rose from his desk. Having donned his coat and scarf, he decided to take a breather in what was a bright, if chilly, day and made his way downstairs to the exit from the building.

Under the tall ceiling of the domed reception hall was a large number of people waiting to be seen. He was squeezing past the queues when he saw Ruth at the end of one of them. Looking up, he saw that the caption above the desk at which she was waiting showed "State Benefits". She was reading some explanatory leaflets as he approached her.

'Good morning,' he said with a warm smile.

'Oh, you're the person I met at the coffee shop.'

'That's right,' said James. 'Fate seems to have drawn us together yet again!'

'Is it still morning?' replied Ruth. 'I've been here for so long it's starting to feel like the afternoon!

'Yes, I am in the right queue,' she said, realising James would have gathered why she was there. 'Being here is no fun but if I am entitled to payments I need to accept them.'

'There are two things I would like to say to you,' said James.

Ruth raised her eyes in anticipation.

'The first is that it's best for you to go away and return later. Judging by where you are in the queue, I can tell you that you will not be seen before the desk closes for lunch. If you leave now and return just before the end of the break, you should be attended to quite quickly.'

'And the second thing?' enquired Ruth.

'Have you missed your gloves?' asked James with a smile.

'Well, yes, I have – I thought I must have left them on the bus. I did enquire at the bus station but they didn't have them. Why do you ask?'

'Because I have them. You left them on the table at the café where we last met. I kept them in the hope that I might see you again. But they are in my office so I'll need to pop upstairs to get them. If you could wait here I'll return shortly and help you pass the time until the desk reopens this afternoon.'

'Thank you. I'll wait at the door.'

James turned and climbed the stairs, pleased to think that Ruth was waiting and did not seem against the idea of spending a little time with him.

Ruth stood near the exit reflecting on the kindness James had shown but apprehensive as to what they would find to talk about.

James mentioned to a junior colleague that he would be away from his desk for a while if anyone was looking for him and hurried downstairs.

He returned to Ruth and handed her the gloves. 'I have an idea if it's agreeable to you.'

Ruth nodded slowly to invite his suggestion.

'The Plough Hotel,' said James. 'Have you been there? – it has a comfortable lounge where we can talk and have some refreshment.'

'That's sounds nice,' replied Ruth, 'but I'm sure you must have more important things to do.'

'It's my pleasure and I'm looking forward to a chat,' said James, guiding her towards the door.

They entered the foyer at the Plough and passed into the large reception room. James spotted two facing armchairs near the fireplace and suggested they might sit there. There was a coffee table between them and James enquired what he could order for her.

'Well, a hot drink would be welcome. I do like Earl Grey tea at this time of the day, but it's not important. Please let me pay,' she said, reaching for her handbag.

'Certainly not,' said James. 'It's my treat.' He beckoned a passing waiter who took their order and retreated reverently.

'I should introduce myself. After all, I know your name but you do not know mine. You are Ruth and I am James – James Stedman.'

'I wonder how you know my name,' said Ruth, her head tilted in an enquiring way.

'When we met at the coffee house, I mentioned I had first seen you at Deepdene Farm when you opened the door to me and my colleague when we came to visit Mr Mortimer. You didn't recall meeting me but I hadn't forgotten you. You were baking bread at the time. I know your name because it came up in conversation later.'

'I expect I mentioned that so many people come and go at Deepdene that names and faces don't always register with me.'

The waiter returned with a pot of tea for two.

'May I tell you a little about myself?' asked James. 'It's not that I think it's all that interesting but you should know something about who you are passing the time with.

'But it will be a potted history – I don't wish to bore you.

'As you would have gathered from where we just met, I work at the government offices. I'm a tax inspector.

'I've been working here for three years having been transferred to Hemport from an Inland Revenue office in Somerset. I live alone in a small, modern house on the outskirts of the town.

'I'm afraid it was a sad event that brought me here. My wife of just two years died suddenly after a short illness. We lived in a village near where I worked. There were so many memories and I felt that moving away might help to put them behind me. There was a vacancy here and my employer agreed that I could transfer to Hemport.

'I am no longer sure that coming here was the right thing, but that's another story and only time will tell.

'So, my life involves my daily 9 to 5 work and the few outside interests I have.'

'I am so sorry to hear that you had such a sad experience,' said Ruth. 'That was an awful thing to happen.' Her expression conveyed her genuine sympathy.

'It's good you have some interests but I can imagine how hard it must have been. I'm sure it's beneficial for all of us to have distractions to balance our daily lives. I wish that I did more in that way but one can easily fall into the work and sleep routine,' concluded Ruth.

'What are your interests?' she enquired.

'Not many worth mentioning,' replied James, 'but I have become involved in a local history society. I'm particularly interested in architecture and also the Roman influence on the history of Hemport but I should be doing more in the way of social activities.

'Also, I have an interest in horse racing which goes back a long way. I couldn't afford to own a horse and pay all the training fees myself but I have joined a small syndicate which makes ownership affordable if only of a small fraction of the horse. It's trained by Charles Edgcumbe, not far from Deepdene.'

'A jumper?' enquired Ruth.

'Yes, and I'm impressed that you know the difference between the flat and the jumps,' said James.

'Well, I should do as my father was very involved in hunting and point-to-point racing when I was growing up. Horses were a feature of our lives and there were always a couple in the stables.'

'Did you ride yourself?' asked James.

'I did and I still could – they say it's like riding a bike – one never forgets. But I was never the horsey type and would sooner do other things.'

'When we first met, I couldn't detect a particular accent in your voice so couldn't even begin to guess where you might have originated,' said James. 'Have you always lived here?'

'No, I spent my life in Oxfordshire before coming down here. Sometimes I can hardly believe the chain of events that brought me to where I am now.

'My childhood was a happy one despite the fact that I had no siblings, not even cousins, with whom to share growing up. But I was fortunate in having good school friends so never felt as lonely as I might have done.

'But I'm sure that none of this is of any great interest.'

'No, please continue,' said James. 'I would like to know more.'

James was enjoying the company of the lady he was coming to like and admire.

'My late father was bequeathed the family home when

his parents died so you might say his background was privileged. It was a large country house with land so I was lucky to have grown up in lovely surroundings. When the times were good, there was a gardener, a maid and a groom for the horses.

'Father wasn't an academic success but found a job as an investment banker through his network of contacts. Gambling was his downfall, first with his own resources and, when that ran out, he made the fatal mistake of using clients' money. Inevitably, it all caught up with him in the end and he died disgraced and penniless.

'Despite all this, I was grateful for being given a good education. There were often visitors at weekends so I got to know some of father's interesting friends, even if some were a little wayward.

'For the last few years of his life my father had a housekeeper. In truth, they became quite close. I got on with her very well. She passed lots of her domestic skills on to me – including bread making! Sadly, she died not long after he did.'

'And your mother?' enquired James.

'More bad news, I'm afraid. She died when I was quite young.

'The death of my father left me without any immediate family at the age of thirty-one and, despite my education, without the means to support myself. I was able to continue living in the house but only until his estate was wound up. The property had to be sold to clear the accumulated debts.

'It is interesting how friends and acquaintances can become scarce when one's circumstances change. Suddenly, I had no money and nowhere to go.'

'Perhaps this explains the reason for your being here,' said James.

'It does. My father was an only child and the family line ends with me. His housekeeper – or lady friend, you might say – had a brother who is Albert Mortimer, the man you came to see at Deepdene.

'I got to know Albert through my efforts to sort out his late sister's estate, not that there was anything of much value. I think she probably gave whatever she had to my father to try to shore him up through his financial problems. It was an indication of her warmth and kindness towards him but was ill-judged as whatever came his way seemed to slip through his fingers.

'Through my contact with Albert he became aware of my situation and that I had nowhere to live after the sale of my father's house.

'He said that I would be welcome to stay at Deepdene. He's a widower and lived alone in quite a large house. I hesitated but there seemed to be no alternative. He did his best to make me welcome. It was quite sweet that he'd made an effort to smarten up the house a bit for my arrival, but he had lived alone for a very long time. There was a great deal to be desired, to say the least!

'What was intended as a short stay grew longer and I found myself becoming a fixture. I cleaned and tidied and even found myself getting out the paint brush, changing curtains and all those domestic things.

'I realised that he was becoming more and more reliant upon me, particularly as his health worsened. I began to look towards another way of life but the more time went on the more difficult it became to contemplate leaving. It must be over four years since I arrived.

'So I am still here, at least in the belief that I am carrying out a useful function in helping Albert. I had never expected this and at times it's difficult to escape the sense of being locked in.'

Ruth drew her handkerchief and dabbed at the corners of her eyes. Her kindly nature had led to her involvement with her adopted uncle, but she had come to feel trapped and unhappy.

'I'm sorry,' she said, 'I do feel lost at times.'

Ruth and Mortimer were such different people. She was educated and at ease socially but Albert was the opposite. They had come together in remarkable circumstances and now inhabited the same small world.

'Ruth, I'm sorry to see you sad. I'm afraid it's my fault for asking so many questions about your past. I can see that it hasn't been helpful to revive memories.'

'No, please don't worry. They say it helps to talk about these things.'

'Perhaps we should take a little air before you return to the government offices. What do you think?' asked James.

'That's a good idea – thank you.'

They walked up the High Street looking in shop windows as they went.

'This reminds me of my one and only real profession,' said Ruth as she looked at the upholsterer's window display.

'My training was in the design and printing of textiles. I was fortunate enough to work in a small studio near Oxford which made bespoke materials for customers. I really enjoyed it and would love to return to it one day.

'I made a good friend when I worked there. Her name is

Annabelle and we still keep in touch. We haven't met for a long while but we write and speak by telephone occasionally. She keeps asking me when I'm coming back! She says there would always be a job for me.'

As they neared the entrance to the offices, James placed a comforting hand on her shoulder. His sympathetic touch spoke louder than words.

He asked the time of her bus back towards Deepdene.

'It should come at about three o'clock. It's just a short journey to where I get off and then a fifteen-minute walk up the lane to the house.'

'Right, if we take you to the counter now we should be able to arrange for you to be seen on the dot when they open. Then there will be plenty of time for you to catch your bus.

'Before we go in, I would like to continue our conversation another day – that is, if you would like to.'

'Yes, that would be nice,' replied Ruth with a faint smile.

'Perhaps if I had your telephone number I could call you to arrange something?' enquired James.

'That's a bit difficult as there's only the business line at Deepdene and it is most likely that Albert would answer in the workshop.

'I usually come into town on Tuesday and Thursday mornings. Perhaps we may meet on one of those days.'

'I'll make a point of looking out for you at coffee time,' concluded James.

That settled, they entered the reception area and went up to the desk where the lady in attendance was finishing a sandwich.

'Alice, when you reopen would you mind taking this

lady through first. She waited a long time without being seen this morning and has a bus to catch soon after lunch.'

'Will do James.'

James guided Ruth towards a seat in the waiting area from where she would be called and returned to his office.

Now alone, Ruth regretted that she had been unable to contain her emotion when telling James her story and fought back another tear. But it was comforting that she had been able to share her concerns with someone who had shown compassion and understanding. She felt she had made a friend.

X

The following day, James had not long entered his office and taken his seat before Brian Day tapped on the door and came in. 'Do you have a few minutes?' he asked.

The interruption to his work was not welcome but James consented to a quick chat.

'I know you're no longer directly concerned with the Mortimer case but I said I'd keep you in touch with developments.'

'Go ahead,' said James, leaning back in his chair.

'Following the meeting we both attended,' continued Day, 'I sent a list of questions to Birch, Mortimer's accountant. To my surprise, he came back almost immediately and, based on what he's come up with, it's clear there'll need to be a follow-up meeting.

'My caseload is quite light until Greenfield has finalised the list of the work to be transferred to me from the other inspectors, so I have time available and would like to get on with it as soon as possible. I intend to ring Birch later to agree a date.

'From what I've seen so far, Mortimer is in for the high jump.

'At the meeting, he said that he had only one bank account which was at the local branch of Westbank in the town. I asked to see the statements for this account and Birch has supplied them.

'Tucked inside these statements was another one in

Mortimer's name relating to a different bank account. It must have been included by accident so it's obvious that Mortimer had attempted to conceal the existence of this other account. It doesn't look good.'

'It may not be quite as it seems,' said James. 'Mortimer has little or no understanding of financial matters. He may well have just overlooked it or thought it was unimportant.'

'Whether by design or omission, we were not provided with a full and complete response to our requests,' replied Day. 'This begs the question as to what other information may have been withheld or misrepresented.'

'What appeared on this other bank statement?' asked James.

'There was an opening balance of a few hundred pounds and a number of credit transactions showing amounts paid into the account during the period. Nothing was paid out.'

'Didn't he mention saving for retirement when we talked to him?' enquired James.

'Yes, but if it's meant to be a retirement fund you wouldn't expect to see it kept in a current account which doesn't earn any interest.'

'Quite so,' said James, 'but I repeat that this man lacks the knowledge to make informed decisions about money matters and it's possible that he doesn't even realise that it isn't an interest-bearing account. What's your conclusion?'

'I think we must make the assumption that this account was used to secrete some of his takings in order to avoid paying tax on them. This will need to be put to him.

'He said that customers visiting his premises usually paid cash for secondhand car parts. This money was put into a box from which he met business and personal expenses. Birch stated that he had made allowances for unaccounted cash receipts but the additions he made were fairly minimal. The existence of another account changes all this and causes concern that the adjustments may not have been sufficient to ensure that the inadequacies in record keeping were compensated for.

'Without the right checks and balances in place, the accounts that Birch prepares can be viewed with considerable scepticism.

'Another point is that, given the loss of his stock in the fire, it is hard to understand how he could have managed to build it up to the value it reached by the end of the year unless, of course, it was being funded by money received which had not been shown in the accounts.

'It is so full of holes that the likely outcome here is for us to estimate what we think that he has made over the last, say, six years and leave it to him to disprove it.'

'Wouldn't that be a little heavy-handed?' asked James.

'That couldn't be said to be the case,' replied Day. 'I work to the book and the kind of approach I'm considering falls well within our official guidelines.'

'Theoretically, it's correct to say that all cases with an identical profile should receive exactly the same treatment,' said James. 'But in my view the broader picture should be taken into account and also the likely degree of impact on the individual.

'For example, some businesses may be sufficiently robust to absorb a charge for back tax and interest and be able to continue to trade. For others, it might mean shutting down or even bankruptcy.

'So it's the proportionate effect that comes into it, not just the amount of tax to be recovered.'

'James,' replied Day, 'you make us sound like social workers. It is our job to apply the law and the way we conduct investigations should reflect that responsibility.'

'In this case, we are considering an individual who is aged and unwell,' said James. 'From what we have seen so far his resources are minimal. If that is true and no concealment of assets comes to light, he would be unable to meet a tax charge of the amount that I suspect you have in mind. What sort of sum are you thinking of?'

'It's far too early to say and obviously I can't produce meaningful calculations at this stage but my initial feeling is that the total tax charge will be substantial,' replied Day.

'You suggested issuing him with tax assessments and asking him to prove that the figures are excessive,' added James. 'We know his records are inadequate and that's why you consider the use of estimates to be the way forward. But for the same reason, the records are so poor that he could not even begin to come up with evidence to disprove your figures. Not even Birch could help him with so little information to work on.

'Let's assume that he doesn't have the amount of money that you claim he owes,' continued James. 'What happens then? We know that he doesn't own any part of the property at which he lives.

'If he couldn't put his hands on more than a few hundred pounds, your demand would be likely to amount to a figure which he could not meet. There seems to be no security against which he could obtain a loan, so what would we gain by asking for more than he could possibly pay? You would have spent a lot of time preparing theoretical calculations only to have to settle for considerably less and possibly only after instigating costly court proceedings. I doubt very much that he has the kind of acquaintances who would be able to help him out financially, so what does he do?

'Having met Mortimer, he does not appear to be of strong constitution. Harsh treatment could have unimaginable consequences. 'I have not detected in him the spirit of a wicked man – misguided, careless, negligent or whatever, but not deserving to be broken.'

'I hear what you say,' responded Day, 'but I am not as sympathetic as you to the plight of a person who may not have paid his dues. Why should an errant individual receive different treatment from anyone else for the same offence? Anyway, I sense that there's more to all this than meets the eye.'

'I have given you my observations,' replied James, 'but now you are in charge and will no doubt proceed as you see fit.' James picked up his pen and turned his attention to the file before him. Day took this as a signal that the conversation was over and left.

James had learned more about his new colleague through this short discourse than he had in the time spent with him previously. Now that Day had full responsibility, his methods had become clear. Compassion was not a word that appeared in the instruction manual and how could he be faulted for carrying out his duties in accordance with the book?

As he reflected on the conversation, it came to James that it was quite possible that it was he who was becoming too relaxed in the application of the rules and that Day was closer to what the official guidelines required of inspectors searching for evasion.

This was not just a contrast between styles of approach. There was no doubt that the "country" way was more relaxed, perhaps overly so, but James knew that this should not influence the application of the rules beyond a limited extent. Day had made a valid point.

XI

After his usual breakfast of a mug of strong tea and some toast, Albert Mortimer had worked steadily in his workshop at Deepdene Farm. The screeching of power tools ceased at ten-thirty precisely. It was time for his break and he retreated to the house, slowed by age and fatigue.

His habits were well known to Ruth who would already have the kettle boiling on the range. Her scones were still warm and the plum and apple jam ready to spread.

After washing his hands – something Ruth insisted upon – he took his place at the kitchen table.

Despite the exertions of his physical work his appetite was modest, more so today on account of his nervousness about expressing himself to Ruth on a matter which had occupied his mind for a long time. He hoped he would be able to find the right words.

As he entered the warm kitchen, Ruth stood with her back to him stirring the contents of a pot on the stove. He took his seat and watched her for a minute or two while sipping his hot drink.

'Ruth,' he said, 'as you know, I'm not a man of many words but it's time I said something about our arrangement, if that's the right way of putting it.

'You ended up here almost by accident and I suppose I've never said enough about how much I've appreciated what you've done for me.

'I expect folk must think it's an odd setup with you here with me like this. We're very different people – I know that – but you've been very good to me. I couldn't have managed on my own and I can never thank you enough. There's a lot I'm unable to do for myself now and I don't think I can go on with the work for too much longer. I don't spend a lot of time at the doctor's, as you know, but I don't need telling that I'm not in the best of shape and something could happen to me at any time.'

Ruth turned to give him her full attention. She could not recall him speaking to her in such an earnest manner and left the stove to sit opposite him.

'Uncle Albert,' – for that was how she sometimes addressed him although they were unrelated – 'it is kind of you to say that but we should remember that you opened your door to me when I had nowhere to go and for that I shall always be grateful.'

'Yes,' replied Albert, 'but I realise that this place is not what you've been used to. You could have left to find somewhere more suitable and been without the burden of having to do things for me. I'd always have understood if you'd done that. After all, we're not blood are we?'

'It's true that we're not directly related but Dad was fond of your sister, as I was. People don't have to be from the same family to feel close. It's about how they get on and how supportive they are of one another. There are lots of people who wish they didn't have the relatives that they do. How many times have you heard someone saying that you can choose your friends but not your relatives?

'We came together through circumstances and what has developed has been helpful for both of us. That's the main thing and your sister would be pleased to know that it's worked out that way.'

The contrast between them was indeed stark. Ruth was a lady of some style who, despite the limitations on what she was able to afford, kept herself stylishly dressed and well groomed. This contrasted with the workman of limited education and horizons who had spent his life toiling with his hands. Yet there was a bond based on respect and affection which transcended the boundaries of their backgrounds.

'Yes, but as long as you're here you can't meet people in the outside world who might change your way of life. In my eyes you are a young and attractive woman and who knows what future there might be for you if you weren't tied to being here?

'I don't want to sound morbid but, one way or another, there'll come a time when we'll part company. I've no heirs so I want to leave something for you to have when I am no longer around.

'On the sideboard over there is a wooden box.'

'Yes, I noticed it this morning and wondered where it had come from,' said Ruth.

Albert reached inside his breast pocket. 'This is the key and I want you to take the box with you when the time comes for you to leave here, whenever that might be. What's inside is then yours. In case there's ever any doubt about it, I'll need to write a note and put it inside to say that it's my wish that you should have the contents. But I want you to promise that you won't open it until then.'

'I love surprises,' she said with a smile, 'but I'm sure it will not be happening in the near future. Thank you, and I promise that I'll do as you say.'

She went to the box and looked at it. Although it had seen better days, she admired what remained of the walnut veneer and inlaid brass.

'How pretty,' said Ruth. 'It's perfect for keeping little treasures. It's very kind of you.'

'Don't lose the key – it's the only one,' said Albert. Ruth hung it on a hook above the fireplace. He was relieved that he had managed to convey what had been on his mind.

'Do you remember the day those tax people came to see me?' asked Albert after a short pause.

'There have been quite a few callers lately and I can't remember which ones you mean,' replied Ruth. 'I'm not sure you ever mentioned anything to do with tax.'

'Well, I've had a call from Birch, the accountant, and these tax inspectors are saying they want to see me again. They've been given a lot of my papers but they've still got more questions. I'm finding this all a bit of a nuisance and I'm going to speak to Birch about it later.'

Ruth rose and gave the simmering pot a stir.

'I'm sure Mr Birch will sort it out for you,' she said. 'He's always been friendly and helpful and has your interests at heart. He's used to dealing with the tax people and I'm sure he'll have the answer.'

'I hope you're right,' said Albert. 'It's worrying me no end. Thanks for the drink and the scone.'

Albert left and Ruth sat at the table, poured a cup of tea from the pot and pondered his remarks. She knew he felt kindly towards her so was not too surprised that he wanted to make some kind of gesture. Why it had to wait until they parted for the final time she didn't know but that was just

Albert's way of doing things, she supposed. The gift could be nothing of great value but she knew he didn't find it easy to express himself and it was a compliment that he had brought himself to do so.

But his remarks about her future introduced thoughts she would normally try to exclude. She had no plans beyond life at Deepdene but there was no point in dwelling on it. Things would fall into place naturally and in time, she reassured herself.

It was Tuesday and the day for one of her trips into town. She did not need to remind Albert who knew her movements as well as she knew his. It would be late afternoon when he next saw her. Ruth put her head outside to check the weather and the shifting bank of grey-white cloud suggested the likelihood of rain.

As she drew a brush through her hair, Ruth wondered whether she might meet James. He had said that he would look out for her on a Tuesday or Thursday, the days on which she went to town, but perhaps he would be too busy or would forget – or even have found another diversion. She was protected by a stoicism born out of life's disappointments.

XII

Greenfield, the District Inspector and senior man at the Inland Revenue office at Hemport, was at his desk awaiting the arrival of Nicholson from the Efficiency Unit at Head Office. He had telephoned only the day before to say that he was coming down and was expected to arrive soon after nine o'clock having travelled down by train from Waterloo.

It would be Greenfield's responsibility to meet with the visitor and attend personally to whatever he wanted to talk about. Although he had never encountered anyone from this particular Head Office Unit before, he had dealt with many incursions from other officials from Somerset House in the past and was experienced enough to handle whatever was thrown at him.

His secretary Joan called to say that Nicholson was in the office and Greenfield asked her to bring him in. He rose and shook hands with the visitor and pointed him to the chair opposite his desk.

Nicholson was tall, angular and immaculately dressed in a pin-striped city suit with shiny black shoes and a briefcase to match. His greying straight hair was swept back, probably held in place by brilliantine, the aroma of which followed him into the room.

Although a good twenty years younger than the DI, Nicholson was his senior by at least a couple of grades. He had obviously risen far and fast to occupy the rank of Senior Inspector.

'You've had a long journey,' said Greenfield. 'Would you like a cup of tea?'

'That's kind of you, but no thank you,' replied Nicholson. 'I had one at breakfast and won't have another until around mid-day. Anyway, time is limited so perhaps we should get started.

'I'm sorry you've been given short notice of my visit but it's the practice of the Efficiency Unit to do things this way and I'm bound by the instructions as they stand.'

'It all sounds a bit clandestine to me,' replied Greenfield, 'but I suppose somebody up there knows what they're doing, or think they do. I'd heard that you don't give much warning.

'How long are you planning to be here? Naturally, given that I have not been allowed the time to reorganise what I have to do, there are other calls on my time today.'

'I need to catch the four o'clock train back to London,' replied Nicholson. 'I'll try not to take up too much of your time. After we've finished, I was hoping to take a look around and possibly talk to some of the staff in the general office.'

Nicholson drew a file from his briefcase and leafed through his papers.

'I'd like to begin by considering your staff complement. What's the total number of people here?'

Greenfield looked at the ceiling and muttered as he did the mental calculations.

'Sixty-eight, possibly seventy.'

'And how many filing clerks are contained within that number?'

'Probably nine or ten.'

'I was hoping for precise figures, but let's work with that for now.

'The national average for filing clerks at Inland Revenue offices is under 10 per cent of total staff employed. Your figure is higher than that. I wonder why that would be?'

'Does it really matter?' responded the DI, hoping that this was not going to be the beginning of a long list of references to trivial matters.

'I'm afraid your reply suggests a lack of understanding of how much it does matter when seen in the context of the overall statistics. If the number of the basic grade of staff can be reduced, money can be saved which then becomes available for investment in more productive resources at the upper end.

'I'll leave these questionnaires with you. Please arrange for them to be completed by each member of the filing staff and returned to me with a description of the work they carry out. Experience tells me we'll be able to take out one, probably two.'

'Do you mean redundancy?' asked the DI with disbelief.

'Of course, how else could we cut the cost?'

'But these are peoples' livelihoods – some of them have been here for decades!'

'That's not our concern,' Mr Greenfield. 'Efficiency and cost-cutting is our objective.

'Leaving that aside,' continued Nicholson, 'who's responsible for stationery supplies here?'

'I'm not sure – I don't get directly involved in that side of things. I've more important things to do than counting paper clips.'

'Well I think it's time you did take an interest. Figures provided to me by Central Supplies show that the per capita consumption of all forms of stationery at this office is 19% over the national average. What do you think this could mean?'

Being interrogated in this manner was not amusing the DI.

'Go on – tell me.'

'Pens, pencils, pads of paper are all the kind of things that people find useful. Pilferage, Mr Greenfield, is on the rise and we need to stop it. I shall be letting you have my written recommendations and they will include reference to having just one key to the stationery cupboard. This would be in the possession of a single person from whom supplies would need to be requested. On each occasion, whatever is requisitioned should then be recorded in a book and signed for. I think you'll be surprised at the results.

'On another matter, one of my colleagues has looked into the costs of running your typing pool relative to other offices. By using simple calculations based upon your franking machine records we can make a reasonable estimate of the number of letters sent out from this office. A simple extrapolation tells us the number of typists required to manage this volume. The answer is 4.2.'

'How can you have 4.2 people?' Greenfield enquired with increasing consternation.

'I can see from your records that you have six recognised typists so we can cut this to four working full-time plus one working two and a half days a week. This is a little more than you need but it will do for a start.

'The lady who showed me in here was your secretary, I think.'

'That's correct – been with me for nearly twenty years.' The DI halted in sudden realisation of what might be coming next.

'She does your typing?'

'Of course,' replied the DI, 'as well as a number of other things.'

'A very positive side about what we do is to invest where long-term cost savings can be identified,' continued Nicholson.

'As far as I can tell, all the typewriters in the pool are outdated. If they're replaced by the latest word processors, the typists would be uplifted by having superior equipment. It's been shown that the new machines are easier to operate and faster to use. The result will be increased output. Over a relatively short period of time, the salaries saved by reducing the number of typists would cover the cost of the new equipment.

'There may be a case for transferring your secretary to the general typing pool.'

'Much of the material I produce is highly confidential,' said Greenfield, stunned by the suggestion. 'Joan has been positively vetted and is totally discreet. She wouldn't have lasted this long if there had been any question about that. We couldn't just transfer this kind of work into the general typing pool which is recognised as the hub of gossip in the office.'

'I realise that she is a trusted and long-serving member of the department,' continued Nicholson. 'Has it occurred to you that it would be possible for her to exercise the same degree of discretion from within the typing pool without taking up a desk space just outside your office?'

'I suppose that could be true but… ' started Greenfield, before Nicholson interrupted.

'Just have a think about it. We don't need to say any more about it now but I shall be including some comments about this in my written report following this visit.

'That covers the more routine aspects I want to mention for now but I've no doubt there will be more to consider as we go along.'

After a pause during which he made some notes, he looked directly at Greenfield. 'I would now like to focus on the investigation work carried out by your inspectors unless, of course, there is anything else you would like to mention at this point.'

The DI declined the invitation not wishing to provoke a further flow of facts and figures. The man from Head Office prepared himself for the next stage of his presentation.

Greenfield knew that Nicholson had the advantage of the well-researched statistics at his fingertips. He could do little more than listen.

'At the Efficiency Unit, we have developed a pretty foolproof way of attributing what we call a "performance factor" to investigating Inspectors,' continued Nicholson.

'This takes into account the number of cases handled by an inspector over a given period into which we incorporate the amount of time spent on each case. This information is readily obtainable from the monthly timesheets you submit to Head Office. The amount of tax yielded as a result of investigations is the final factor in the calculations.'

Greenfield managed to stifle a groan.

'The system would not be complete if it did not make allowances for experience. At one end of the scale is the most senior investigating inspector from whom we would expect the maximum output. Conversely, there is the recently appointed person who will have much to learn. All this is taken into account by making the necessary adjustments to our workings.'

The DI was leaning forward over his desk with hands clenched tightly as he waited for the next revelation. He picked up his pipe from the ashtray and put it down again.

'Combine all this information and we can attribute a rating to every one of the four investigating inspectors working here over the last twelve months.'

'Shall we look at the final ratings?' enquired Nicholson, beginning to show signs of self-satisfaction that Greenfield found unappealing.

'Their names are Ashworth, Blackwell, Davies and Stedman. Their ratings out of 100, in that order, were 32, 44, 52 and 62. As will be immediately obvious, this represents an average of less than fifty per-cent.

'Let's consider Ashworth a little more closely as he is clearly lagging behind the others. He is one year from retirement and his best work seems to be behind him.'

'Did you take into account the fact that he was off sick for a couple of months?'

'Good question, Mr Greenfield, and that has been factored in. We incorporate periods of absence which we are able to extract from personnel and attendance records. Had we not done so, his score would have been even lower.

'Blackwell's history suggests a gradual decline in his performance. I haven't met him and may wish to do so but can you offer any explanation?'

'Blackwell is in his late fifties and is another one who will be retiring before too long,' replied Greenfield. 'He is conscientious and thorough but works at his own pace. He may be a bit on the slow side but he takes pride in accurate and well-presented calculations.'

'I can see he's a plodder,' said Nicholson. 'There is room for the dependable and unspectacular within a team provided that it does not represent too high a proportion of the overall complement. I'm not sure we have the right balance in this office.

'I wonder whether it might be of benefit to send him on a course to introduce him to some modern working practices?'

'That's down to you,' said Greenfield, 'but I doubt it would make much difference.'

'There is a certain mentality that considers the Civil Service to be a job for life, and that's one of the challenges we face on an almost daily basis,' concluded Nicholson who then went on to consider Davies, the second-rated of the four Inspectors under review.

'I don't think there is much to say about this man,' said Nicholson. Only two years into this kind of work, the indications are that he is probably heading in the right direction.

'Although Stedman is your top-rated man, he seems to have reached a plateau in terms of output.'

'He came here following his request to be transferred out of the office in which he was then working,' observed the DI. 'This was connected with family bereavement and he felt it would be best if he had a change of scene to help him cope with his loss. The department was understanding and consented. We shouldn't underestimate the impact of what he went through.

'Nevertheless, it's probably fair to say that his approach in investigation cases may have been a little too lenient at times and I have discussed this with him. I believe it will come right.'

'The overall performance of the group is below par,' announced Nicholson.

'We shouldn't overlook,' observed Greenfield, 'that the population in this district has increased significantly. The growing number of taxpayers has created extra demands on our resources.'

'I know that a man named Brian Day has been transferred here recently,' said Nicholson, 'so he will have boosted your numbers and his reputation for penetrating work suggests that he will be a valuable addition to your investigative function.

'With the strength of the investigators up to five, the results should be marked and I would like to review matters again in six months. By that time we should have sufficient data to measure the effects.

'I would be grateful if you could discuss matters with Ashworth, Blackwell and Davies and perhaps you will be able to persuade all of them to sharpen up their ideas. Stedman needs to continue to build on his foundations and you have indicated that this is in hand.

'I would like to meet Day. It seems to me that he's a key element in the short term plan to step up the pace in this district. As much as anything, his fresh approach may inspire the others. His internal progress reports have been made available to me so I know quite a bit about him but there is nothing like getting face to face. Where is he now?'

'As far as I know, he's in the office today.'

'Let's get him in.'

Greenfield pressed a button on his telephone and a loud buzz could be heard somewhere outside his door.

'Joan,' said the DI, 'please see if you can find Brian Day. Let me know if he's unavailable, otherwise ask him to come my office as soon as he can. Thank you.'

Not having an agenda for this meeting with Nicholson had unsettled Greenfield. He would be glad when it was all over. The prospect of drawing his pension now seemed even more attractive.

Day soon appeared displaying his usual early morning brightness. 'Good morning,' he announced, fixing his eyes on the stranger seated opposite the DI whose identity had already been made known to him.

Nicholson rose and shook hands with the young man. Day pulled up a chair and the DI indicated to him to place it alongside his so that they were both facing the visitor.

Day knew of the Efficiency Unit which was within the same building where he had worked when in London. He had carried out his basic training with another recruit who was later posted to the Unit. They had kept in touch so he had a good idea of what went on there.

Looking directly at Day, Nicholson said, 'You are ambitious and seem to have the ability to go far.'

Day was not short of self confidence but this statement was indeed praise from a senior establishment figure.

'It must have been considered that both you and this office would benefit from your coming here. It should be valuable experience for you to work outside the metropolis and the returns from the investigation function here are not what they should be. It's true that the level of work has increased due to the influx of new residents and I'm expecting the extra pair of hands to make a significant difference.

'Your posting will increase the number of inspectors on investigation work from four to five. That's a good start but is only of value if the nature of the addition to the ranks is of the required calibre. It's believed that you have the credentials to increase the average performance quotient here.

'If you can come up with the results, this is a project which should do no harm to your promotion prospects.

'Just tell me where you are with what you've been doing since you got here,' asked Nicholson.

'I am grateful for your comments,' replied Day, 'and it's pleasing to know that I was considered the right man for the job.

'After a period of general familiarisation during which I worked alongside other inspectors, I have now been given my own allocation of cases which I am looking forward to getting on with.'

'Give me an example of one,' said Nicholson.

Turning to the DI, Day said, 'I suppose I could mention Deepdene Farm.' The DI nodded his approval and Day prepared to continue.

'A farm?' asked Nicholson. 'I am not too familiar with agricultural businesses.'

'Nor I,' replied Day, 'but it's not a farming enterprise.'

'That's interesting.'

'It's a scrap yard.'

'That's a real challenge,' continued Nicholson. 'Businesses dealing with the processing of scrap are notoriously difficult to pin down. I've had some experience and, traditionally, most transactions are conducted in cash. As a consequence, audit trails are often non-existent.

'I was hoping to follow your progress through a case and this sounds a suitable one,' said Nicholson. 'At what stage is the investigation?'

'There has been one meeting at the business premises which I attended with James Stedman who was handling the case at the time. Following that, I raised some queries with the taxpayer's accountant and the responses have come in. There is a clear requirement for a second meeting. I am in the process of trying to arrange for this to be held at the accountant's office shortly.'

'I need to return here in the very near future as there will be matters to follow up with Mr Greenfield,' said Nicholson. 'If you have no objection, I'd like to join you at the next meeting. Perhaps you could let me know when you have fixed the date.'

Day readily agreed and was quick to realise that this would create the opportunity for him to impress the senior man from the Efficiency Unit.

As Day left, Nicholson rose and shook his hand confirming that they should keep in close touch about the arrangements for seeing Birch and Mortimer.

After watching Day leave the room, Nicholson turned again to Greenfield. 'I'd also like to take the opportunity to meet Stedman. Not only is he a key member of your investigation team, he was party to the first meeting at Deepdene and I would like to hear his views on the case.'

Like everyone else in the office, James was by now well aware of the presence of Nicholson and it was no surprise when Greenfield called for him to join them. He paced towards the DI's office wondering what kind of interrogation would be awaiting him.

'Good morning, Mr Stedman,' said Nicholson as James entered. 'I've heard quite a bit about you.'

'Nothing too awful, I hope,' responded James, attempting to inject a note of levity. Nicholson's passive expression told him that this was not going to be an amusing experience.

'Your colleague Brian Day is now running the Deepdene case,' stated Nicholson. 'I'm planning to join him for the second interview with the taxpayer and his accountant. From the first meeting you attended, is there anything you suggest that I should look out for?'

'Brian Day now has the file and the transcript of the first meeting,' replied James. 'I have already given him my view on how we might proceed. My suggestion was that we should tread carefully bearing in mind that Mortimer is unwell and elderly and has little understanding of financial matters.'

'Thank you for that,' replied Nicholson.

'In the course of every examination I carry out,' continued Nicholson, 'it is vital to know the people involved who are, after all, key to any operation. For this reason, I'm glad to have the opportunity to meet you.'

'Mr Greenfield had informed me that your department would probably be taking an interest in procedures at this office,' said James, 'but I didn't know you were coming today.'

'Nor did I,' muttered the DI with a strained smile.

'We have discussed a number of administrative matters,' continued Nicholson, 'but these are subsidiary to the main business which is the matter of tax yielded from investigations. Do you have a view on this?'

'Being just part of the team, an overview is not something I can provide. I would have thought that only Mr Greenfield is placed to do this.'

'Yes,' said Nicholson, 'but I imagine that it would not be impossible, for example, for you to compare the function at this office with how things were done where you worked previously.'

'I suppose that's a fair comment,' replied James, reluctant to give opinions where he did not consider it his place to do so.

'I think it's perfectly fair,' snapped the man from Head Office. 'Why wouldn't it be?'

James took most things in his stride but the sharp response took him by surprise.

'There's a manual which gives guidance to staff engaged in this kind of work,' said James. 'The same publication is used in every office throughout the country so the instructions are the same for everyone. Given that we all follow the rules there shouldn't be any difference.'

'I see,' said Nicholson looking at his notes. 'Do you have a feeling about your own recent performance?'

'I am not the best judge of that,' said James thoughtfully. 'A subjective view is not necessarily useful. There are plenty of people out there who think they are doing perfectly well yet may be falling short of what is expected of them.

'It's also inevitable that someone's productivity will become geared to the tempo of activities around them.'

'I'm not sure what that means,' commented Nicholson with a puzzled expression.

'You can't work so quickly that others can't keep up with you or so slowly that everyone else is held back,' explained James. 'It's important to be in step with your colleagues.'

'So you are content with the current standard of your work?'

James was becoming irritated by the directness of his interrogation.

'I am doing my best as I hope I always have done,' said James. He knew that the continuing struggle with his recent personal tragedy remained a distraction. He was making progress but there was some way to go.

Greenfield leapt to intervene.

'Don't forget how important James is to this office,' he said. 'It has been shown that he has been as competent as anyone, if not more so.'

Nicholson made no comment and turned again towards James. 'Unless you have anything to add, Mr Stedman, I think we can conclude our chat – thank you.'

James rose without speaking and left the room.

Nicholson once again focused on the DI. 'Before I leave, and as mentioned earlier, I would like to go to the main office, talk to some of the staff and try to get an idea of what they do. It's also interesting to know whether they may have any suggestions about the general running of the office. Is that all right with you? There's no need for you to accompany me.'

Greenfield nodded his agreement and left him to it.

XIII

The Haldon Hills are a magnificent setting for what is the most elevated racecourse in the country as well as being one of the oldest established. To the west are the barren hills of Dartmoor and to the east the Exe estuary leading to the sandstone cliffs of Lyme Bay.

With the windscreen wipers at full speed against the driving rain, the horsebox from Lower Barton stables climbed the precipitous Telegraph Hill to its destination at the summit. Two horses were being carried to the race meeting, Southern Pride and Majestic Lady. The former was to represent the owners' syndicate in the third event of the afternoon, a contest over hurdles confined to horses which had not yet won a race.

Majestic Lady was now eleven years old and getting on a bit in racing terms. She was a consistent and genuine mare who had repaid her owner by managing to win a race or two each season. Her genuine and kind temperament made her a favourite with the stable staff. A handicap steeplechase over three miles in the second race would be her target today.

There were three people in the cab of the vehicle. Gloria was at the wheel with the chattering Gary sitting between her and amateur rider Sam Fitzherbert.

'How much longer is there to go?' called Gary, known neither for his patience nor his punctuality. 'I fancy a horse in the first and I want to be there in time to get my bet on and watch the race!'

'It's pointless you going on and on like that,' replied Gloria, now tired of the perpetual banter of her restless passenger over the last forty miles. 'I'm glad you don't come to the races regularly. Just keep quiet, I'm going as fast as I can.'

Leaning against the passenger side window, Sam sat quietly leafing through his copy of the Racing Post. Pensive and detached, Sam attempted to ignore the chatter between his fellow travellers and studied the opposition in the race in which he was to ride Majestic Lady.

Silence prevailed for a minute or two and Gloria dropped another gear to negotiate the steepest part of the incline to the top of the hill.

Gary drew a small tin from his pocket and started rolling a cigarette while considering Sam's placid demeanour. Sam's short hair and clean-shaven appearance was in stark contrast to the untidy man to his right.

Gary lit up and blew a cloud of sweet-smelling smoke towards the ceiling of the cab at which Sam recoiled and grimaced. 'Do you have to do that in here,' he said. 'None of us wants to inhale whatever fumes are coming out of that thing.'

'Hang loose,' replied Gary with a look of amusement. 'Open the window if it's bothering you.'

'You should realise that I can't do that without letting the rain pour in,' said Sam.

'Hang on mate, I'll turn up the blower on the heater,' a measure which served only to cause the smoke to swirl around the cab at greater velocity.

'What with the rain and your smoke, I can hardly see out,' said Gloria, glowering at her inconsiderate passenger.

'It's gone out now anyway,' replied Gary looking disappointedly at the extinguished stub between his fingers.

'Are you going to win on this thing today?' he enquired, turning to Sam.

'This "thing", as you call it, is a fine horse and a pleasure to ride. It always runs to its best and has never fallen. You can work out the rest for yourself.'

'It doesn't win very often, does it?' enquired Gary.

'You probably wouldn't understand that winning is not everything. The owner and his friends always have a good day out watching their horse run. If she returns safe and sound that's the main thing – earning some prize money is a bonus.'

'If I were an owner, I'd be looking upon it as an investment and want to get my money back and a lot more,' replied Gary. 'There's no point in having a horse if you can't get hold of a bit of privy information and pile your money on when it's supposed to win.'

'Obviously you have a different outlook from most owners, thank goodness,' said Sam.

'I can't afford to think the way they do, can I?' replied Gary. 'The kind of person who owns a horse has plenty of readies and if it costs them a bit it won't make a lot of difference. It's all right for those who inherit pots of cash – I have to work for what I get.'

Gloria elbowed Gary sharply to indicate that enough was enough.

The rain had eased by the time the vehicle reached the brow of the hill. Gloria steered down a narrow lane through the forest of conifers leading to the racecourse. After entering the horsebox compound, Gary hauled on a waterproof he found hanging at the back of the cab, jumped down and wandered off into the drizzle. Gloria helped Sam lower the rear door of the box and they each led a horse to the racecourse stables. Leaving Sam to settle the horses, she made her way to the paddock where the pre-race parade for the first race would take place. On the way, she met Jeff Cameron who was carrying his saddle and riding gear towards the jockeys' weighing room.

They exchanged greetings and Gloria enquired after his health.

'I've been better but that's nothing unusual these days – feeling a bit creaky after riding out this morning. Not as young as I was.'

'You're riding one in the first, aren't you?'

'Yes, but I'm not looking forward to it as much as I might be. On more than half the times it's run, the horse has fallen or failed to complete the course. I wouldn't have taken the ride but I've known the owner for goodness knows how many years and I like to repay his support when I can.'

Gloria called, 'Good luck, and see you in the paddock before the third race.' Cameron went on his way to the weighing room to complete the pre-race formalities.

Seconds later, Charles appeared alongside her.

'I was hoping to speak to Jeff,' he said, 'but I'll be able to catch him later. If not before, we'll see him in the paddock just before Southern Pride's race. Let's go inside for a hot drink. I expect you're in need of something after driving the box all that way.'

'The drive was OK,' replied Gloria, 'but I did wonder for a moment whether we were going to get that great big thing up the hill – and Gary made a nuisance of himself all the way, as usual.'

'Let's hope ours runs well and then it will have been worth the effort,' said Charles. He put his arm around her shoulders and guided her towards the lounge reserved for owners and trainers.

Some of the members of the syndicate owning Southern Pride were inside enjoying a drink provided with the compliments of the management of the racecourse. Charles and Gloria acknowledged them before moving to the bar to claim their welcome beverage.

Bright sunshine appeared as a bank of cloud moved away. Charles and Gloria went to look at the runners being led around the paddock for the first race. At the sound of a bell, the jockeys mounted in readiness to make their way to the starting line.

Charles looked across at the bookmakers' boards and reported to Gloria that Jeff's horse was third favourite at 5-1 with two of the others vying for favouritism at around 2–1.

'You reckon he's got a chance?' came Gary's voice from somewhere behind them.

'Your guess is as good as anyone's,' replied Gloria. 'Knowing your luck, anything you back is probably best avoided. How much are you planning to put on?'

'Well, that would be telling but I'm saving my biggest bet for your horse in the third. Good idea?'

'We know no more than what the form guide in your newspaper tells you,' said Charles. 'You pay your money and you take your chance, as they say.'

'Fair enough,' said Gary and moved away and towards the line of bookmakers.

The runners left the paddock and made their way across the centre of the course to the starting post on the far side. Jeff's yellow silks and cap would be easy to pick out during the race. Horses and riders circled in sight of the starter who had mounted his rostrum and was examining his watch.

With seconds to the off, the starter raised his flag and the eight horses began to walk towards him in a close group. At the drop of the flag, the field moved forward at a trot then quickly bounded into a full gallop. Two miles and twelve fences lay ahead of them as they jockeyed for early position.

While most of the runners were restrained and allowed to settle, the two most fancied horses were given their heads and raced off in front leaving the others trailing a dozen or more lengths behind. At what seemed an alarming pace they skimmed over the two fences in front of the grandstands. The crowd roared their appreciation of the spectacular sight of horses and riders in full flight.

Jeff was sharing third place with another runner and called across to the young jockey on board. 'They're going too quick in this soft ground – they'll tire and come back to us.'

The leaders' dash in the early stages was indeed ill-judged and energy was being sapped that would have been best conserved for the final slog through the sticky ground.

At the rear of the field, two of the horses were pulled up by their pilots who had decided there was no point in driving their mounts which were clearly not up to the task on the day.

The leading pair continued to jump in tandem, neither willing to give way to the other. At the third fence, a straggler at the rear of the field lost its footing, slithered and capsized on the drenched turf.

After the fourth fence, Jeff and the rider alongside him continued to travel comfortably and matched strides behind the first two. The riders knew that it was to their mutual advantage to race in tandem so that their mounts would be encouraged forward by the horse alongside. After another rider had given best to the conditions, there were only four remaining. It was becoming difficult to distinguish between the jockeys as their coloured silks were turned grey by the mud thrown from flying hooves.

The pace slowed as the heavy ground continued to take its toll on stamina and the field turned into the home straight with two fences to jump. The front-running leaders were now asked for a final effort to take them towards the finishing line.

At the penultimate fence the front pair struggled to get over and landed at almost a walk. The relentless duel had sapped their resources.

Better leaps from both Jeff and the only other remaining contestant took them nearer to the heels of the leaders who had led from the start and had little more to give.

The leading pair was passed easily by their two pursuers as the final fence came into view. Jeff was upsides with his only rival as they cleared the last obstacle at which both slipped and skewed on landing. After bumping together and veering off a true line for a few strides, balance was regained and the drive for the finishing line was on.

The crowd rose and cheered on the last remaining contestants in the struggle for the spoils.

Jeff had ridden a patient and watchful race and glanced at his opponent only a couple of yards away to his right. The jockey was already throwing all his effort into pushing his mount towards the winning post, now only half a furlong away. Jeff waited, knowing that timing was everything, but there was a risk - countless races had been lost by leaving the final effort until too late.

He tucked his mount in behind the other horse to gain shelter from the buffeting wind and, with just a few lengths to go, pulled out and made his move. His arms pumped as he drove from low in the saddle. It was close and, for a moment, it looked as if he might not make it but the sheer determination of horse and rider put them a short head in front at the line.

The stirring contest was over and the appreciative crowd had witnessed a memorable display of courage and tactics.

'That was masterful,' said Charles to Gloria as he dropped his binoculars – 'judged to perfection. That's why he's still the best in the business.'

Loud applause greeted Jeff as he was led into the winner's enclosure not least from the owner and his entourage.

After the customary photographs had been taken, Jeff hurried across the paddock to the weighing room to deal with the post-race formalities. He could then take a breather before his next ride, Southern Pride in the third race. Several calls of congratulation came from punters at the paddock rails but he'd been around long enough to know that you were only as good as your last ride. It would have been a different story had he failed to make it to the front.

'That told us a lot,' said Charles to Gloria as they left the stands. 'It's heavy ground and only those with plenty of stamina will get round. Conservation of energy is everything and that's what won the race on the day.'

Gloria felt a tug at her sleeve as a grinning Gary appeared. 'Were you on that one?' he asked excitedly. 'It seemed an obvious choice to me so I put a good wad on.'

'Good for you,' responded Gloria, 'but I expect you'll give it all back to the bookies before the next race.' Gary continued on his way to collect his winnings.

'That was a good start for Jeff,' said Gloria as they watched the horse unsaddled. 'Let's hope he can do the same for us. Majestic Lady doesn't mind the heavy ground so perhaps she'll run well in the next.'

High up in the stands, Miles and James had watched the race together. James was studying his race card and the form figures for the horses in the race just completed.

'The retrospective view is always interesting,' said James, 'working out why horses finish in the order they do, particularly when all the form indicators suggest something different.'

'I suppose the betting market is probably the best guide,' replied Miles. 'Knowing where the money is going must mean something.

'It's a real advantage to have information which is not available to the general public,' he continued. 'Stable staff spend every working day of their lives with the horses and are probably better placed than anyone to judge the well-being of an animal. The lads and lasses are not well paid and probably like the chance to make a few extra quid. They can't really afford to lose so need to be pretty sure before they put their money down.'

The number of runners in the second race was reduced as several trainers made the decision that the soft ground was unsuitable for their charges. In a field of six that went to post, the dependable Majestic Lady was considered to have a reasonable chance and the bookmakers offered odds of 4–1.

Jockey Sam Fitzherbert decided to travel at a steady pace over the three-mile trip knowing that the testing conditions would catch out a few of the opposition. His plan was to wait towards the rear and try to forge ahead a couple of furlongs from home.

Having jumped the third–last fence, two horses edged ahead of Sam on the 11-year old. A quick glance over his shoulder told him that he had no immediate challengers. He urged his mount to quicken but there was no response and it was clear that he would not be able to reach those in front of him. Having accepted that he could not improve his position, he eased down to settle for third place. The horse had run creditably and the owners would be pleased with the performance.

The starting time for Southern Pride's race was approaching. The horse had been tacked up and was being led around the parade ring.

'He seems relaxed and quite happy in himself,' said Charles, 'but he's never run in ground quite this soft and we won't know whether he can handle it until about twenty minutes from now.'

'Whatever happens,' said Gloria, 'we'll learn a lot and should remember that we expect him to be more suited to jumping fences than the smaller hurdles he faces today. I see that the bookmakers are not giving him much of a chance. He's quoted at 10-1.'

The ten runners were led around the parade ring as the crowd at the rails looked for pointers to aid their selection of the likely winner. In the distance, the bookmakers called out the odds as the punters moved around looking for the best value for money. Gary was among them searching for the highest available odds for his planned wager on Southern Pride.

The trainer was joined in the paddock by the members of the ownership syndicate who were discussing excitedly the prospects for their horse.

Miles and James were in conversation with a fellow member of the syndicate, a local farmer and seasoned follower of the racing game.

'I won't be putting a bet on ours today,' he said. 'A lot of folk think that they must put something on just because they're owners. There are plenty of horses that never win so that can be an expensive hobby. They say the bookies never lose and there's some truth in that – I've never met a poor one.'

'I've heard that said about farmers as well,' chipped in Miles with a wide grin.

'Working the land,' replied the farmer, 'we're subject to all kinds of uncertainties beyond our control, not least the weather and the prices we can get for our produce. If all the elements are against us we can make a loss over the course of a year. Then we hope that it can be turned around in the next year but you need an understanding bank manager in the meantime.

'The bookie will always come out on top as long as he balances his book on the race.'

'What does that mean?' asked Miles.

'As the bets are coming in for a particular race, the bookmaker is constantly adjusting his calculations so that he knows what he would have to pay out on whichever one wins. He needs to make sure that the money he has taken on the horses which don't win is more than the amount he will have to pay out on the one that does. It sounds simple but it needs an agile mind.'

'I think we're all here for an enjoyable day out and if Southern Pride does win, or even gets placed in the first three, we'll each receive a small share of the prize money,' said James. 'We don't have to bet on the outcome.'

Jeff arrived and shook hands with the members of the syndicate before entering into discussion with Charles.

'Brilliant ride in the first race,' said the trainer. 'Well done.'

'I'd have won if I'd been riding the horse that finished second,' replied Jeff, with his usual deadpan expression. 'When I can't beat a young lad in a finish I'll give up.'

'I don't need to say anything about tactics,' said Charles. 'You've ridden the horse before and you know the conditions out there, not to mention the fact that you've been around this track countless times and know it like the back of your hand.'

'I think I'll know quite early on how it's going to end up,' said Jeff. 'A lot will depend on how he jumps out of this tacky ground. We'll just have to see how he handles it.'

Sam legged Jeff up and he joined the other runners on the way to the starting post.

Three miles and sixteen hurdles awaited them as they left the start on the far side of the course. Down the back straight, the group moved at a steady pace and all crossed the early hurdles without difficulty. At this stage, it was about settling into a steady rhythm and being placed to have a clear sight of the obstacles as they came up.

By the end of the first circuit, the pattern of the race had unfolded. Some found themselves unable to keep up with the pace and drifted behind. At this stage, Jeff's horse was one of only five with a realistic hope of passing the winning post in first place.

At the next jump, one of the runners departed after brushing through the top of the birch and capsizing on landing. Both horse and rider were on their feet quickly as the remainder plugged on.

All were continuing at a moderate pace aware that they needed to keep something in reserve for the final sprint for home. Southern Pride was tackling the hurdles with ears pricked and was settled in fourth place within sight of the leaders. None of the jockeys was yet showing any anxiety about the way their mount was travelling.

Turning for home on the final right hand bend, they were close up when the last quarter of a mile and the final two jumps came into sight.

The last hurdle was cleared with the five challengers upsides as they landed. Now the jockeys threw all their energy into the drive for the line. Southern Pride was left in third place as the front pair sprinted on at a pace that could not be matched by the others.

Realising that his mount could not reach the two leaders, Jeff had eased when the horse behind him suddenly found an unexpected burst of acceleration and went past him with just twenty yards to the finish. Southern Pride had finished fourth so was out of the prize money.

Back in the paddock, Jeff was unbuckling his saddle when Charles arrived alongside and asked for his comments.

'It never felt likely that he would win,' said Jeff. 'It was a good show but certain things were against him. He went through the mud with determination but he'll be suited by better ground.

'The horse hasn't always jumped his hurdles with confidence but today he crossed every one without touching a twig. I don't know whether you could make it out from the stands but he was giving them a couple of feet of daylight. The others were skimming the hurdles so he was losing a length or so at every one.

'Jumping the larger obstacles will suit him. He's finished the race in good heart and isn't too tired. He's probably as fit as he needs to be after that run and I wouldn't hesitate to enter him for the Wincanton race. Just confirm the date to me as soon as you can and I'll make sure I'm available.'

There was an excited buzz among the syndicate members as Charles relayed the jockey's comments. They hadn't won today but the omens were promising for the next outing. 'I'll assume that you'll all be coming to Wincanton unless you say otherwise,' declared Charles as the group made its way to the paddock exit.

As Jeff started back to the weighing room, a message crackled over the public address system. 'Stewards' enquiry – Stewards' enquiry – Jockey Cameron to the stewards' room – This enquiry will not affect the placings in the race'.

Not for the first time, Jeff found himself on his way to be interviewed by the stewards, seething at the idea that he might be charged unfairly with some perceived offence. In his mind, it was the Press who had labelled him with a certain reputation and he had become an easy target for stewards who might be looking for a way to display their vigilance.

He toed the line in front of the panel of three stewards and the middle one spoke after consulting some notes on the table before him.

'On reviewing the last race, it appears that you did not ride your horse out for the best placing that could be achieved and, as you know, this is an offence under the rules of the Jockey Club. In short, we believe that you eased up after the last hurdle allowing the horse behind you to take third place in front of you. What do you have to say about this?'

In his younger and wilder days, Jeff would have told them in clear and colourful terms what he thought of them and their opinion but experience had taught him to contain his sentiments. These were amateurs having the temerity to question his professionalism.

'It's about judgement,' Jeff commenced, in his blunt manner, 'although I am not sure you would understand that. My horse was beaten having travelled three miles in heavy conditions. There was no way I was going to push him any harder when he'd done all he could. He has a future ahead of him and I wouldn't be the one to break his spirit.'

The three heads went together and there followed a few seconds of muttering before the chief steward spoke again.

'We find you guilty of failing to ride your horse out. You should remember that there are ordinary members of the public out there placing a pound or two of their earnings on races like this. Had you been placed third, those who had backed your horse each way would have had some return on their money.

'You are stood down for three days starting tomorrow.'

'And what about my earnings?' said Jeff angrily. 'I need to make a living like everyone else and now I'll earn nothing for the next three days. You lot might not need the money but I do.'

The chairman exchanged whispers with his fellow stewards either side of him. Following a short pause, he announced that the suspension would be increased to four days to take account of his disrespectful remarks.

The jockey resisted voicing the range of expletives that entered his mind knowing that further comment might result in the sentence being increased to five days, or even more. Returning to the weighing room, he changed and left without answering his colleagues' questions about what had happened at the enquiry. On the way to his car he disregarded some requests for autographs and drove off.

Charles and Gloria were making their way back to the horsebox when Gary made his usual appearing act.

'I've just heard the result of the enquiry. I told you all along Cameron wasn't straight and I blew all my winnings on that horse. Why you use him I do not know.' He marched on towards his free ride home in the horsebox.

'I don't think I can stand all that nonsense on the way back,' said Gloria. 'Do you think Sam can drive? He's probably more capable of ignoring Gary than I am.'

'Yes, come with me in my car,' replied Charles. 'We'll need to think hard before bringing him again!'

XIV

It was just over a week since the Inland Revenue office at Hemport had been visited by Nicholson, the man from the Efficiency Unit at Head Office.

Without any great enthusiasm, District Inspector Arthur Greenfield had implemented Nicholson's suggestions for economies to be made in relation to stationery and supplies. At least the DI would be able to confirm that this had been dealt with when he came back. No doubt the man from Head Office would have dreamt up further recommendations during his absence.

On the previous occasion, Nicholson had turned up at short notice. Today, his visit had been known about a little further in advance and Greenfield sat waiting for him at the appointed time of 10.30.

The visit had been timed to coincide with the morning of Brian Day's interview with Albert Mortimer at the offices of Birch and Company in the High Street. Nicholson had asked to join him as an observer at the meeting.

'More of the same from this man from Head Office, I suppose,' said Greenfield to James when they had met a little earlier. 'We've put in place his ideas about the control of stationery so that should keep him quiet for the time being but, as you know, he wants to attend the meeting with Birch. Day seems to be regarded as something of a rising star and I've no doubt Nicholson will be taking the opportunity to watch how he handles things and making a report to someone further up the ladder.

'By coming back so soon I've no doubt the idea is to remind everyone to keep on their toes.

'I wasn't at all happy with the way that he dealt with you. Although he must have been aware that you were performing well enough, he still wanted to use his own questionable methods of putting a squeeze on you. It rankles, but there's nothing we can do but grin and bear it for now.'

'It wasn't a very enjoyable experience,' said James, 'but it certainly gave me food for thought. Talking it over with a colleague later helped me to see things in a more positive light.

'The statistics show that I'm not doing a bad job,' continued James, 'but we should all be open to re-examining the way we do things. I'm giving it some thought and accept there's probably some truth in what he said.

'I don't think I'm doing any better or worse than before although I understand that someone could conclude otherwise. It's true that I have become inclined to take a softer line than some and recent events in my life may have influenced my outlook.

'It seems to me that having objectives and purpose in life is what fuels the spirit. My journey had been pretty conventional – education, exams, first job, financial security, all leading to settling down and, eventually, marriage. The last stage was cut short for me with the loss of my wife and I'm still searching for the way forward.'

'Look, I'm no counsellor but take your time before making any decisions about your future,' replied Greenfield, concerned that James might reach a hasty conclusion that he might come to regret.

'There's no doubt you're a valuable member of staff and there are times for all of us when we need to ensure that we're continuing to comply with the requirements of our paymasters. We need to play their tune rather than our own version of how we think things should sound.

'Look at me! Retirement looms yet I am still being chased to keep in line. How do you think that makes me feel? Take your time and things should settle down.

'Perhaps you could do with a break from the office. That reminds me, aren't you away on a course shortly?' James confirmed that he would be away from the office on Monday of the following week.

'It's only one day but at least it will be a diversion. What's the course about?' enquired the DI. 'Not more incentives to extract maximum returns from errant taxpayers, I hope! We've all had enough of that for the time being.'

'No, something a bit different this time. The title of the lecture is "Aspects of International Taxation". I'm not sure what that means but I've been sent some notes which I'll be reading over the weekend.'

'I should know more about that myself,' said the DI, 'but I expect they've given up on me. I have a feeling that the international dimension will take on greater importance in the years ahead. The wily so-called professionals will go on searching for ways to beat the system and cross-border arrangements could well form part of it. The backroom boys in London will be working hard to establish treaties with countries whose tax regimes are less transparent than ours.

Some countries invite people to deposit their money with them on the basis that they can be assured a veil of complete secrecy.

'Anyway, James, not exactly a holiday for you but at least you'll have a change of scene. Come and see me when you get back and let me know how it went.'

Not long afterwards, Nicholson arrived and was taken through to Greenfield.

'Did you look into the stationery and supplies matter that I mentioned last time?' he enquired.

'Yes, that's all in place. No doubt you'll be telling me if you've thought of anything else.'

'I will indeed,' said Nicholson, 'but, as you know, the main reason for my visit today is to accompany Day when he goes to see Mortimer and his accountant.

'How's Day been getting on?'

'He hasn't yet taken a case from start to finish so I can't say,' replied Greenfield. 'Having got to know him a little, I am expecting him to be pretty tenacious with his enquiries. But I imagine that's what you want to see from him, isn't it?'

'That's quite correct,' said Nicholson. 'I'm hopeful he will make a difference in this office and contribute significantly to the amount of tax recovered from evaders.

'He should be along soon,' said Nicholson, examining his watch, 'if we are to get to this meeting on time.'

'One thing I have learned about him is that he's a good timekeeper. I've no doubt he'll arrive on the dot,' observed the DI.

True to form, Day knocked a minute later and entered carrying a large file of papers.

'All prepared, then?' asked Nicholson.

'I'm sure you'd agree that preparation is everything,' replied Day. 'It's taken some hours to assemble all the notes and queries but I'm confident everything is ready. Is there anything you would like to ask me before we leave?'

'No, I'm coming along with a clean sheet and an open mind. I'm happy to leave it all to you. If I think of anything pertinent I'll cut in.'

'We're due there fairly shortly so we'd best make our way,' said Day, showing no signs of nervousness that he was about to come under the scrutiny of a senior man.

A short distance down the High Street, the pair arrived at a door alongside the shop window of a ladies' outfitter. "Birch and Company – Accountants" was gold-blocked on the glass panel. They entered and climbed the steep narrow stairway to the first floor.

In what appeared to be the reception area, a typewriter sat on an unmanned desk. Day looked around at the tired décor and noted the faint odour of damp. This was not at all like the slick professional offices of the metropolis.

'I suppose somebody will turn up in a minute,' said Nicholson who prided himself on his punctuality and disliked being kept waiting. 'We are spot on time.' After checking his watch he paced towards the window overlooking the High Street.

'That door probably leads to where we need to go but there's no bell or anything on the desk and we can't just walk through,' said Day, himself becoming impatient.

'What do you think of this town?' enquired Nicholson, turning back from the window.

'It hasn't taken me long to realise that I wouldn't want to spend the rest of my time here. There are attractions in rural life but I'm not ready for it in the long term.

'Unless I've misread all the signs, I've been sent here for a reason and I intend to do my best to achieve what's expected of me. I've no doubt I'll be moved on in due course.

'I'm glad for the opportunity to work in a different environment. London is likely to be more stimulating due to the larger scale of everything, but it's interesting to experience how a rural office works.

'Whether it's a big case in London or a market gardener in Devon shouldn't make any difference. The objective is the same.'

A door handle squeaked as it was turned and the men looked to see who would appear from the inner office.

Birch stepped through and greeted the two inspectors. 'Good morning, I'm sorry there was nobody here to meet you. The receptionist works part-time and she isn't in today.'

He approached Day and shook his hand.

'And you are Mr. Nicholson, I presume. Mr Day mentioned that someone from Head Office would be with him today.'

'I hope that's acceptable to you,' said Nicholson.

'It's all the same to me,' said Birch.

'I expect you'll want to get on. The client is in my office and I'll take you there in a moment.

'Before we go in, I'd like to mention that Mr Mortimer is finding this whole affair very trying. You may well say that it's the same for everybody but it's proper that I should draw your attention to the fact that he is not a well man and I really don't know how he manages to carry on with his physical work. His mental condition is quite fragile and the smallest things seem to disturb him.

'It wouldn't be right for me not to say this as you will, I'm sure, want to take it into account in your approach towards him.'

Neither Day nor Nicholson commented but both nodded to acknowledge what Birch had said.

Birch led the pair down a narrow corridor and opened a door to the left into a small and cluttered office. Mortimer was perched on one of several chairs lining the perimeter of the room. Birch sat behind his desk in the centre of the room and pointed the visitors towards two chairs arranged to face him.

Mortimer did not rise from his chair and remained silent, dwarfed by a large, soiled red pullover. His forlorn expression did not change as he considered the two men.

Birch made no introductions to his client and Day opened his file and set it on his knees. The accountant spread some papers on his desk and was the first to speak.

'For the benefit of everyone, particularly Mr. Nicholson who did not attend the first meeting, I shall sum up the position as I see it.

'I met with Mr. Day and his colleague, Mr. Stedman, at Mr Mortimer's premises a short time ago. Following that meeting, I was left with a number of questions most of which have been responded to.

'A second meeting was requested by Mr Day and today he is accompanied by Mr Nicholson,' said Birch, turning to Mortimer whose eyes were fixed on his shoes. 'I understand that Mr Stedman is no longer involved in the matter.

'My client and I will do our best to answer any further questions you may have.'

'There are a number of matters that I need to address,' commenced Day.

'Primarily, there is concern about the amount of

estimation in the figures you produced. You have said yourself, Mr. Birch, that you could not be certain about the amount of income shown and that you had included an additional sum to allow for this. You said that your estimate was based on your long experience of the workings of the business.

'With respect to you,' continued Day, 'I'm not happy about this. It seems to me that the total income shown is little better than guesswork. If this is so, I put it to you that it would be no different if I were to give my estimate of what has been undeclared and leave it to you to disprove it.'

'You miss the point,' replied Birch. 'I have prepared annual accounts for this business for many years and know how it operates. I am familiar with the records and know Mr Mortimer's personal circumstances. If I decide to include an estimate to compensate for what I consider to be shortcomings in the accounting records, it will take into account my knowledge of the whole picture including my client's normal personal ougoings and way of life. This is very different from you dreaming up a figure without any sound basis of calculation.

'I reject your suggestion that it is just a guess which I regard as an insult to my integrity and professional standing,' continued Birch. 'Your colleagues at Hemport office will be well aware of my policy of co-operation with the Inland Revenue.'

'Now that you have mentioned your professional status,' said Day, 'I see that the lettering on the door to your premises describes your firm as "accountants". I have carried out some research and can't trace your name on the membership lists of any of the recognised professional institutions. To which accounting body are you affiliated?'

'Whether I belong to a professional body is irrelevant,' replied Birch, his voice rising.

Day and Nicholson exchanged glances. Although it was quite possible for an unqualified accountant to carry out perfectly satisfactory work, such an individual would not be subject to the stringent rules that membership of a professional organisation would impose.

'What matters is the competence of the practitioner whether accountant, solicitor or whatever,' continued Birch. 'I have no need to defend myself as I'm confident that my work is to a more than satisfactory standard. I could give you the names of a couple of firms around here whose work is lamentable, despite claiming to be highly qualified.'

Day's tactic was to unnerve Birch and undermine his authority. Having achieved his aim, he switched his approach.

'I need to take a view on this,' Day continued. 'There is no dispute that there are accounting failures and this needs to be dealt with. The only way to approach it is to add an estimated amount to your client's declared profit for income tax purposes. This is no different to what you did in an effort to attempt to regularise the deficiencies but I shall be assuming that the understated amount is considerably greater than you proposed.

'I intend to take the view that your client's takings have been understated by £1,000 over each of the last six years. You are free to contest this in which case I would be asking for evidence to support any reduction you consider appropriate.'

Suddenly, Mortimer entered the conversation. 'How can

you say I earned money I haven't got?' he blurted, clearly distressed at what had been said. 'This can't be right Mr Birch, can it?'

'I hear what you say Albert,' replied Birch, 'and any proposals will be scrutinised very carefully before we even consider agreeing to anything.'

'To move on to another matter,' continued Day, gathering momentum, 'it seems that your client may not be familiar with the definition of what constitutes an employment. Someone who pays remuneration to an employee must make deductions for tax and national insurance before handing over the remaining amount. The money retained must be paid to the Inland Revenue at the end of each month. I have found no evidence that remittances have ever been made to the Collector of Taxes under the Pay as You Earn regulations. This suggests that there are no employees.

'Yet the nature of the relationship with Mr Irvine calls this into question.'

'What about him?' said Albert. 'He does some work for me and I write down what I pay him. What's wrong with that?'

'When we last met,' said Day, 'you said that you had been paying him as a self-employed person, in other words the gross amount with no deductions for tax and national insurance at source.'

'That's correct. He told me he was self-employed so there was no need to keep anything back.'

Day continued to develop the point. 'It's not the case that workers can just choose whether they are employed or self-employed, Mr Mortimer. It is a question of fact based on the type of arrangement with the person who pays them.

'The principles behind this are well established by cases decided in the courts. In my view, he should have been regarded as an employee and statutory deductions made from his remuneration before it was paid over to him.'

'What makes you think he should be treated as an employee?' barked Birch, beginning to share his client's annoyance with what was being put forward.

'I would have thought that you might have known the answer to that, Mr. Birch,' stated Day, sensing that his man was cornered.

'Irvine has worked regular hours at Mr. Mortimer's premises over a long period of time and at a fixed hourly rate. What else would you call it?'

Birch searched for words but gave no response.

Day had looked at Irvine's file at the office and knew that his only income came from Mortimer, a fact that would further support the contention that the basis of the relationship had been that of employer and employee.

'As I have said, deductions should have been made and paid over to the Collector of Taxes. This did not happen and I have prepared detailed calculations of the amount that should have been accounted for over the years. It would be possible for me to go back longer but I have decided to limit my figures to just the last six years. The total loss to the Inland Revenue is about £1,000 and interest will need to be added and compounded. As you appreciate, Mr Birch, there is a right of appeal to the courts but, frankly, I think you would be unsuccessful.'

'That's robbery,' spluttered Mortimer his face reddening with anguish 'I paid the man a fair wage and left it to him to pay his own tax.'

'Don't get too excited, Albert,' said Birch. 'We'll have time to think about all this.'

Nicholson remained silent as Day paused and leafed through some notes before speaking again.

'There is also the matter of the bank account which was not disclosed at the last meeting,' said Day. 'I have since been provided with further statements relating to this account and have noticed that several hundred pounds was banked during the last accounting period. This will need to be added to the declared profit and subjected to tax on the assumption that it was income which was not included elsewhere. Of course, I shall need to assume that the same thing happened in the past. I intend to produce similar calculations for the previous five years and include the results in the final settlement figure.

'I would also like to refer to the lady you called Ruth. You said that most of what was paid to her was to cover housekeeping, presumably groceries and the like. You have mentioned that she helped with some administration for the business and I would like to know what portion of the amount paid to her related to that work. Then we can look into the likelihood of a failure to deduct tax and national insurance, as in the case of Irvine.'

Mortimer's head reeled at the offensive being launched on him by this man and the implied commission of offences, but there was worse to come.

Nicholson spoke for the first time.

'I have listened carefully to the discussion and no doubt, Mr Birch, you will wish to digest what has been said and discuss the implications with your client. Once you have reached your conclusions about the points raised so far, we shall look forward to receiving your offer in settlement of the tax lost.

'Mr Day has outlined his findings and has made it clear that account will be taken of any evidence you wish to submit which might persuade him to reconsider or adjust his proposals. My colleague has indicated that he would be looking back over a period of six years and I should remind you that we may need to consider years earlier than that if evidence of fraud is discovered.

'But there is another point that I would like to raise.'

Suddenly, Mortimer rose from his chair. 'You're out to finish me,' he shouted. 'I don't know what I've done to be spoken to like a criminal. I meet some rough types in my line of work but I've never been treated like this in all my life. I've had enough.'

With that he made for the door and left, his ravings still echoing as he thumped down the stairs.

Birch put his head in his hands. The two inspectors remained impassive.

'I think it's as well Mr. Mortimer has left as there is something further I have to say which, given his loss of composure, is probably best explained to him by you, Mr. Birch,' said Nicholson.

The accountant raised his head but did not speak. He had also had enough for one day.

'At the previous meeting at his premises, I understand that reference was made to Mr. Mortimer's claim that the vehicles affected by fire at his scrap yard were taken to a local landfill site. On the assumption that the local council makes a charge for this kind of tipping, sight of the invoices was requested so that we could ensure that Mr Mortimer was receiving the appropriate tax relief on the payments made. Have they come to light?'

'I asked Mr Mortimer to look for them but I haven't heard anything yet,' replied Birch.

Nicholson stared at the accountant for a few moments before continuing.

'I've had some experience of the kind of business carried on by your client.'

Birch lifted his eyes in anticipation of where this might lead.

'The stock at the commencement of the accounting period in question was valued at £5,000 and this related to the collection of scrap vehicles in the yard. I see that this sum has barely changed over the years so suspect that this is another estimate without a formal valuation being obtained. Would that be correct?'

'That is so,' replied Birch.

'As Mr. Mortimer has said, and as we know from Press reports at the time, the whole of his stock was consumed by fire on that unfortunate summer's day. Your client stated that the remains were disposed of without anything being received for them. Is that true?'

'That's what he told me and I had no reason to doubt him. What can you expect to get for charred remains?'

Nicholson turned momentarily to Day who was listening intently to his line of enquiry.

'I happen to know that the scrap value of a vehicle is greater when it has been burned out.' He paused to allow time for a reaction. Birch looked puzzled and said nothing.

'In the normal conduct of a scrap metal business,' continued Nicholson, 'the whole vehicle is taken away and crushed. The objective is to end up with a block of unadulterated metal. During this process, the non-metallic components need to be removed. The likes of plastic, rubber and glass are worthless and need to be extracted so that only metal remains. The process of removing this material is costly and is reflected in what is paid for the scrap vehicle.

'If, on the other hand, a vehicle is taken to the conversion plant without any of the unwanted elements present, weight for weight its value is greater. This would have been the case with the vehicles incinerated at Mr Mortimer's premises. In effect, the fire would have dealt with the removal of the valueless material. The reduction to its more valuable state would already have taken place before the scrap was sold on.

'I suggest to you that this is common knowledge in the scrap metal business and that Mr Mortimer must have been aware of it. If his stock was worth more than it was before the fire, it's unthinkable it would be simply taken to a council dump, and at some cost. It would have amounted to throwing money away.

'The indisputable conclusion is that he did receive cash for the disposal of the scrap cars. The receipts seem to have been unrecorded so no tax would have been paid. The questions that arise are how much did he get and who paid him, not to mention where the money went. Would you like to comment?'

Shaken by this revelation, Birch thought deeply before answering.

'We are in the realms of serious allegation and it would be wrong of me to attempt to answer without giving the matter careful consideration and discussing it with my client. My first thought is that legal advice may be needed as this is a subject that goes beyond my expertise. I must, therefore, reserve comment.'

'I respect your judgement and would adopt the same stance in your position,' responded Nicholson.

Day was in awe of Nicholson's shrewd and piercing intervention.

'It seems to me that you are planning to bring the full force of the legislation into play without regard to the individual and his means,' said Birch. 'Receiving a wave of tax demands in the kind of figures you are suggesting might drive him to desperate measures but I suppose that wouldn't matter to you.'

'I would have thought it obvious,' said Day, 'that it is our duty to extract the correct amount of tax or are you thinking that he should pay less than his due? If we allowed this kind of thing to happen, other taxpayers would need to pay more to make up for those who do not pay what they should. That wouldn't be fair, would it?

'As to his means, if my colleague is correct and there were proceeds from the sale of the fire damaged scrap, no doubt he would be able to meet any tax bills out of that money, wherever it may be,' added Day with a smug expression.

'But what if he doesn't have the money to pay what you believe he owes?' snapped Birch.

'That's of no concern to us,' replied Day. 'Our work is complete when we have arrived at the amount we believe to be due. The Collector of Taxes then takes over and asks for settlement. If payment is not made the case would be passed to our Enforcement Office who would consider the instigation of court proceedings to recover the debt.'

'I suppose they would strip him of everything he owns,' said Birch.

'Those are your words not mine,' said Day as he gathered together his papers.

Nicholson rose. 'We are grateful to you for your time, Mr Birch. My colleague will be preparing notes of the meeting and providing you with a copy.' The men departed leaving Birch at his desk where he remained pensive for some minutes.

He had been presented with a deep dilemma. He could not ignore the demands of the Inland Revenue for more information about what happened to the fire-damaged scrap vehicles, but he was concerned about questioning the troubled Mortimer further. His client had already stormed out of the meeting with the inspectors and he did not know how much more pressure he could take. Another layer of concern might be one too many.

It had to be faced and there was nothing to be gained by delaying the inevitable. Perhaps there was an explanation as to why no money had been received when the stock was disposed of. If so, it had to be established.

There needed to be a discussion with Albert. He telephoned Mortimer's number and Ruth answered.

'Ruth, it's Birch here, the accountant.'

'Hello Mr. Birch. I am afraid that Albert isn't here. I thought that he was visiting you.'

'He has been with me but left a short time ago.'

'Shall I give him a message?'

Birch decided against doing so as Mortimer would probably not call back for fear of receiving more unwelcome news.

'Please tell Albert I'll call to see him in the morning at about eleven.'

'I shall – I'm sure he'll be here. I'll let you know if not.'

'Before you go, Ruth, how has he been lately, health-wise? I didn't mention it to him when I saw him but he seems to have lost weight and looked very pale.'

'For a long time I have urged him to visit a doctor, but he refuses to go,' replied Ruth. 'I doubt he'll change his ways now. I am guessing he feels something is wrong but doesn't want to know what it is. There is no point in my pressing him.'

'Thank you and I'll see you tomorrow, no doubt,' said Birch, replacing the receiver and reflecting on just how he could best handle this delicate matter.

XV

Ruth sat wondering how Albert would be feeling after the ordeal of his meeting with Birch and the Inland Revenue officers when she heard movement at the back door.

Albert came in looking tired and distressed. He dropped into a kitchen chair drawing deep breaths as he collected himself. Ruth allowed him time to recover and went to fill the kettle. No words passed for a minute or two.

'I've put the kettle on – would you like something to eat?' asked Ruth.

Albert raised his head to look at her. After what I've just been through, I couldn't eat a thing but a hot drink would be just the job.'

Ruth placed a mug of tea before him and drew up a chair opposite. 'Do you want to tell me about it?'

'I don't understand these things but all I know is that the Inland Revenue wants me to pay a lot more tax for years gone by,' gasped Albert, struggling to get his words out. 'They made lots of accusations and said I haven't been paying enough. They're going to guess a figure and send me a bill. From the way they were talking, I won't have the money to pay what they'll be asking for.'

'What did Mr. Birch have to say?' enquired Ruth.

'They came up with a lot of questions and he answered them as best he could. He said we'd have time to think about it.

'I lost my temper and walked out – couldn't take any more of it. Birch will tell me how it all finished up when I see him.

'The way they spoke made me feel like a convicted criminal. I suppose I haven't always been whiter than white but I don't think I deserved that. I'm drained by it all.

'I'm well past retirement age and you know better than anyone that I'm finding it harder to do the work. I'll need to let it all sink in but I don't know whether I'll want to carry on after this.'

'Mr. Birch telephoned when you were on your way back from the meeting,' said Ruth. 'He's calling to see you tomorrow at eleven.'

'That's good. I suppose I need to know how it ended up today and to work out where I go from here. I'll go and lock up the doors to the workshop and then go for a lie down. I feel worn out.'

Ruth watched him as he crossed the yard, moving slowly and uncomfortably. She welled with compassion for this man who had little to look forward to more than seeing the sun rise the next day.

Suddenly, she felt the need to talk to James about what had happened. Although he was no longer involved in the handling of the Mortimer case, he had attended the first meeting at Deepdene and knew the background. She hesitated at the thought of asking him to talk to her about a matter being dealt with by his own department but needed his words of advice.

Mortimer passed through the kitchen and towards the staircase. Ruth called after him as he went.

'It's not a day I usually go into town but I might need to later. Would you rather I stayed if you're not feeling well?'

'No, you go on,' called Albert as he started to climb the stairs. 'I'll be out of the way for a while.'

Ruth filled a cup with what remained of the tea in the pot. What was happening had brought not only Albert's future into focus but also her own. Many times she had pondered what might lie ahead but now the reality might be coming closer.

James had become a friend and perhaps he would be able to help without compromising his official position. Having located the Inland Revenue offices at Hemport in the telephone directory, she paused and reconsidered but went ahead and dialled the number.

'I would like to speak to Mr. Stedman, please,' she said to the operator who then asked for her name. She remembered that she had never told James her surname and that it would mean nothing to him. There was no alternative to giving her first name although she had wished to avoid any suggestion of familiarity.

In seconds, James answered.

'Ruth?'

'James, I didn't want to trouble you… I tried to stop myself from ringing you, but… I hope it doesn't cause too much difficulty.'

'Not at all. It's a lovely surprise to hear from you. Gossip spreads like wildfire in the office and there's probably already speculation about the identity of the lady who called me! But that's the least of my worries.

'I hope all is well,' he said, having detected the anxiety in her voice.

There was a short delay which told James that she was trying to contain her emotion.

'Ruth, please tell me what's worrying you. I'll do all I can to help if there's a problem.'

'I didn't know what else I could do,' she replied. 'There's something I would like to talk to you about but it follows Albert's meeting today with your Inland Revenue colleagues. I wouldn't dream of asking about what took place. It's not my affair. It's really about Albert's reaction and whether there's anything I can do to make him feel less worried. He seems to think his world is about to collapse.

'There's nobody else I can turn to,' she said, her voice faltering as she spoke.

'Ruth, I'm pleased that you felt able to call me and have the confidence to think that I can help. As you suggest, I need to be a bit careful in my position but I see no reason why I can't talk to you as a friend. I have no knowledge of what happened at the meeting and don't really want to know. Your concern relates to Albert's state of mind and how he can best face a challenging situation like this. I can easily imagine that it's all been quite distressing for him.'

'Oh, James... thank you so much.'

'This is obviously something we can't discuss over the telephone so we'll need to decide where and when to meet. As something is bothering you it needs to be soon. It isn't a market day so you wouldn't normally come into town. I finish at five today – could we meet somewhere after that?'

'It's a nuisance but the buses become very unpredictable towards the end of the day so it would be difficult to promise a particular time.'

'I know that you wouldn't be keen for me to collect you from Deepdene but it occurs to me that the Pot Inn is quite near you, that's if you don't mind making your way there in the dark. Do you have a torch?'

'I do and I am quite used to walking down the lane to the main road.'

'See you at six?'

'Thank you, James, I hope you won't think I'm making a fuss and wasting your time.'

'Not at all,' replied James. 'I look forward to seeing you.'

James had been well aware of the visit of Day and Nicholson to the offices of Birch and Company earlier in the day. It was not difficult to imagine that Mortimer had been given a hard time. Day would have been keen to impress the man from Head Office who, from what James had learned of him, was also unlikely to have shown much sympathy.

James went to the Pot Inn in advance of the appointed time to be sure he would be there when Ruth arrived.

As he walked to the entrance, Miles Kemp emerged from inside shielding his eyes from the bright light thrown by the lantern above the door. James recognised his fellow member of the racing syndicate. His loudly checked tweed garments and plus-fours left no doubt about his activities.

'James,' he called loudly, 'what are you doing here? Probably the same as me, I expect!

'I've been out with a shooting party and we ended up here. All the others have gone and I stayed on for a couple of swift ones before going home. It's a jolly good way of meeting people and a couple of them asked for more information about my investment services.'

'Where's your car?' asked James looking around the car park.

'Left it at home – I've called a taxi. It should be here any minute. I'd come in and join you but I'd better get back.'

The beams of bright headlights swept across the car park as Miles's transport arrived. He gave James a hefty slap on the back and walked shakily towards the taxi. 'Bye old boy.' James hoped to himself that Miles had been more in control when taking aim with his gun earlier in the day.

James entered the premises and the usual bartender awaited his order.

'Had a busy day?' enquired James.

'Those shooting boys spend more time in here than they do out with their guns – they can certainly hold their drink!

'Let's hope they all find their way home safely. I'm pleased that Miles has chosen the taxi route.

'He's the life and soul is Miles. What can I get you?'

James studied the beer pumps and chose the local brew.

'On your own?' enquired the landlord as he filled the glass.

'I've come to meet a friend here. It's a lady named Ruth who lives not far away. Perhaps you know her.'

'If it's the one I think it is she's a lovely lady. We don't see her very often. She lives with old Albert at Deepene. Girlfriend, is she?'

'We have some common interests and meet occasionally,' replied James who took his drink and went to a banquette in a bay window. From here he watched the stream of traffic heading home at the end of another working day.

James looked at the clock above the fireplace and checked his watch. It was a couple of minutes past six. The bell above the door tinkled and he rose in anticipation that it would be Ruth.

She entered, at the same time removing her hat and shaking her hair free.

James waited while she spoke to the landlord who smiled and welcomed her.

'Good evening, madam,' he said, with a note of conviviality previously unheard by James. 'And how are you?'

'I'm well, thank you – feeling quite refreshed after stepping out in the cool air.'

'You've walked down from Deepdene?'

'Yes, it isn't far and at least there's no traffic to dodge.'

'How's Albert? – I haven't seen him for a very long time.'

'Not at his best, I'm afraid, but he isn't getting any younger.'

'What can I bring you?' enquired the host.

'Anything hot,' said Ruth, 'but I'd prefer tea if you have it, please.'

'Right you are – I'll find the tea bags.'

'James,' said Ruth, turning towards him. 'Thank you for coming.'

James led her to the window seat where she stretched to remove her windcheater and scarf to reveal a plain blue woollen dress beneath. She passed her hands through her brown hair and leant back.

'How are you?' enquired James.

'Speaking with you today helped and I was relieved you could meet me. I still feel guilty about troubling you but I'm concerned about Albert.'

'Does Albert know you're here? No, that's a silly question; of course you wouldn't go out without telling him.'

'After the meeting with Mr Birch and the tax inspectors he returned exhausted and went to bed shortly afterwards, but I mentioned I would probably be going out.

'At that point, I was already hoping that I might be able to talk to you about it although I'm very conscious that it's a matter being handled by your own office. Please just tell me if that makes it difficult for you – I shall quite understand. I was just hoping for a few words of advice as to how Albert might cope with what he's facing.

'It seems he lost patience during the meeting and walked out. I'm sure that wouldn't have helped but he probably couldn't take any more of the questioning. He's just not used to that kind of thing. He won't yet know how the meeting ended but Mr Birch is calling to see him in the morning and he'll find out then. His main worry is that he'll be asked to pay more money than he can possibly afford.'

A mug of tea was brought to her. She took her first sip and began to feel more relaxed.

'Before I continue with my story, how has your day been?' she enquired.

'Pretty routine. Trying to catch up with the ever-increasing stream of paper that crosses my desk. It was a welcome relief when you rang!'

'Did your colleagues work out who I was?' she smiled.

'One or two looked at me later, perhaps thinking I might tell them more, but I decided to keep them guessing. It will give them something to talk about for while!'

'As I mentioned, I had reservations about contacting you,' explained Ruth, 'but you said you might be able to comment in a general way.

'As you know, Albert is in poor health and I fear it's worsening.

'After the meeting at the offices of Mr. Birch this morning

he came back quite distressed. He was very upset by the way he'd been spoken to by the men from the Inland Revenue who seem to have been quite tough with him – made him feel like a criminal, he said.'

She paused for a few moments as the landlord cleared empty glasses from a nearby table.

'Obviously, people have their jobs to do but I am concerned about how it will all affect Albert.

'After he walked out of the meeting, Mr. Birch was left alone with the tax people. We don't know what happened but he will no doubt have more to say when he comes tomorrow. I hope it's not more trouble.'

'I met Albert once, as you know,' observed James. 'It was on the day I saw you for the first time. In our work as investigating inspectors we meet all types some of whom are outright rogues. But Albert strikes me as a basically decent man. I am sure that you wouldn't be associating with him if that weren't the case.

'A lot of people are negligent with their tax affairs. There's always something more interesting to do than filling in tax forms and adding up columns of figures.

'I very much doubt that Albert is the type to orchestrate his activities with the deliberate intent of evading tax but obviously my colleagues have unearthed something which has given them reason to believe he hasn't paid as much as he should. I don't know what's behind it.

'The Inland Revenue is empowered by law to charge penalties and interest where it can be shown that tax has been evaded. The amount levied takes into account the seriousness of the offence. It may be down to just carelessness or, at worst, deliberate fraud.

'But there's no point in worrying about any of this now. Let's be positive and hope that Mr Birch will come up with answers which will satisfy the Inland Revenue.

'I don't know Albert well but I am aware of his situation. It's unfortunate that something like this has come up at this stage of his life.

'If it does reach the point when the Inland Revenue asks for a sum of money, it would be down to Mr. Birch to make every effort to keep the sum payable to a minimum. It will count for a lot if he co-operates fully with the enquiry and responds promptly to any questions.'

Ruth continued to listen carefully, admiring the clarity of James's thoughts and expression, already feeling encouraged that things might not be as bad as she feared.

'It's the uncertainty that's a bother but there's no short cut,' continued James. 'It requires patience and the hope that the conclusion will be a fair one. That's easier said than done but there's nothing to be gained by worrying.

'I know you appreciate that I'm unable to intervene directly. I would, however, be glad to be kept in touch with developments in case I can offer any suggestions.'

'Thank you very much, James. I did not expect a magic wand to be waved. I'm grateful for your words of encouragement. We'll just have to wait and see.'

James reached and squeezed her hand. 'That's the spirit,' he said. 'We'll be optimistic.'

'The other day, Albert gave me a present but did so in a very unusual way,' said Ruth. 'An old wooden box had appeared in the kitchen. I didn't take much notice as Albert often brings in bits and pieces that he comes across in the course of his work.

'He surprised me by saying that there was a present inside for me. The curious thing was that he said I should not open it until I left the house for the last time. He gave me what he said was the only key.

'It's good of him to be thoughtful in this way and I've no idea what it could be. What worries me is that he's never given me anything before so I hope it's not an indication that he feels his time is limited.'

'Does he ever go to the doctor?' asked James.

'I have suggested many times that he should do just that. He shrugs off my suggestions and distrusts "quacks" as he calls them.

'But what do you think could be in a fairly large box which doesn't weigh that much?' asked Ruth.

'The first thing that comes to mind is that it might be some kind of documentation. Perhaps it's his will,' observed James.

'I hadn't thought of that,' said Ruth, 'but he's never mentioned a will. I wonder whether the box might contain his final wishes and directions for me to carry them out.'

'From what you've said, it sounds like there may not be much to leave.'

'I doubt there's much of value,' replied Ruth. 'There's the scrap metal in the yard which I suppose someone would buy. Neither the land nor the property belongs to him. He's told me that, on his death, everything will revert to the landlord.

'When he told me about the gift, he also made a little speech about how he feels guilty that he might have held me back from making more of a life for myself.'

'Ruth, you won't know about the contents of the box for

some time so it's best to put it to the back of your mind for now,' said James. 'I expect it will be a nice surprise.

'I can understand that he's concerned about your future and I'm sure that one day you'll have the opportunity to become more independent.'

'It's quite something to have to declare oneself penniless but that's what it amounts to. As you know, I'm a regular visitor to the State Benefits office. Albert thinks that funding my trips to the shops for provisions covers everything I need but there is a little more to my requirements. I have not let on that I make visits to collect the handouts – he would be upset at the thought.'

'You are unselfish and loyal and have made all the difference to his life. I know that everything will fall into place for you.'

Ruth seemed calmer now and James felt able to change the subject.

'On a happier note, it's not long until the race meeting at Wincanton. I hope you're still able to join me.

'Actually, one of the members of the racing syndicate was leaving here as I came in, so it would have been an opportunity for you to meet someone else who will be there on the day of the races. I don't suppose you know Miles Kemp.'

'I know him to be an estate Agent in the town although I have never met him. In my situation, I have never needed to consider the buying or selling of property,' she said with a wry smile.

'If the time arrives for you to move on from Deepdene, are you planning to stay in the area or do you have something else in mind?' asked James.

'My options are limited so I don't spend too much time thinking about it. I do like it around here but I'm a bit detached from the town and haven't really got to know that many people.

'After this period of uncertainty in my life, I would be happy with anywhere that provided me with a home I could call my own.'

'I understand, Ruth, and I'm sure that you will find the peace and security that you deserve.'

'At the moment I have warmth and a roof over my head so shouldn't complain too much,' added Ruth.

'As for the trip to the races,' she said, smiling, 'I'm looking forward to it immensely.'

XVI

The day after the meeting with Nicholson and Day, Birch drove to Deepdene to see Albert Mortimer.

Try as he may, he was unable to shed the sense of responsibility he felt for the predicament in which his client now found himself. He had carried out his duties in preparing the annual accounts of the business in the same way he always had. In previous years, the figures submitted had been accepted by the Inland Revenue without amendment. On this occasion, questions had been raised.

The Inland Revenue held a list of accountants whose history suggested that their work should be regarded with circumspection. Birch was not in this category and his dealings with the Inland Revenue office at Hemport had been generally uneventful over the years, an indication that the standard of his work was acceptable to them.

Now he asked himself whether he had done enough. He had been articled to a large firm of respected accountants. The training had been thorough and it did not seem to him to be of great importance that he did not manage to pass the final examinations leading to a professional qualification. He believed he knew the mechanics of audit and accountancy as well as anyone, even those former colleagues who had passed their exams with ease and risen through the ranks. In his mind, it was more about being able to do the job competently than just having a string of letters after one's name.

But as a sole practitioner, Birch had no colleagues with whom to discuss problems or share ideas about current working practices; no points of reference in relation to his own level of competence. The problem could only be exacerbated by the passage of time.

What should have been obvious to him had now become patently clear. He had become out of date and entrenched in the old ways and this was no longer good enough in the changing and more demanding environment of professional practice.

He knew now that he had not been sufficiently penetrating in his examination of Mortimer's records. The Inland Revenue had come up with valid reasons why the accounting profit should be questioned and he knew that he could have anticipated this beforehand.

Now there was the need to tell his client that the Inland Revenue was asking for more details concerning the disposal of the fire-damaged vehicles. Mortimer said nothing had been received for them and that they were merely dumped at a council site. Nicholson had advanced reasons why he believed there would have been proceeds of sale.

He drew his car to a halt at Deepdene and parked in the same place that he always did. Drawing out his handkerchief, he cleaned the lenses of his spectacles and stepped out. Tall and dark-suited, he made his way towards the house with satchel in hand. Having been many times before, he knew to go to the back door.

'Good morning Mr Birch,' said Ruth, 'Albert's in the kitchen.'

'Are you well?' enquired the accountant as he entered the passageway inside.

'I'm well enough but poor Albert is not in the best of shape.'

'I'm sure he's not feeling much like talking to me so I'll keep it as brief as I can,' said Birch as he continued towards the kitchen.

Mortimer was at the table with a mug of tea in front of him.

'How are you today,' asked Birch.

'Not good. Now my back's gone,' he said, reaching both palms to the base of his spine. 'I'm not having the best of times at the moment, am I? I lifted something in the workshop earlier on and now I can hardly move.'

Ruth had entered with Birch and observed, 'You must get it seen to, Albert. It looks like you won't be able to work for a while so you won't be able to make the excuse that you can't afford the time off.'

'Perhaps I will,' replied Mortimer, wincing as he attempted to alter his position on the chair.

'Would you like a cup of tea, Mr Birch?' enquired Ruth. He declined and Ruth left the kitchen asking that she should be called if needed.

'What would you do without Ruth?' asked Birch as he settled in the chair opposite his client.

'Don't ask me,' replied Mortimer. 'With all the worries I have at the moment, I don't want to start thinking about how guilty I feel that I'm stopping her from getting on and making a better life for herself. I know I need to do something about it.'

'You left the meeting with the tax people before the end,' said Birch.

'I couldn't take any more of it.'

'I understand – you're not used to that kind of interrogation.'

'What happened after I left?' asked Mortimer. 'Not that I'm very keen to find out.'

'I don't think we need to go over everything that was said. The tax inspectors will have gone away to plan their next move. When they've done so they'll contact me but it probably won't happen that quickly.

'But there was one particular question I need to ask you. Do you want to talk about it now or another time?'

'Carry on.'

'When we first met with them in the workshop, they were asking whether there were any invoices from the council for the tipping of the scrap cars into the landfill after the fire. They asked about it again after you'd gone.'

'I've looked through all the paperwork I have,' continued Birch, 'and can't find a record of any documentation to back up the payment of anything to the council. I don't expect you've had time to take another look.'

Mortimer raised an unsteady hand and took a sip from his mug. He looked directly at Birch for a few seconds before speaking.

'You're my professional adviser, aren't you?'

'Yes – it's been a long time,' replied Birch.

'If I understand things correctly, that means I can talk to you in confidence, doesn't it? I mean, you don't have to pass on to the tax people everything I say if I don't want you to.'

'If we agree that something should be kept between us then there's nothing wrong with that,' said Birch, interested to know what was coming next.

'Ruth can't hear us but we both know what she's sacrificed by helping me out. She won't hear of it and always says she's grateful to me for providing her with somewhere to live. Her background is very different from mine.

'Whatever happens I want to see her right and I've done something for her for when I've gone. That won't surprise you, will it?'

'I can well understand that, Albert.'

'I am feeling worn out and haven't felt well for a long time. Now this back problem could stop me working altogether.

'It looks as if I'm worth less than nothing. On my death, the whole of this property goes back to the landlord and Ruth couldn't stay on. There's nothing valuable in the house and my things would probably end up being chucked out. The equipment and tools in the workshop are outdated and patched-up and probably wouldn't meet Health and Safety requirements.

'It's my guess that there wouldn't be enough to pay the bills that the Inland Revenue comes up with.'

Birch had already reached the conclusion that insolvency seemed likely.

'All of this conversation is in confidence including what I'm about to say,' continued Albert. 'Agreed?'

'It goes without saying,' said Birch. 'Client confidentiality is paramount.'

'There are no bills from the council for the tipping of the burned-out cars and that's because they weren't taken to the landfill,' said Mortimer, looking at Birch for his reaction.

The implications of what had been said hit Birch like an electric shock. It was hard to believe that what Albert had said to the tax inspectors was a deliberate deception.

Throughout their relationship, Mortimer had occasionally shown himself to be careless and unreliable but never other than honest and trustworthy. Birch struggled to come to terms with this admission which meant that he had deliberately misguided both him and the Inland Revenue.

'I can see you're shocked and I expected that,' said Mortimer. 'I'm not proud about what I've done but it was the only way.

'There are lots of people out there who own a lorry and do their business in cash – pound notes, no bills, no paperwork. They're very clever in covering their tracks and I doubt the Inland Revenue is even aware that most of them exist.

'There were two or three of them who were more than happy to give me bundles of notes in return for the scrap. They gobbled it all up in no time – like a flock of gulls.'

'And where's the money now?' asked Birch, becoming more grave with the passing moments.

'I'm not going to tell you. Although we are talking between ourselves it's best you don't know.'

Mortimer looked down, heaved and sobbed.

'It's been very hard for me to tell you this,' he continued. 'You've helped me for a long time. I've always trusted you and I think you've had faith in me. Now I've admitted that I've not been honest with you. But you must understand that it hasn't been for selfish reasons. I've had no benefit from the money myself.'

'Albert, I'm grateful to you for confiding in me,' said Birch and reached a hand across the table towards him. Mortimer took it and held it for a few moments before dropping his head disconsolately.

Birch knew there was nothing more to say. It had been difficult for Mortimer to make his confession and further questions would be inappropriate at this time.

'I'll come back in a day or two – just to see how you are. In the meantime, don't worry too much. There's always a way.'

As Birch left the kitchen he met Ruth at the foot of the stairs.

'Not only am I worried about Albert, I am concerned about you. The way he is at the moment will bring an increasing burden upon you.'

'Thank you for your concern,' said Ruth. 'I'm sure we'll get by.'

Birch sat in his car and went over the conversation with his client. Albert's confession had created an insoluble problem. If nothing else, the Inland Revenue would need to be told that no records could be found of payments to the local council for taking away the vehicles. The assumption would be made that he had received something for their disposal but had concealed the amounts. He had pledged confidence to Albert and was not bound to disclose what he had learned about the cash received from the scrap dealers. Birch had been in practice long enough to know what would happen next. The inspectors would not be pleased that an attempt had been made to mislead them and would come down on him heavily. Swingeing tax assessments would be raised upon him leading to demands that there would be no possibility of meeting.

Mortimer said he had received no personal benefit from the money. If that was the case, where did the money go? Even if it had been given away charitably, it would not alter the view of the Inland Revenue that a fraudulent submission had been made.

XVII

James had made the journey to London by train to attend a training session at Head Office in the afternoon.

The eight-thirty from Hemport arrived at Waterloo station on time two hours and forty minutes later.

The journey passed first through the green and undulating landscape of rural Somerset and Dorset. Leaving behind the conurbations of North Hampshire and Surrey, the train slowed as it passed through the densely populated approaches to its final stop.

There was not much call for knowledge of the workings of International Taxation in Hemport. Nevertheless, James found his lecture notes enlightening. As Greenfield had said to him, perhaps this was a subject which would assume greater importance as time went by.

James waited for his carriage to empty before disembarking on to platform 14 at Waterloo. Barely intelligible announcements crackled and echoed under the glass canopy high above as James consulted his street map and made for the appropriate exit. It was just a few minutes' walk to his destination.

On arrival at the lecture room, he was issued with a name badge and, over a cup of tea, chatted with colleagues from across the country who had also come to learn more about the subject.

On the desk allocated to him was a white envelope

bearing his name. As the group assembled and took their places, James opened it and drew out the single sheet of paper.

It read:

Mr Stedman

I would be grateful if you could meet me after your course has finished. There is something of importance I would like to discuss. If it's convenient, I suggest meeting at the Fitzroy Arms which is about ten minutes' walk from where you are. Look forward to seeing you – I shall recognise you.

Thank you.

Mr Meade

'How strange,' thought James, 'that it doesn't say what it's about.' As the message had appeared on his desk in the meeting room, he could only imagine that it must have been put there by a member of staff in the building. He put his thoughts to one side as the lecture began.

After the closure of the session, some of the attendees were planning to continue the discussion at a hostelry across the road. James made his excuses and expressed his regrets that he would be unable to join them. His curiosity had been aroused by the note on his desk and, not without misgivings, he would be making for the Fitzroy Arms to seek out Mr Meade and find out what it was all about.

With the aid of his map, he arrived at the Fitzroy Arms in light drizzle at about twenty-five minutes to six. The pavements were busy with commuters on the way home and others arriving for the wide choice of the early evening entertainment: theatres, cinemas, and restaurants catering for all tastes.

The Victorian edifice of the Fitzroy Arms stood prominently on a corner, the entrance lit by a large carriage lamp.

James paused to admire the elaborate carved stonework surrounding the windows. Etchings on the frosted glass declared that fine wines, beers and spirits were available within. Despite the inclemency of the weather, the double doors at the corner were wide open and bright chandeliers shed light into the gloom outside.

Why this had been chosen as a place to meet he could not imagine. Not only was it crowded with people, the babble of voices would make it almost impossible to hold a conversation. Nevertheless, and having come this far, he pushed his way through the drinkers huddled inside the door and into a small clearing at the centre of the room.

The walls were decorated with framed and fading monochrome photographs of luminaries who, he presumed, were erstwhile regulars – Augustus John, Dylan Thomas, George Orwell and others – all of whom were likely to have sought inspiration in a glass or two.

His view was limited to the body of people immediately around him and he guessed that the absence of tables and chairs was to maximise the standing room and, thereby, the number of paying customers who could be crammed in.

It was starting to seem like a bad idea. Disinclined to push his way through the crowd to get to the bar and unable to sit down, his patience was running out. He was beginning to consider heading back the way he had come when he felt a hand on his shoulder.

He turned and looked at the man who had touched him. Almost as tall as James, his thin and pale features were topped by receding, wispy black hair. James put him at over fifty years of age but he may have looked older than he was.

'Mr Stedman?' enquired the man.

'I am,' replied James. 'You're obviously Mr Meade.'

'Yes, but I'll say more about that shortly. Thank you for coming to meet me.'

'I don't know what this is about but this doesn't seem the best place to talk,' said James. 'You must have known it would be jam-packed at this time of day.'

'With this in mind,' said Meade, 'I've found a cubicle where we can talk more comfortably. I have already opened a bottle of wine so we won't need to join the queue at the bar. This way, please.'

James followed as Meade made his way through the crowd, at the same time taking the measure of the man leading him. He had pictured someone in a suit and tie but this person was dressed flamboyantly in an open-necked mauve shirt under a light brown leather jacket.

They arrived at a quieter area where there were some screened seating places. Meade appeared to nod to someone, possibly as an acknowledgement for ensuring that the seats had been kept for him. They sat opposite one another on a semi-circular bench and on the round table in front of them was an uncorked bottle of white wine with two glasses.

'I believe that wine is not your favourite tipple but, in the circumstances, I thought it would be easier than queuing up for the real ale.'

James was disconcerted by the idea that this man knew anything at all about his personal tastes. He was already starting to view Meade with suspicion and waited for what he had to say next.

'You'll have a train to catch and we both need to get on so I'll try to come to the point,' said Meade, half-filling the two glasses.

'Please feel free to ask any questions that come to mind and, in the meantime, I'll begin by explaining my position. On behalf of clients, I've been instructed to meet you and deliver a proposition.' James recoiled at this statement and what it could possibly mean.

Meade seemed to James well-balanced and educated and the clarity of his speech suggested a professional background, perhaps in the legal sphere.

'That's the extent of my brief and there will be no requirement for us to be in contact again after today,' continued Meade.

'Why can't whoever they are speak for themselves and why have I been chosen to receive what you describe as a proposition?' asked James. 'Is this some kind of a joke?'

'In your position, you'll be well aware that people often appoint agents to act on their behalf in relation to their dealings with the Inland Revenue,' replied Meade. 'Why do they do so? It's because they feel more confident if they are represented by somebody with more knowledge of the subject than they have. In this case, I have been asked to act as an intermediary. There are other potential advantages in indirect communication, particularly where there may be delicate aspects to a matter.'

'Just stop for a moment,' said James. 'I came here in good faith and in response to the request I found on my desk in the lecture room. I had assumed that it might in some way relate to my attendance at today's meeting. I want to know a lot more about all this before we go any further. I am far from convinced that you are genuine and my coming here was almost certainly a mistake.

'For a start, who are you and where do you come from?'

'I am a professional person, Mr Stedman, and can only ask that you trust me. I have no vested interest in what I have been sent here to do. When this conversation is over my job will be done and you'll be entirely free to decide what further action you take. There will be no attempt at persuasion on my part.'

'Before you say anything else,' said James, 'I would like to know the source of the information which led you to me. You knew how to contact me. You recognised me although we have never met before and even seem to know that I prefer beer to wine!'

'Mr Stedman, it's true I have been supplied with information about you but I'm unable to say how it was gathered. I can only comment in general terms.

'I think that both you and I would be surprised to know just how many people there are within Government circles who are prepared to help in return for some form of consideration.'

This was a new and intriguing world for James who had never imagined this kind of thing went on within the Inland Revenue and certainly not in East Devon.

'An example might be the envelope that awaited you on your desk today. Somebody knew where you were going to sit and managed to put it in the right place. I don't know how that was achieved but it's a remarkable piece of planning.'

'What is your background and experience?' interrupted James.

'There's only so much I can say but as I'll become anonymous after this conversation it does allow me a little more scope.

'I was once employed in a government department, a subsidiary of Her Majesty's Treasury. The activities of that branch are not totally unrelated to those carried out by the Board of Inland Revenue. At that time, like you, I was required to sign the Official Secrets Act.

'Since leaving that employment a number of years ago, I've worked in a freelance capacity, giving advice to individuals or companies needing help with understanding their legal obligations in relation to the UK tax system.

'Sometimes, I'm asked to undertake assignments which are not directly connected with my mainstream work. If I can be certain that my professional standards will not be compromised, and I have the time, then I may accept. This meeting with you today is an example.

'It's unimportant whether I agree or disagree with the line being taken by whoever appoints me. My role is purely to carry out instructions. If I'm confident that what I'm asked to do is within the law, it presents me with no difficulty.

'If you have no further questions at the moment, I would like move on to what I have to put to you. You'll want to get away as soon as you can. I expect you'll want to catch the next train to Hemport which, if I'm correct, leaves in about an hour and thirty minutes.'

There was silence as Meade drained his glass. He looked down at the table before starting to speak again, this time in lowered tones.

'When you return to your office, you will learn of an

event which has taken place in your absence. It will concern the unauthorised removal of documents by an unknown person.

'Those papers contain material of a sensitive nature.'

Stunned by this astonishing revelation, James struggled to think which papers within the office could be of any importance. It was true that security at the government offices was not watertight but dusty files containing routine records of members of the public would be unlikely to interest the criminal. Surely, there was more to be made by lifting jewellery or electrical goods.

'Yes,' said James, 'it's true that all the information held in the public sector is confidential but it certainly doesn't follow that it's of any interest to anybody else.'

'Allow me to move on,' said Meade.

'In a certain office within your department and in the bottom drawer of a particular filing cabinet was a file containing loose confidential papers.' He paused.

It didn't take James long to realise that he was probably describing the District Inspector's office and the filing cabinet in the corner of that room. The informers' letters were – as all the inspectors at the office knew – in the bottom drawer.

'We both know the nature of what was in that drawer,' said Meade, looking enquiringly at James.

The use of the past tense was startling and James waited for whatever was to follow.

'Let's assume that the papers got into the wrong hands,' continued Meade. 'Someone in possession of that material could create an almighty stir if, for example, details were passed to the Press.'

'Who has these papers,' cut in James, 'if they have indeed been taken?'

'I am able to tell you that the file will be in the possession of the joint owners of a business known as Nelson Properties. In the past, you have made efforts to locate a Mr Skinner in his capacity as Company Secretary.'

James knew that one of the informers' letters concerned Nelson Properties but Meade was suggesting that the whole lot had been taken. He didn't know how many letters were in the file but dozens would have accumulated over the years. If the names of those informed upon were made public it would be calamitous for the department which would be accused of failing to maintain confidentiality.

'I believe it's possible that the company may have failed to comply with its tax obligations,' continued Meade, 'to the point where they would prefer that the whole matter was put behind them. This is particularly so as their activities will soon fall outside the United Kingdom tax jurisdiction and will then be of no further interest to your department.

'What they request is a positive assurance that the name of the business has been wiped completely from all Inland Revenue records so that their slate will be clean. While there's a file in your office, which I'm sure there is, or if the name of Nelson Properties appears on any lists or registers that you maintain, there remains the chance that an enquiry might be generated by your department.

'Your name has been forwarded as the person best placed to ensure that this is taken care of.'

Meade halted and waited for James's comments.

James already knew of the steps taken by the directors to relocate the company offshore and that there was the strong possibility of tax being due on the undeclared profits of previous years. Not having paid their dues and scenting that the Inland Revenue were on their trail, it seemed clear they had decided to flee the country and leave their liabilities behind.

'It is unthinkable that I would erase files and records so that the company can escape their responsibilities,' replied James. 'If I did so and it were to be discovered, I would be in the deepest trouble. Without question I would lose my job and the stigma would ruin my future employment prospects. What on earth makes you think that I would want to become involved in anything like this?'

'It's down to you to decide,' said Meade, 'but what's at stake is the reputation of the Board of Inland Revenue. All the informers' letters will be in the possession of individuals who would go to some lengths to get what they want.

'If you do not carry out what is being asked of you, the directors will conclude they still remain open to pursuit for their UK tax liabilities for the years when they were resident in this country. They will also remain well aware of the impact of making the contents of the informers' letters public.

'If the information were to be released, accusations of failure to preserve the confidentiality of taxpayers' records would bring the Inland Revenue to its knees. There would be resignations up to ministerial level. The identities of those informed upon would be revealed. It's not hard to imagine how those people would react.

'If you do as requested and delete all remaining references to the company in the Inland Revenue records, the matter would become history and nobody would be the wiser.

'To reiterate, the company will continue to hold the letters taken from the filing cabinet. If they are pursued by the Inland Revenue at any time in the future, they would be released into the public domain.

'To go to these lengths the scale of evasion must be massive,' said James, 'and why choose me? Given the gravity of the threat, they could have gone straight to the top.'

'I don't know what's involved in terms of tax but I draw the same conclusion as you,' said Meade. 'But it's academic. There's no price on avoiding the discrediting of a government department, possibly even the government itself.

'Why they have chosen someone at your level and in the very office which holds their records is not easy for me to discern. Given the amount of planning put into this, I can only imagine that it has been carefully thought out and all other options considered.

'If I didn't do what they want me to, how would they know?' asked James his voice rising.

'Without wanting to sound glib,' said Meade, 'probably in the same way they know your preference for real ale.

'I think there's no more I can add. I hope I've provided enough information to enable you to make your decision.'

'Oh, and by the way,' he said quietly as he glanced from side to side, 'my name isn't actually Meade. I was required to have a handle by which I could be called. I apologise for the deception but I know you'll understand.' At this, he stood, shook hands with James and passed through the throng towards the exit.

James sipped at his remaining drink and deliberated over

this unexpected and extraordinary encounter. Perhaps the wise thing would be to pretend this evening had never happened. Or should he stick his neck out and wipe Nelson Properties from the records so that the good name of the department would be preserved? But if he were caught in the act of doing so, how would his employer view what he had done?

XVIII

Earlier that same afternoon, Miles had been awaiting a visit from Shaw and Greene.

Coming at such short notice and so soon after their last visit, Miles was worried that they wanted to see him again. His concern was that they might want to talk about the repayment of the money he owed them.

At least there wasn't much time to spend thinking about it. They had telephoned an hour earlier and would be arriving in fifteen minutes. Thinking of an excuse to put them off was not an option. He would rather face it now than live with the uncertainty and, whatever his shortcomings, he was not without courage.

He told the ladies in the outside office that the directors of Nelson Properties were coming and that no telephone calls should be put through to him until after they had left. Both grimaced knowingly and went back to their work.

Miles had told Shaw and Greene that he would try to come up with new marketing strategies for the letting of their flats but had given little time to it. Aside from splashing out on newspaper advertising, he couldn't think of anything. He knew that the real problem was their reluctance to spend on keeping the properties in good order but they wouldn't accept that.

How Miles wished that his accidental meeting with them at the Plough had never taken place for it was that encounter which led to their business association. Although their fees provided a lifeline and a steady income, it seemed increasingly likely that it was only postponing the inevitable and, worst of all, he was now in the grasp of these individuals whom he had come to detest.

Sometimes he considered giving it all up, declaring himself insolvent and facing the consequences. Ultimately, it was the desire to perpetuate his father's legacy that drove him on.

The time of the meeting was nearing and he braced himself, resigned to an uncomfortable experience.

Shaw and Greene arrived and were shown in by one of the ladies. The door was closed behind them and they took their customary positions opposite Miles in the back office. Shaw spoke first.

'Are you well, Miles? You're looking tired.'

'I suppose I'm not at my best. I've had a couple of late nights this week, not purely social - a mix of business and pleasure. Unfortunately, it's all part of the job, meeting people and developing contacts.

'But to what do I owe the pleasure of your early return to my office? Good news, I hope,' said Miles, knowing this was extremely unlikely to be the case.

'When we last met,' replied Shaw, 'I said I would take a look at the figures relating to the loans we advanced to you. It's been a long time since I did so and it makes interesting reading.

His eyes narrowed. 'I blame myself for not doing this sooner but what I've found is worrying.'

Miles froze at the prospect of what was about to be disclosed.

'There have been four advances at different times and, without adding interest, the total is around £15,000.' He pulled a calculator from his pocket and stabbed at the buttons. 'Roughly speaking, accrued interest over the years would increase this sum by about a quarter.'

'We'll come back to that in a minute,' interjected Greene, 'but before we go any further I'd like to bring you up to date with current developments with ourselves and our business.

'As you know, we've been going on holiday to the island of Grand Petra in the West Indies for several years. The last time we saw you we mentioned we were working on some business opportunities there. Unlike the planning authorities in this country, the people in charge over there have been very encouraging about our ideas for property development. It's the beginning of something quite exciting.

'After much deliberation, we've both decided to make a complete break and relocate there. The wives love the idea and can't wait. We'll be leaving within the next couple of days.

'We've dealt with the formalities and now have all the necessary permissions to live and work there. Of course, with a move like this we need to ensure that all the loose ends have been tied up in this country before leaving. Neither of us owns a house in this country now and the registered office of Nelson Properties has been repositioned to Grand Petra.

'We've had some advice from tax specialists and they tell us that to remove ourselves entirely from the United Kingdom tax net, we need to ensure that we have no remaining interests in this country.

'With this in mind,' said Shaw, 'we took the decision to

sell the blocks of flats and this has now been achieved. Completion will take place in a couple of days. We didn't mention this to you before as nothing is certain until the signatures are on paper and the money has changed hands. The new owners may or may not honour the existing tenancies but we'll have no control over that once we've gone.

'We've been grateful for your help in managing the flats but now we've no choice but to terminate our agreement with immediate effect. You'll remember there's a no-notice clause in the agreement.' He paused to allow Miles to comment.

Miles was not shocked – he had been prepared for anything and there was an underlying sense of relief that he would not have to deal with these people again, regardless of the loss of income that would result. But the loans had been mentioned and this was of serious concern.

'There's not much I can say,' said Miles. 'Nothing lasts forever and I suppose this day had to come. I'm glad to have had the opportunity to be of assistance over the years.'

'Obviously, we don't know your financial position, and it's not our affair,' continued Shaw. 'Our advisers say that we must sever all ties with this country if we are to become non-resident for tax purposes. Unfortunately, we'll need to include the loans made to you as part of our winding-up arrangements. We are left with no choice but to decide how to deal with them.'

Miles was cornered. As well as the borrowings from Nelson Properties, his own house had been remortgaged with the bank and he was up to the limit of his overdraft facility. This spelt the end for him.

'I wouldn't be in a position to repay the loans at the present time,' said Miles, deciding to leave it at that and see how they responded.

'We'd guessed that you might not be too well placed at the moment,' said Greene, 'and would hate to think that the consequences of our moving abroad might cause you any problems.'

The lack of sincerity in Greene's words was obvious and Miles expected no quarter.

'We had concluded that immediate settlement of the loans might be inconvenient for you. With this in mind, and taking into account our long association, we have been trying to think of ways to make it as easy as possible for you.'

Perhaps, after all, these men were more humane than Miles had thought. Were they going to suggest some kind of severance package in recognition of his services over the years which might ease the situation? He waited to hear more.

'We have a little problem we think you may be able to help with,' said Greene. 'If you can, it would give us the opportunity to do something in return.

'Mistakenly, we had taken the view that no tax was payable on the rents arising from the flats. We had set up an overseas trust to receive the rents. We are the joint trustees and sole beneficiaries.

'We thought that was the end of the matter as far as the UK tax authorities are concerned. But we are now given to understand that we could be liable to tax on the rents arising over the years on the basis that the properties generating the income are located in this country. This was another reason to dispose of them before the past, as it were, catches up with us.'

Miles was ahead of them and reckoned it was likely that they had known the correct tax treatment all along but kept quiet about it in the hope that the Inland Revenue wouldn't find out.

'I'm sure you can understand that we need a nice, clean break. But as things stand there is an obstacle which continues to present some difficulty.' Greene turned to Shaw who took over.

'There is a document in the possession of the Inland Revenue which we would prefer wasn't there. As long as it is, there would be the chance that it might surface after we've left. This could cause us some inconvenience.'

'What is it and how do you know it's there?' asked Miles.

'I don't think you need to know the exact nature of the document. Suffice to say that if it was no longer in their hands it would eliminate any possibility of a misunderstanding arising at a later date.

'To address the second part of your question, we know it's there because we have an acquaintance who has told us so.'

'This means you have an insider at the Inland Revenue office,' said Miles. 'I can't believe this could happen in a town like Hemport.'

'I suppose there's some similarity with the way you conduct your business. You mix with people and generate contacts in the hope that they may bear fruit in the fullness of time.

'We like having contacts in strategic places so that we can call upon them as and when the need arises.'

'I imagine that such people do not make their services available to you voluntarily,' observed Miles with a wry smile.

'Do you know, Miles, sometimes people don't want payment as such. For example, there may be someone with the need of a little help with their financial affairs, perhaps the restructuring of loans which may have become unmanageable. We try to help if we can and, on those occasions, we look for a way that the person may be able to reciprocate by offering us services of some kind in return.

'It's helpful for us to know what goes on in the Inland Revenue offices at Hemport given their possible interest in our affairs. We have a friend there who has been able to help. Civil servants are not well paid, Miles, and our man has greater demands upon his income than he's able to meet. We have been able to come to a mutually beneficial arrangement.'

Miles considered the men across his desk. The money they had made probably amounted to a fortune in the eyes of most men. Yet here they were finding ways to continue with the irrepressible drive to increase their wealth.

'We have a proposition which could benefit both of us,' said Greene. 'Sadly, our relationship with you will terminate as from today. We are grateful for what you've done but, regrettably, this means the management fees we pay you will come to an end.

'However, and in consideration of your services over the years, we are prepared to consider the cancellation of the outstanding loans and the continuation of payment of your fees for a further three months in lieu of notice.'

Miles was staggered by the degree of generosity on offer

but knew there must be a price to pay. The only question was how much?

'In return for these gestures, we would need you to carry out one more commission for us.'

'And what is that?' asked Miles

'Are you aware of the layout of the Inland Revenue offices?' asked Shaw.

'I don't know why it matters but, yes, I have been there several times to discuss my tax affairs and also to raise the odd question about the operation of Pay as You Earn against the salaries of my employees.'

'The Inland Revenue offices are on the top floor of the government buildings, aren't they?' asked Greene.

'That's correct, the second floor,' replied Miles, trying to make sense of Greene's line of questioning.

'Do you remember a long corridor running the full length of the main office?'

'I do, and the District Inspector's office faces directly down the room. I remember that in particular as the door is solid oak, ornately carved and quite imposing.'

'That's fine – you know enough for our purposes.'

'Why is any of this important?' demanded Miles.

'From what you have said, it's clear that you know your way from the main entrance to the building and all the way to the District Inspector's room.'

Miles remained bemused and could not imagine where this was leading.

Shaw reached into his jacket pocket and produced two keys attached to a leather fob.

'This is a key to the front door to the government offices,' said Shaw, pointing to the larger one. 'And this is the key to a filing cabinet in the corner of the District Inspector's office. It's a grey three-drawer cabinet which is in the corner of the room, behind the desk to the right as you look at it.'

'Wait a moment,' said Miles, 'what on earth are you trying to suggest?'

'We are suggesting that you might like to help us. In return, we will help you by writing off your debt. We would also pay your management fees for the next three months even though you won't have to do any further work. That's a good deal, isn't it?

'If this cleans the slate for you and puts you in a position to stay in business and keep paying the wages of your employees, then surely it's something you would wish to consider very carefully.'

Miles felt the net closing. He rose and paced the small area behind his desk.

'What, exactly, are you asking me to do?'

'We believe there is a thin brown file in the bottom drawer of the filing cabinet I mentioned,' said Shaw, becoming more earnest. 'Between the hours of six and midnight this evening, you would enter the premises using the front door key I've just placed on the desk in front of you. No other doors within the building will be locked including the door to the office of the District Inspector. Enter that office, go to the filing cabinet and open it using the smaller key. Take the file, lock the cabinet and leave the building closing the front door behind you. That's all there is to it.

'At just after nine the next morning, a courier will arrive at your office in the High Street. After you have given him the file, he will hand you a document signed by us as directors of Nelson Properties stating that the loans have been cancelled. An electronic transfer to your bank account of a sum equivalent to three months' management fees will be made within minutes of this taking place.'

'Why doesn't your accomplice on the inside do this for you?' asked Miles.

'We can rely on him for certain things but this is beyond what we could ask of him,' replied Greene. 'We all have our limitations.'

'And why this evening?' enquired Miles, still hardly able to believe what was being asked of him.

'There's no time like the present and it needs to be done without delay. We wouldn't want you to have too long to think about it.

'Just think, in the space of twenty-four hours you could be solvent and clear of all debts to us. There would also be a nice credit to your bank account to go with it.'

'These papers must be pretty important for you to go to these lengths,' said Miles.

'It doesn't take a genius to work out that there is something in that file which we would prefer wasn't there. We're about to start new lives and we don't want anything coming out of the past that could be a nuisance to us. You can understand that, can't you?'

'I may have bent the rules on the odd occasion but I have never deliberately got myself into anything illegal,' said Miles, tensing with the gravity of the matter.

'The decision is yours,' said Shaw. 'After we have left today, we shall never meet again. Whatever you decide, we suggest that you dispose of the keys. It is in your interests that they do not remain in your possession. When we go, I'll leave the keys here on your desk so you can do as you see fit. We have a spare set in case we are forced to think of another way.

'As soon as we know that the file has been handed to the courier, we'll arrange for our pledges to be carried out.

'Conversely, and if our requests have not been complied with, the offers will be withdrawn. I am afraid that we would then have no alternative but to instruct our solicitors to proceed immediately for recovery of the outstanding loans.

'We use a firm in London who are pretty tenacious with this kind of thing. Their tactics can be pretty scary and I have known them leak information to the Press if things don't go their way. The local paper would love a story about the failure of a long-established local business. We wouldn't want this to happen.

'I don't know how your mother would take it if a scandal broke, or what your late father would have thought.'

Miles's eyes blazed. 'What do you know about my mother? Leave my family out of this.'

'Let's just say we do our homework.'

The men rose and moved to the door. 'We'll see ourselves out – hope to hear in the morning that all has gone to plan.'

Miles slumped in his chair, dazed by the ordeal and its implications.

XIX

The bar at the Plough had not long opened when Miles entered, his mind still whirling after his conversation with Shaw and Greene. He was alone as he mounted a stool at the long oak bar and waited to be served.

It had not been difficult for him to come to the conclusion that there was no alternative but to comply with the demands of the directors of Nelson Properties. Although he shook at the thought of the daunting task facing him, the consequences of failing to do so were even more worrying. If he did not carry out their wishes, the directors would move quickly to commence proceedings to recover the loans advanced to him. Financial ruin and disgrace would follow. He could not contemplate his family name being dragged through the courts.

Having been supplied with a glass of single malt whisky, Miles applied his mind to the task before him. He went over everything repeatedly so that there would be no hesitation as he took the steps leading to his goal. He pressed the zipped pocket inside his jacket to reassure himself the keys were still there. Without them his mission would be fruitless.

It was only a quarter past six but Miles was already ordering another drink and beginning to feel a little calmer. 'This must be the last one,' he thought to himself. 'That's enough to set me up for what I have to do but I must keep my wits about me.'

Some regulars entered and called to him as they headed for the bar. He acknowledged them but was in no mood for conversation. In a passing moment, it occurred to him that it was probably no bad thing he'd been seen at the Plough. The theft from the government buildings would be public knowledge once it had been reported and the police became involved. The fact that he was known to have been in the Plough might provide some sort of alibi if it came to people being asked to account for their movements on the evening of the crime.

This glimmer of encouragement soon faded when he reminded himself that it would all count for nothing if he were caught in the act, a not unlikely outcome for an amateur making his first attempt at the commission of a robbery.

He downed his second drink and eased himself off the stool. In the foyer, he pulled on his jacket and passed through the revolving door into the damp, dark atmosphere outside. Shops were closing and there were long queues at the bus stops on either side of the road. Homebound traffic buzzed in both directions.

His expression was taut with nerves as he strode up the High Street, his collar turned up to reduce the possibility of recognition. There could be questions later about who had been seen in the vicinity.

Near the top of the High Street, it was a short dash across the road to the unlit government offices. Civil Servants were apt to leave on the dot of five and everybody would have gone home.

Mounting the steps to the entrance, he fixed his gaze directly ahead to avoid meeting the glance of anyone who might know him.

Having arrived at the door, Miles looked about before inserting the larger of the two keys into the lock. He attempted to twist it left and right but it remained in the vertical position.

Under the light thrown by a street lamp behind him, he could see that the key looked new and had probably only recently been cut. Not long ago, Miles had bought a replacement key for his own front door. It would not work and he needed to take it back to the locksmith for an adjustment. If this was the case with the key now in his hand, it would be all over. If he couldn't get in, there would be no alternative but to abandon his mission. His blackmailers would assume that he had not even tried and proceed to carry out their threats.

There was now a steady drizzle which was beginning to cause a trickle of water to run down his neck. Seconds passed as he tried again and again to make the key turn. The tension mounted and his heart pounded. The longer he was here, the greater the possibility of being identified. He couldn't risk it for much longer.

'Having a bit of trouble?' came a voice from behind him.

Miles spun around, fearful of who it might be. It was a tall, thin man wearing a flat corduroy cap and a long grey raincoat. By his side was a lady of shorter and rounder proportions whose hair was sheltered from the rain by a pink plastic bonnet tied under her chin.

'We're always having trouble with the front door to our chapel,' continued the man in the unmistakable brogue of the Welsh valleys.

'If it weren't for us nobody would be able to get in on a Sunday.

'Do you want me to have a go?' asked the man, glad for the opportunity to display his prowess in this kind of situation.

'Yes,' stammered Miles, looking about, 'if you like.' He was worried that what was becoming a gathering outside the door might attract others curious to know what was going on.

The Welshman drew out the key and looked down its full length to ensure it was truly straight. Seeming to be satisfied, he drew a handkerchief from his pocket and started to wipe it.

'It probably hasn't helped that it was wet,' he said, turning to his wife who smiled her approval of his assessment.

'My name's Clem,' he said, continuing to dry the key, 'and this is my wife Bron. That's short for Bronwen, not an uncommon name where we come from. We're from Pontygwynlais – I expect you've heard of it.'

'Well, actually, I don't think so but I expect it's a very nice place,' replied Miles, trying to control his rising sense of panic.

'No, it's awful. That's why we try to get away as much as we can. It's a hotbed of malicious gossip and whining dogs. The furthest most of them have been is Barry Island.

'We're on holiday in a caravan down by the coast. With all this rain, it's been like trying to sleep inside a drum, hasn't it Bron?' His wife, who had not left his side, nodded.

'That's a nuisance,' said Miles, 'but I'm in a bit of a hurry to get in.'

After looking again closely at the lock, Clem slowly introduced the key and then shoved it hard. He turned to Bron who was glowing with admiration of the exploits of her man.

'It's gone straight in,' said Clem to Miles who didn't know whether this was good news or bad.

'This is what we find with the chapel key. It's no good messing about with it. You have to ram it in.'

Clem twisted the key sharply in a clockwise direction. The lock turned and he threw his weight against the door at the same time. It sprang inwards and the momentum took him with it. Bron trotted in behind him.

'There you are, boy, easy when you know how!'

Miles stepped in quickly pushing the door behind him.

'No lights in here then?' asked Clem.

The last thing Miles wanted was to advertise their presence by turning on the lights.

'Well,' stuttered Miles, quickly inventing an excuse, 'there's been a power cut and we're waiting for the electrician who said we mustn't try to turn anything on until he gets here.'

'Actually,' said Clem, 'there's a bit of light coming through the windows from the road outside and I can make out those fancy architraves around the edge of the ceiling. I spent my life in the building trade so I know a tidy bit of work when I see it. I'd like to have more of a look around.'

'It would be much better in daylight. Perhaps you could come back when it's open to the public,' replied Miles, anxious the couple should get on their way.

'We won't be able to do that as we have to clear out of the caravan early in the morning and go home.'

'That's a pity but perhaps the next time you come,' said Miles.

'Terrible weather isn't it,' said Clem as he and Bron continued to look around the room. 'We'll think again before coming on a winter break down here, won't we love?' His wife took his arm as they passed through the door and disappeared into the darkness outside.

Miles called his thanks after them, closed the door and sank back against it, breathing heavily. He was careful not to shut it tight in case there was a repeat of the difficulty in opening it when he came to leave. Looking around, he saw an umbrella stand and leaned it against the door to hold it in place.

Despite having gone over everything in his mind repeatedly, he realised he had forgotten his torch but he would be able to find his way across the reception hall in the semi-light thrown from outside the building.

He could make out the narrow strip of carpet running from the front door to the foot of the stairs on the far side. Before setting off, he recalled that the artful trespasser always removes his shoes to avoid leaving footprints. He took them off and placed them on the doormat.

From the bottom of the stairs, there would be two flights to climb to the top level where the Inland Revenue offices were located.

Guided by the handrail alongside the stairs, he climbed to the landing on the second floor. He could just manage to read the words "Inland Revenue Enquiries" written large on a sheet of white paper stuck to one of the double doors leading into the main office. The hinges creaked as Miles pushed against the resistance of the closing mechanism.

Inside the windowless room there was darkness but for a series of tiny red and green lights flashing on dormant electronic machines on rows of desks. Aided by this runway of lights and his memory of the layout of the room, Miles walked tentatively towards where he knew Greenfield's office to be.

After tripping over an unseen object and stumbling headfirst, he decided to remain on hands and knees for the remainder of his journey in order to avoid a recurrence.

He crept slowly in the direction of the DI's door with his hands reaching in front of him. In the gloom, the door could not yet be seen but it wouldn't be far ahead. For a few moments, he became disoriented by the darkness but a look back at the lights on the desks behind him confirmed that he had been travelling in a straight line.

Having made contact with the door, he rose to his feet and felt for the handle which turned smoothly and quietly.

Inside, he returned to his knees and inched towards the shadowy shape of the desk which he could just make out a few feet ahead. Soon his hands were on the front panel. He knew that the filing cabinet was behind the desk and in the far right corner of the room from where he was crouching. He moved slowly to his right ready to move straight ahead when he reached the corner of the desk.

Leaving the desk behind, he followed his mental image of the route to the cabinet. He collided with a metal waste paper bin which was heaved to one side. An effort to disentangle his feet from a bundle of cables on the floor set off a series of beeps from something on the desk above him. Probably barely audible in the daytime among the background noise of the office, the sound pulsated and echoed in the dark silence. Miles yanked randomly at the wires until the noise stopped.

Having reached the back wall, he began reaching to right and left for the cabinet. It was a relief to feel the cold metal surface. Climbing to his feet, he ran his hands up and down to ensure there were the expected three drawers. This confirmed, he took out the small key and inserted it into the lock at the top. The barrel revolved smoothly and he dropped to pull out the lowest drawer. There was a cardboard file which seemed to contain a sheaf of paper and he knew this must be what he'd been sent for. The drawer was otherwise empty.

He locked the cabinet, returned to his knees and began crawling back to the door. As he did so, the file slipped from his hand shedding some of the loose documents inside. A circular sweep of the hands gathered all he could find and he could only hope that nothing had been missed. After stuffing everything back into the file, he continued scampering back the way he had come.

'Oh, no!' murmured Miles to himself, 'I forgot about fingerprints.'

'Nothing I can do now,' he thought and kept going.

The journey to the exit was quicker and easier with the benefit of his experience of the trip in the opposite direction and soon he arrived at the front door. After replacing his shoes, he moved the umbrella stand to one side then opened the door slightly and peered through the crack. Outside, a scattering of people was passing in the gloom. When all was clear, he stepped outside quickly, pulled the door behind him as quietly as he could and hurried down the High Street towards his office.

Back at his desk, his head ached and his legs shook uncontrollably.

Once calmed, he straightened the file and placed it on his desk. He had no desire to look at the contents. There would be enough nightmares without adding further fuel to the imagination.

The next morning, Miles sat exhausted at his desk. It had been impossible to sleep with his mind continuing to race with the events of the previous evening. He had left the file locked in his desk drawer and decided to go in early to await the anticipated arrival of the courier.

It was dark when he arrived in town but the High Street was already busy with preparations for the day ahead. Brightly lit windows were being dressed and delivery vans unloading fresh stock.

It was not his usual practice to engage with the outside world this early. Normally, the premises of Kemp & Company were cosily warm when he arrived in the morning. The two ladies were always in before him with the radiators turned on and the kettle filled ready.

Today, the office was cold and damp when he arrived. While shivering at his desk waiting for the room to warm up, he looked at the file in front of him. Perhaps it should be wrapped up and addressed. He decided to leave it unsealed in case the courier wanted to verify the contents. It was now less than an hour before he was due to arrive.

He felt a little better for a hot cup of tea and was beginning to come to terms with the day. Over the last twelve hours or so, he had been a character in an unreal drama and the final scene was about to be enacted. For a fleeting moment, he felt a glow of achievement for the satisfactory completion of his task. This was soon replaced by the sobering realisation that he could have been caught in the act. Even more worrying was the lingering possibility of detection after the event.

Before long, the front door was pushed open and a short, slight man entered wearing orange and black leathers and a visored crash helmet. Miles advanced from his office towards him and waited for him to speak.

'Good morning – would you be Mr Kemp?'

Miles confirmed he was and looked past the courier to the kerb outside where a powerful-looking black motorbike was parked.

The courier looked at a piece of paper in his hand and announced that he had come to collect a package for Nelson Properties.

'I've been told that you'll be giving me something in exchange for this file,' said Miles.

'That's correct. My instructions are to hand over this envelope in return for what I receive,' replied the courier.

'The file contains loose papers,' said Miles. 'Do you need to see what they are?'

'No,' replied the courier, looking again at the note in his hand. 'There's nothing here that tells me to check the contents, but I have been directed to ensure that what I take is sealed down.'

Miles located some wrapping paper and a roll of brown tape on a desk in the main office and quickly made up a secure parcel. The exchange was made and the courier left. He returned to his desk, his fingers trembling as he opened the envelope and examined the contents. He could only hope that Shaw and Greene had sent what they had promised.

He unfolded a document inside which confirmed that all his liabilities to Nelson Properties had been discharged.

There was a separate letter, also signed by both directors, indicating that a bank transfer of £2,100 would be made immediately on receipt of confirmation that what they wanted was in the possession of the courier.

Miles sat and heaved a deep sigh of relief. He was still very tired but the completion of this stage of the process had relieved him of much of the stress. Soon it would be time to confirm that the transfer to his account had been made.

He left his office at a couple of minutes before nine o'clock and went to the bank. Lights beamed through the windows. He stood outside until the door opened.

'Good morning, Mr Kemp,' said the pretty young clerk who looked as fresh as Miles was weary. 'You're early!'

'Do you know,' replied Miles, 'you're the third person who's said that to me this morning. People must think I spend half the day in bed.'

Looking around the banking hall, he saw that only one teller's window was open. George Riley, the assistant manager, was busy counting notes and securing them within elastic bands.

'A bit early for you, Miles,' observed the unsmiling Riley while continuing to count.

'I suppose it might be a bit earlier than usual, but I'd appreciate your help.'

'What can I do for you?' asked Riley, having finished stacking the bundles of notes into neat piles.

'I'm hoping that a bank transfer has been received into my account this morning. I'd be grateful if you could check.'

He watched Riley's expression as he tapped the buttons on an electronic machine in front of him.

Riley occasionally halted and studied whatever was on

the screen before restarting. After what seemed like several minutes, he looked up at Miles.

'Nothing coming up – the overdraft is exactly the same as it was at close of business yesterday.' Miles turned away fearing that this was where everything would start falling apart.

'Oh, wait a minute, something's churning through – this machine can be a bit slow to get going in the mornings. Yes, a cleared payment of £2,100 is showing. Is that the amount you were expecting?'

'You'll be pleased to know that this has cleared the overdraft. Let me see, you now have a credit balance of £612.84.

'Can I help you with anything else?'

'Yes please, just one more thing,' said Miles, stifling his excitement at hearing the news. 'I want to take out £1,000 of the £2,100.'

'I am afraid that you can't do that.'

'Why not? – it's my money.'

'Well, actually it isn't. £612.84 is yours and the rest has been mopped up to clear the overdraft. It's obvious that any credits will be set first against any debit balances. You could apply for another overdraft if you wish but, for the moment, that's how it stands.'

'More bureaucracy and form-filling,' replied Miles. 'We can cut all that out if you just give me the amount I'm asking for.'

'Can't be done,' said Riley firmly. 'I can give you the application forms for a new overdraft but it could take a couple of weeks until the decision comes back.'

Miles went away with £600 of the new credit balance,

disgruntled that the main beneficiary of his windfall was the bank.

The circle had been rounded and things were looking better. He had cash in his pocket. The overdraft had been eliminated, at least for the time being, and the substantial loans cancelled. For the first time for as long as he could remember, he was able to enjoy a sense of financial buoyancy.

His remaining concern was that he would be brought to book for entering the government offices and removing items which did not belong to him. Now was the time to draw on his eternal optimism and believe that he would escape the attention of the authorities. After all, he was a well-known local figure with no history of misdemeanour and would surely be unlikely to rank as a suspect if it came to a hunt for the culprit.

XX

It was the morning after his trip to London. James had been in his office for only a few minutes when the telephone rang. He lifted the receiver and heard the voice of the DI's secretary.

'Good morning, James. Mr. Greenfield asks if you could join him in his room in about ten minutes.'

'Will do,' replied James.

'I'll confirm that to him. 'Bye James.'

On his arrival at the office, James had expected there to be a buzz of chatter about the theft which, according to what he had been told, would already have taken place. As nothing was mentioned to him by any of the staff he passed on the way in, he could only assume that the DI had decided to keep things to himself until he had made an announcement to his senior staff.

James tidied his desk and made his way down the corridor to the office of the top man. He looked around as he went expecting to see colleagues heading in the same direction. Seeing none, he paused outside the door and listened for voices within.

All being silent, he tapped the door and the DI's direction to enter was immediate.

James was still considering the implications of his meeting with the man called Meade the previous day. What Greenfield would have to say about the events of the previous evening might have some bearing on how he would react to the proposition presented to him on behalf of Nelson Properties.

The DI sat straight-backed behind his desk and invited James to sit opposite him. Strong tobacco fumes hung in the air and his pipe was still smouldering in the ashtray.

James took his seat and waited.

'Thanks for coming,' commenced Greenfield. 'I want to talk to you about informers' letters but, before I do, what happened about that Nelson Properties matter? Did you have any luck in tracking them down?'

James knew much more about Nelson Properties than when he had last discussed the subject with the DI but felt, as yet, limited in what he could disclose. 'I've done all I can,' replied James. 'It's on hold at the moment until I can decide on the next move.'

In the course of his preliminary enquiries, James had made all the checks he could think of and had even visited the address of Skinner, the one-time company secretary. Since then, there had been the meeting with Meade and the request that he should delete all references to the company within the Hemport office. He needed to keep the content of that discussion to himself for the time being and, perhaps, forever.

'I see, but we need to reach some sort of a conclusion. As you know, there's been an enquiry from Information Services at Head Office and I need to fill in this form and send it back to them.' After a few moments' consideration, he pushed the form across the desk to James. 'I'll give it to you so you can deal with it when you're ready. That gets it off my desk.'

James knew of the plan to steal the file from Greenfield's cabinet but why had he not mentioned it? Perhaps the DI may not yet have discovered that anything was missing.

'When I first came here, I inherited a long-established practice in relation to informers' letters,' continued Greenfield. 'There are historic reasons for this but we won't go into that now. In the first place, mail addressed to me goes to my secretary outside. She sifts though it and passes me anything requiring my individual attention. This would, of course, include any letters from informers. The next stage is for me to appoint a member of staff to look into each one and report back to me. The original letters are retained by me and kept under lock and key.

'The statistics make it clear that these letters are vital to our efforts in tracking down tax evaders and recovering what they owe us. By comparison with cases selected randomly for investigation, the returns in terms of tax are much higher when based on information supplied by informers. We may view some of these communications with distaste, but they are of material value.'

There was a tap at the door and James turned expecting them to be joined by other staff members. It was the DI's secretary who placed some typing for signature on the desk and then left.

'I'd like your view on a couple of things, James, but it needs to be in confidence. Do you feel comfortable about that?'

'Yes,' replied James. 'Carry on.'

'It's best if what I want to talk about is kept between the two of us. It's not that I don't trust the other inspectors, but the more people who know the greater the chance of things slipping out. Before you know it, what started as confidential can become common knowledge. Even worse, wagging tongues can distort the facts.

'I have reason to believe that someone in the office is leaking information,' announced Greenfield. 'There's been nothing too worrying so far but it shouldn't be happening at all.'

'Can you give me an example?' asked James.

'There are several but there was something in the local newspaper the other week referring to the circumstances surrounding a member of our staff who left at short notice. I got Joan to ring them to ask for the source of their information but, of course, they wouldn't comment.

'All the staff here have signed the Official Secrets Act and my strong suspicion is that someone is not sticking to the rules. If it's proved, instant dismissal would be automatic.

'The local paper seems to be very anti-establishment and we wouldn't want them latching on to anything more controversial.

'What I'm asking you to do is to keep your ear to the ground and let me know if you hear any talk suggesting who might be doing this.'

James felt dutiful towards Greenfield, a man whom he admired and respected. He would have no compunction about providing him with the identity of anyone he believed to have engaged in the illicit passing of information.

'There's another matter which is a bit more startling,' continued the DI.

'I just mentioned informers' letters and how they're kept in my possession. All the inspectors have been told that they're kept locked in the bottom drawer of that filing cabinet.' He pointed over his left shoulder to the corner behind him.

'What would you say if I told you that the letters are not in there at all?'

'Naturally, I would be surprised. There's never been any secret about where you kept them. I would be at a loss to understand why we'd all been told otherwise.'

'In the interests of security, it is sometimes necessary to – shall we say – give out misinformation.' He paused and stared at James who tried to fathom out what he meant by this.

'What I am actually telling people is where the letters are not kept, although they don't know that. It's a tactic from my Army days when deception was an essential ploy in warfare. The idea is to make the enemy believe what you want them to, not necessarily what is truly the case. Do you understand?'

'If the letters are not where people have been told they are, where are they?' asked James.

'That doesn't matter but you can be sure they're in a safer place than the bottom drawer of that cabinet.'

'Then what has been kept in that drawer, if anything?' asked James.

'It's an ordinary file containing loose papers of no interest to anyone. I filled it with a number of routine and out of date inter-departmental memos. From the outside, it looks identical to the one in which the informers' letters are kept.

'Yesterday evening, someone entered the offices and came into this room. They opened that drawer and took what was in it,' continued Greenfield.

It was starting to fall into place. James knew that Nelson

Property's plan was to steal the file from the bottom drawer of the cabinet and take possession of the informers' letters. It was now clear that what was taken would not be what they had expected.

Meade had told James that the papers would be passed to a firm of solicitors. They would not be seen unless called for by Shaw and Greene. They would do so only if the Inland Revenue began to issue enquiries into the activities of Nelson Properties.

As long as the papers stayed within the stolen file, the directors of Nelson Properties would remain ignorant of their true nature. If they were ever motivated to look at them, they would see that they had no bargaining value.

'How do you know that this took place last evening,' asked James as he assessed this remarkable turn in events.

'When I came in today, I noticed that the tangle of electrical cables alongside my desk had been disturbed. Some plugs had been removed including the one leading to my old electric clock which had stopped at about six-thirty last evening.

'There was something else. As I looked down to the cables on the floor, I saw the edges of some sheets of paper protruding from under the desk. I picked them up and recognised them as a couple of the memos I'd put in the file in the bottom drawer of the cabinet. It's obvious that these must have dropped from the file when it was taken out. I checked and the drawer was empty.

'There's no doubt in my mind that whoever took what was in the drawer believed they were taking the collection of informers' letters. There is no other logical explanation.

'Neither can we escape the conclusion that whoever did

this had inside information. How else would they know where to find the file?'

'Was anything else taken?' asked James.

'I've accounted for everything in this room. There's been no report of anything missing in the general office so we can assume the sole objective was to get to that drawer.'

'It also follows that they must have had the keys,' said James. 'Where did you keep them?'

'The keys to the cabinet are kept here, in the top drawer of my desk. It isn't kept locked so anyone could have got to them, but they seem to be in the same place they usually are.'

'And what about the front door to the building?' asked James. 'That's always locked overnight.'

'I don't have a key for it. Somebody in the main reception area has responsibility for locking up after the last person leaves at the end of the day. I took a close look at the lock earlier and it's not damaged.'

'I suppose that someone sufficiently determined could find a way of getting hold of the keys and taking copies,' observed James.

'Exactly,' said the DI, nodding his agreement.

'To sum it up,' announced Greenfield, 'this was a targeted theft by someone who knew what was believed to be in that drawer. Who would want those letters? Most likely, it would be a person or persons who might be adversely affected by something contained within them.

'I'm glad to be able to say that we still have the informers' letters. If my theory is correct, one of those letters will bear the identity of whoever was responsible for the break-in.'

'I think that's possible but there might be another angle,' said James.

'I don't know how many communications were in the file or who they related to,' he said, 'but the possession of those letters would put someone in a strong position if the intention was to carry out some form of blackmail. This would apply regardless of whether or not they had been named in one of the letters.'

'That's perceptive of you and may well be true,' replied the DI, 'but I'm still persuaded to follow the assumption that whoever did it would have been the subject of one of those letters. Not only would the potentially incriminating information have been removed but, at the same time, they would be empowered by the wider ranging confidential material in the file.

'I conclude that this is a cleverly worked double indemnity. They retrieve a communication which casts doubt on their activities and, at the same time, acquire a quantity of potentially embarrassing material relating to other people.'

James was seeing the DI in a new light. The head of the office was a steadying influence and it was testament to his style of management that he remained of even temperament whatever came up. Some saw him as just seeing out his time until his pension scheme bore fruit, but his incisive comments showed there was plenty in reserve when needed.

It was known that he had served with distinction in the Second World War and been decorated for his achievements. Mention was never made of what earned him this recognition but his true mettle was now apparent.

'Looking through the letters, the most recent one was in relation to Nelson Properties, the company I asked to you to look into. This was the first informer's letter received for over a year. The immediately previous ones related to local tradesmen who were being accused of relatively minor misdemeanours such as asking for cash in hand, no paperwork, that sort of thing.

'This leads me to conclude that these Nelson people are behind it. I don't know how substantial this company is, but it seems that they are the only ones that might be of sufficient scale to merit the seriousness of the steps they, or their appointed person or persons, took in entering the premises.'

'But, with respect,' said James, 'the evidence is circumstantial.'

'That may be so,' said Greenfield, 'but we are not attempting to prove a case, merely establishing the most likely suspect. The problem can only be solved by using the balance of probabilities.'

'Can you say any more about what was in the informer's letter?' asked James.

'I mentioned previously that it had been produced on an old typewriter, an obvious effort at concealment of identity. The spelling was inaccurate and the phraseology almost infantile. I believe that this was the common man feeling hard done by and seeing it as a way to get his own back. I didn't mention this to you before but scrawled at the bottom were words to the effect that money was being sent out of the country.'

James recalled Miles's words when he had quizzed him about his dealings with Nelson Properties. He had been involved in the collection of rents for the company arising from blocks of flats in the area and had mentioned that an overseas trust had been the ultimate recipient.

It had also been made clear that the flats were in a poor state of repair and that the occupants' requests for updating were ignored. It seemed likely that a dissatisfied tenant had sought retribution by writing the anonymous missive.

Having delivered what he considered to be a plausible explanation, Greenfield eased back in his chair and waited for James to speak.

'I can see why you have not reported this incident to the police,' said James.

'Indeed,' continued Greenfield. 'If what happened became public, all kinds of problems would arise. The newspapers would have a field day: lack of security at government offices, confidential material taken, details of people's financial affairs made public – it goes on. It's irrelevant that we know there is nothing important among what they took. Just the idea that people could walk in and take away what they wanted would be enough to send the balloon up.

'It's also why I've asked you to listen for chatter in the general office. If I'm correct, there must be someone out there wondering why what has happened has not become common knowledge. It could be that the insider may be unable to contain his curiosity and identify himself by careless words.

'Let's talk about where we go from here,' said Greenfield. 'What exactly did you manage to find out about Nelson Properties?'

'I made enquiries of Companies House, among others, and discovered that the registered office of the company had been at a private address in the town. I sent an enquiry form to the address to ask for more information about the company's activities. At the same time, I decided to visit the property. There was no sign of occupation although I discovered that we were not alone in sending letters to the company secretary at the same address.

'Recently, the registered office was changed and transferred overseas. No officer of the company now resides in the United Kingdom.'

'This wouldn't be uncommon,' said Greenfield. 'It is a classic evasion tactic which involves severing all ties in this country and moving everything abroad.

'To which country has the company relocated?' asked Greenfield, eager to know more.

'The registered office has been moved to the island of Grand Petra in the Caribbean.'

The DI allowed himself a smile as he leaned back in his chair. 'That's good news – these people may not have been quite as clever as they thought.'

As the island was such a long way away, James wondered why.

'Cross border tax evasion has become big business,' continued Greenfield, 'and companies will take every opportunity to evade tax including changing place of residence and manipulating the rules so that they pay little or no tax under any jurisdiction.

'Fortunately for us, they've chosen the wrong territory. It may once have been a suitable location, but not any longer.

'You probably won't know this, James, but we have a small department located in Liverpool, away from prying eyes and ears. The channel of communication with this department is available only to someone of my seniority, in other words at District Inspector level and above. It is known simply as "International Services", a title that does not fully explain its function, and deliberately so.

'As a department, we have been slow to react to the loss of revenue arising from the exploitation of overseas loopholes and there has been intense activity over the last year or so with a view to confronting the problem.

'For such measures to be effective, there has to be international co-operation. Unsurprisingly, not all countries want to participate as they prefer things the way they are. Some are dependent on processing questionable financial transactions to keep their economies afloat.

'Fortunately, a fully reciprocal agreement has very recently been put in place with Grand Petra. This is not yet known to the general public. There is a small group of people within the Liverpool office dealing exclusively with the island, a sign of the importance attached to the connection. When the word gets out, I have a feeling that some of the people who went there to escape tax will be fleeing like rats from a sinking ship. Unfortunately for Nelson Properties, they have chosen the wrong time and the wrong place.

'The island's ruling party is now absolutely committed to stamping out artificial tax evasion schemes which are dependent on using their territory as a haven for business. It may have suited previous administrations to encourage this and reap the financial rewards but this is no longer the case. Companies sheltering there have been charged hefty annual sums by the government and they did very well out of it. Wisely, the Grand Petra administration has decided to start with a clean sheet and develop long-term and legitimate relationships with the international community.

This will bring them greater benefits in the long term.

'Our government is, of course, keen to encourage this change in approach and is assisting with the elimination of the old practices. We have some people working with the authorities on the island and there is a direct link with the International Services department.

'Please let me have a report of everything you managed to find out so we can pass it on. I know that the Liverpool office is fully staffed so you be can sure they'll be on to it immediately. The game is up for these people.'

'What if the directors of Nelson get wind of what's happening and just leave Grand Petra and find somewhere else suitable?' enquired James.

'I think you'll find that our counterparts on the island will take a very tough approach. They want to send a strong message that the fun is over.

'When they learn of our suspicions they will detain the people concerned until we confirm to them that any tax evaded in this country has been settled. During this transition period they'll be taking no chances. They have suspended the principle of innocent until proved guilty for the time being. All suspects remain under virtual house arrest unless and until all charges against them have been fully investigated and any tax liability settled.

'Of course, we won't be able to finalise our calculations of what they owe us overnight. You can be sure they won't have a very comfortable time until then.

'After that the future of the directors of Nelson Properties would not look bright. They'll be kicked off the island and wouldn't be allowed back into the United Kingdom. They would become stateless and have no legal nationality.

'I expect there's a country somewhere that would take them, but it would come at a cost – quite probably everything they have left.'

Meade had done his job and done it well. In his professional manner, he had made the alternatives clear to James. The directors had skilfully planned and executed a theft from the government offices. This was no mean feat in itself.

But Shaw and Greene had overlooked something. They had assumed that the dependable legislature of their homeland would be replicated elsewhere. Although they had taken full advantage of the stable and predictable economic environment of the United Kingdom, they still chose to avoid paying their dues. Now the price would have to be paid.

There was no longer the need for James to give any further thought to the proposition made to him by Meade. Before long, the directors of Nelson Properties would be receiving a letter of enquiry from the Inland Revenue, sent to their new location in Grand Petra. According to what James had been told, this would prompt the directors to retrieve the stolen papers from their solicitors. Only then would they realise that the documents in the file were of no value to them. They would be powerless to repel the inevitable probe into the conduct of their financial affairs.

XXI

It was the day of Wincanton races and Miles would be in his office for only a couple of hours before leaving to make the journey to Somerset's only racecourse.

After arriving in town, he walked past the government buildings, half expecting to see activity related to the theft from Greenfield's office. There might be comings and goings as the police gathered information and evidence.

There was nothing unusual to be seen. This did not mean that everything had died down. On the contrary, it was more likely that the DI had not yet discovered the theft from his filing cabinet. When he did, thought Miles, everything would erupt and questions would be asked.

Seated at his desk, he attempted to set aside the haunting feeling of guilt and drew out his wallet. He counted out £400 which should be more than enough for the afternoon's entertainment.

One of the ladies in the outside office called through to say there was a telephone call.

'I need to get off to Wincanton before long but I'll take it quickly. Who is it?'

'I didn't quite catch the name – something about construction.'

Miles picked up the telephone and announced himself.

'Good morning Mr Kemp. If I'm not mistaken, you're the proprietor of Kemp and Company, aren't you?'

'I have that pleasure,' replied Miles in his usual jaunty style.

'I'll come to the point. I'm sure you're very busy.'

'Well, not too pressed at the moment,' declared Miles.

'My name is Farrell and I am the Sales Director of Barford Construction. You may have heard of us.'

'Yes, I have,' said Miles. 'Keeping my ear to the ground as I must, I believe you've acquired the large development site to the north of the town.'

'That's correct and all our proposals have now been accepted in principle by the local authority. We have the all-clear to build two hundred houses, a mix of detached, semi-detached and terraced, as well as several retail units. It's a big project which will take well over two years to complete.

'We need an agent to help us to market the properties, set up an on-site sales office and so on.

'At a board meeting yesterday, the directors of the company decided that we should appoint an established local agent to represent us rather than one of the national firms, a number of which seem to have sprung up in the town of late.

'We want to win the trust and support of local people and for them to know we are conscious of the need to take their interests into account as we proceed with the development. The success of a project like this means involving the public and listening to what they have to say.

'For example, we are not one of those companies which moves their own workforce from one location to another. As far as we possibly can, we employ local tradespeople to ensure that a fair proportion of the proceeds generated from the sale of our houses feeds back to the community.

'Recruiting a national firm of estate Agents might give the impression that the commission they earn would be channelled to some central operation. We want them to know that it will be staying locally and contributing to the local economy.

'Our function is to make profits for our shareholders, Mr. Kemp, but we pride ourselves on an ethical approach. As part of our plans, we have already agreed to construct a much-needed extension to the playground facilities for the local primary school.

'In summary, we have concluded that your agency is the one best suited to our needs. I believe that you are now the only truly local firm. We've looked into your history and reputation and you seem to fit the bill. You are also in the High Street which is where we need to be.

'Our normal practice is to offer support to our appointed agent by way of an initial investment to make sure the premises are suitable for the necessary marketing displays.'

Miles listened agape to this offer which would be impossible to refuse. An exclusive agreement with no competition! His father's lifetime commitment to building the reputation of the firm was about to pay off.

'Coincidentally, I'm in the course of reviewing my business plan for the immediate future and it wouldn't be too late for your requirements to be incorporated,' said Miles, trying to conceal his elation.

'That seems ideal,' said the caller. 'We would like to meet you as soon as possible to ensure that the necessary arrangements can be put in place without delay. I'll call back later once I've worked out a date with my marketing manager who will accompany me when I come to see you.'

'That's absolutely fine,' replied Miles. 'I'll be out this afternoon but you can make an appointment through one of my staff.'

The telephone replaced, Miles sat back, took several deep breaths and managed to contain the desire to shriek with delight.

So much had happened in a short few days. His liabilities to Nelson Properties had been wiped out and the bank overdraft cleared. Now it seemed there would be a source of income from Barford Construction which would ensure financial security for years to come. Being associated with a national housebuilder could only enhance the reputation of his firm. There would be spin-offs and those wanting to buy a new house on the development might ask him to sell their own, thus generating even more commission. When people eventually moved on from the development, they might again call on his services. The potential was unlimited!

It was time to set off to Wincanton to see Southern Pride run. He smiled to himself as he replaced his wallet in his inside pocket. As good fortune seemed to be on his side, perhaps he should ride his luck and put a good wager on the horse later in the day.

Trainer Charles Edgcumbe's only runner at Wincanton was Southern Pride in the second race.

The box carrying his charge had left in good time for the 40-mile journey from East Devon to Somerset. His sister Gloria was driving and Charles was the sole passenger in the cab.

Gloria's friend Gary had persuaded her to allow him to come along. She was not prepared to contemplate a repetition of his incessant banter of the last occasion and consented on condition that he travelled in the back with the horse. With only one of the two stalls occupied, there would be plenty of room for him to settle down on a bale of hay. Realising there was no alternative, Gary reluctantly agreed to do as he was told.

'It's nice and quiet with him out of the way,' said Charles, indicating over his shoulder to the back of the vehicle. 'Luckily, Southern Pride seems to have accepted him,' he laughed. He was amused at the idea of Gary being shut in with the horse.

'The ownership syndicate has been pretty patient,' continued Charles, 'so let's hope we can give them something to cheer about today.

'On paper, the previous form has not been exactly scintillating. Failing to complete the course on the first two outings followed by a tiring fourth does not make encouraging reading.'

'Yes, but we know there's more to it than that,' replied Gloria. 'It's been a learning curve for the horse and we have also been finding out more about him along the way.

'His previous races have been over hurdles and Jeff Cameron thinks he will be much better suited by fences which he'll tackle for the first time today.

'But the most important factor might be the going underfoot. All his previous runs have been on soft or heavy ground. With little rain over the last week, the going today will be much more to his liking. It should be perfect racing ground.'

'I think everything is in place for a good run,' observed Charles. 'We just need that essential bit of luck.'

Deep down, Charles knew that time was running out. There had been impatient murmurings from some of the owners which could gather momentum if the horse continued to underperform.

Their journey along minor country roads had been tiring. Gloria was glad to swing into a parking place alongside the other horseboxes at the racecourse and turn off the engine. Leaving the cab, she took in the fresh air and stretched her limbs. Set high above the market town, strong winds often prevailed at Wincanton and today was no exception. Charles and Gloria buttoned their coats to the collar and surveyed the scene.

Gary, too, was relieved to find that the box had come to a halt and wanted immediate release from his confinement. He banged the sides of the vehicle and called to be let out.

Charles and Gloria exchanged mischievous smiles and waited for a minute or two before letting down the ramp.

Gary descended stiff-legged pulling on a black woollen overcoat a couple of sizes too large.

'Where did you get this?' asked Gloria pulling at the sleeve of his coat.

'It's as warm as toast,' said Gary, 'one of the best investments I ever made. I only paid a few bob for it – a pal of mine was a bit short so I did him a favour and took it off his hands.'

'Pity he wasn't nearer your size,' commented Gloria.

'Blimey, it's freezing here,' he said as he adjusted his eyes to the bright light. He was not too well suited by outdoor activities, preferring the warmth and comfort of the betting office or watching the racing with his feet up in front of the television.

'That was a nightmare,' he said, 'and the horse kept giving me threatening looks. I'd rather use public transport than go through that again.'

'I made it quite clear,' replied Gloria, 'that you could only have a lift if you travelled in the back. Perhaps you'll think twice in future about prattling on and distracting the driver.'

Gloria and Charles watched with amusement as Gary brushed hay and dust from his clothing. In his hand was a tattered copy of the *Sporting Life*.

'At least you've had plenty of time to study the form,' said Charles, taking the publication from him.

The newspaper was open at the page showing the day's runners at Wincanton and Charles skimmed over the entries for the second race.

'Ten runners in our race, so let's see what the opposition looks like.

'A couple of the horses have won over fences in the recent past and the betting odds suggest one of them will win today's race. The rest of the field is quoted as 6-1 or more and Southern Pride is estimated at 16-1. They're big odds but everyone will be looking at what he's done in the past and reckoning that he won't have much of a chance.'

Gary collected himself and set off towards the grandstands and the adjacent facilities. 'I need a drink,' he said as he marched purposefully away.

Southern Pride was let out and checked over. Unlike Gary, he seemed undisturbed by the journey and appeared relaxed and supple as he was led around. Having settled him in one of the stables provided by the racecourse, Charles and his sister went to see if they could find the owners.

Gary arrived at the public bar and saw Miles Kemp

chatting to a group of people at the counter, ruddy-faced men in tweeds and green wellington boots.

'We've got one in the second race and I fancy his chances today,' announced Miles to the gathering.

'Don't take too much notice of the price. He's been laid out for this one.'

There may have been some exaggeration in his claim but he was enjoying playing the role of an owner, leaving the assembled company in no doubt that he was not just an ordinary punter.

The group departed and Miles was looking for someone else to chat to when Gary arrived at the bar.

'What ho!' said Miles, unable to remember the name of the man who he last met at Lower Barton stables.

'How are you, mate?' responded Gary, pausing to allow Miles time to offer him a drink.

When Miles had a well-filled wallet, he was the epitome of generosity. He ordered Gary a pint and requested a refill for his own glass.

'You seem in good form,' said Gary as he took his first draught.

'I'm feeling good,' replied Miles. 'I've had one or two things go my way lately and I'm looking forward to the day out.'

Gary looked from side to side before speaking. 'I've got a bit of information I'd like to share with you.

'When we were at the stables, I got to know one of the lads and I've kept in touch with him. I called him yesterday for an update on the chances of Southern Pride today and he told me to leave it alone – doesn't think he's ready.'

'I'm getting different vibes,' said Miles. 'The word is that the horse is going to win one day and that it could be today. I'm going to have a decent punt on it.'

'Yes, but you can't beat inside information,' replied Gary, 'and the lad I know sees the horse every day. Nobody's in a better position to make a judgement than he is. The third favourite is a horse called Mighty Red and he reckons he could skate in. That's where my money's going.

'The snag is I'm waiting for a cheque to come in so I'm a bit short of readies at the moment. It's a pity because this one's nailed on.

'I don't suppose you could let me have a score until I see you next?'

This was a good time to catch Miles who was replete with goodwill and well fortified.

'I'll give you twenty-five,' said Miles after some consideration. 'Put five pounds on Mighty Red for me. That gives me some insurance in the unlikely event that my horse doesn't win. If your horse wins, you can give me back the twenty I've lent you plus my winnings on the fiver. How's that?'

'Perfect,' said Gary who was delighted with the deal and happily pocketed the notes.

Charles and Gloria went to the weighing room to see if Jeff had arrived for his ride on Southern Pride. Moving among the other jockeys preparing for the first race, Charles asked whether anyone had seen him. It was clear he had not yet turned up and there was little time left for his rider to book in and go through the preliminaries in time for the second race.

They left and stood outside looking in the direction of the car park. There was still no sign of their jockey.

'This is the last thing we wanted,' said Charles anxiously. 'Everything is in place but for the rider and he's essential if we're to get the best out of the horse.

'We'll need to start thinking about a replacement in case he doesn't show up but there's nobody comparable. His knowledge of the horse is vital. So much time and effort would have been wasted.'

Gloria remained silent, sharing in her brother's concern.

They continued to search for Jeff but without success. 'This would be a downer all around,' said Charles, 'not only for us and the owners but also for Jeff himself. The press would have a field day reporting that he had failed to turn up and putting their own interpretation on why.'

They wandered back towards the weighing room pondering who might take his place on the horse. There would always be jockeys who would be glad of the riding fee, but none with Jeff's ability.

Suddenly, there was the pattering of running feet from behind them. They turned to see Jeff, somewhat out of breath, carrying his saddle and bag of equipment.

'Sorry,' said Jeff, 'roadworks on the A303 and long delays.'

Much relieved, the trainer went with Jeff to the weighing room to smooth the way through the pre-race procedures. They located his silks and ensured that everything was in place for him to get ready in the few minutes remaining before he needed to weigh out. The discussion of race tactics would have to wait until they met in the parade ring.

James parked his Ford Escort within sight of the stands and opened the passenger door for Ruth who had gladly accepted his invitation to join him for the day.

Their journey had been uneventful and they had agreed that, for today, domestic concerns would not be discussed. This was an outing to share and enjoy.

'With your experience of horses, I expect that you'll be able to judge the well-being of a runner by the way it moves in the paddock,' said James.

'All that was a long time ago,' replied Ruth. 'I am as likely as anyone to pick a horse because of its name or the colours worn by the jockey. But selecting a winner is not everything – I am just glad to be here. It's such a long time since I've been to the races.'

'The race will be starting soon,' said James, 'and as owners – in your case, the guest of an owner – we'll be able to go into the paddock before the race, meet the trainer and jockey and see the horse at close quarters.'

The first race was over and the bookmakers were now forming a market for the second, the race in which Southern Pride would be taking his chance.

Gary moved along the bookmakers' boards in the betting ring looking for the best odds for Mighty Red, the horse he had been tipped as the likely winner. So strong had been the betting on the two most fancied horses that his selection had drifted from the early morning forecast of 6-1 out to 9-1.

Gary had taken with him £5 to cover his bets for the afternoon. He added this to the £25 given to him by Miles and put the whole lot on Mighty Red. At 9-1, this would mean a profit of £270 if the horse won, more than had passed through his hands for a very long time.

By now, Miles was not in total control of his faculties but had not lost sight of his purpose to put a bet on Southern Pride to win.

The only question was how much. 'Why shouldn't I have a good bet,' he muttered to himself. 'If I lose it won't break the bank and if I win I'll go home with a very tidy sum.'

Given the support for other horses in the race, the price of Southern Pride had also drifted and was generally quoted at 20-1. He passed along the row of bookmakers' boards and noticed one of them increase the price to 25-1.

He drew out his wallet and riffled through what was inside. Most of what he had started with was still there and prudence guided him to reserve some of it. He gathered a handful of the notes and handed them to the bookmaker offering the best odds.

'All this on Southern Pride,' he announced.

'It's your choice, sir,' said the bookmaker, 'but you know it's an outsider, don't you?'

'It might be outsider to you, but it's not to me,' replied Miles. 'How much have I given you?'

'It adds up to £260, and at 25-1 that means that you would win £6500 – if it passes the post in front.'

'That'll do for me,' said Miles, who took his betting slip and moved away.

Information circulates quickly in the betting ring and the price of the horse was already being marked down with the news of this sizeable wager. Without realising it, Miles had influenced prices across the board. But he had secured good odds and that's all that mattered to him.

After the initial panic of Jeff's late arrival, all was now calm in the parade ring as the trainer and owners of Southern Pride discussed the forthcoming race.

'I don't think I've had the pleasure of meeting this lady,' said Charles of James's companion.

'This is Ruth, a friend of mine. May I introduce Charles, the trainer. Ruth used to ride but hasn't been to the races for some time. I'm looking forward to having the benefit of her knowledge of the racehorse.'

'Delighted to meet you,' said Charles – 'hope you have an enjoyable day. Perhaps we may see you with James at the gallops next time.'

'That would be nice,' said Ruth, 'but don't ask me to sit on one – it's been a long time.'

'Wouldn't dream of it – unless you'd like to, of course.'

Fully kitted, Jeff Cameron entered the paddock and headed towards the group. On the way, he shrugged off the attention of reporters looking for a quote. He had a long memory and would never forget what he perceived to be their fabrications about his private life.

With his frayed jeans and more than ample overcoat, Gary did not quite fit the bill but managed to get himself among the owners of Southern Pride. He arrived alongside Miles who smiled benignly.

'All sorted Miles,' said Gary. 'Your fiver's on Mighty Red.'

'It's nice to have two in the race but I'd rather Southern Pride won considering the amount I've put on it,' replied Miles.

Charles addressed the owners and said how pleased he was that Jeff had agreed to take the ride and that all the preparations for the race had gone well. For the first time, the horse would have suitable ground conditions.

'I see that the price of the horse has dropped within the last few minutes,' said one syndicate member. 'I wonder what that means?'

'It means that the horse has attracted support in the betting market,' replied Charles. 'In other words, someone has put their money down. I cannot imagine why or who it could be.'

Miles shifted a little uneasily but surely his £260 could not have made that much difference. The fact was that in a market with limited turnover the sum he had placed had done just that.

'Well, Jeff,' said Charles, 'are you fit and well?'

'I'm OK now,' he replied, 'but sitting in traffic for an hour wasn't much fun. How's the horse been?'

'He's been handled quietly. Seeming to have reached the peak of his fitness, we didn't want to overwork him. He comes up against fences for the first time today and, as we all know, our hope is that he will fare better over these obstacles than he did over hurdles.'

Inwardly, Charles hoped that his optimistic words would be justified.

'Having ridden him a time or two, I think I've worked him out so we'll see,' concluded Jeff, in his familiar non-committal style.

The ten wind-blown runners reached the starting line on the far side of the course and assembled ready for the off. Anticipation grew and binoculars were raised in the stands.

Soon the race was under way with two miles and four furlongs to travel and ten fences to negotiate.

The pace was steady as the jockeys allowed their mounts to settle into a rhythm. Jumping is the name of the game and it was important to allow the horses to find their stride and avoid errors at the fences.

As the runners passed the stands at the end of the first

circuit of the course, the crowds whooped and cheered for their fancies. At this moderate pace, the horses had remained in a close group and not one jockey had yet made the effort to try to outpace his rivals.

As they quickened with over a mile to run, the field began to change order as first one, then another, lost ground. The urgency shown by their riders was an indication that neither horse was able to keep up.

It was becoming clear that the winner was likely to come from the four horses leading the field which were beginning to draw away from the others.

Jeff Cameron was in fourth place about ten lengths behind the leader and appearing to be going comfortably.

Charles assessed the placings through his field glasses. 'The three in front of ours are the two most fancied horses and the one called Mighty Red. I wouldn't like to say which is going best – they all seem to be travelling well within themselves. Here comes the water jump.'

At this most challenging of obstacles, Southern Pride made an error. He cleared the fence well enough but his rear legs trailed in the water on the landing side. Jolted to his left, Jeff lost a stirrup iron and took several strides to regain it. He reined back to allow sufficient time for his mount to recover its balance but by then the three horses in front had moved well ahead.

With half a mile to go, Jeff knew that hurrying to catch up with the others would be unwise. Experience told him to allow his mount to make up the lost ground gradually rather than expend valuable energy in rushing to try to close the gap.

Southern Pride was going better than in his previous

races and it was clear that the firmer ground was proving to be advantageous.

At the next fence, one of the leading horses toppled. It had cleared the obstacle satisfactorily but lost its footing on landing. Now there were only two in front of Jeff's mount, Mighty Red and the horse best supported in the market. The leaders were now clear of their pursuers by three or four lengths.

Keeping a close eye on the leader, Jeff nudged forward to come alongside Mighty Red. All three horses jumped the next fence fluently and now there were only two remaining obstacles in the home straight.

At this point, the jockeys could hear the mounting roar from the crowds in the stands as all three moved forward in line to the second last fence. It was impossible to tell which horse was most likely to win. It was anyone's race. All cleared the fence and landed upsides.

With only one fence remaining to negotiate, the race was on in earnest and the pilots drove furiously towards the last.

There was a loud gasp from the spectators as the leader brushed through the top of the last fence. He had been in the lead for much of the way and the effort was starting to take its toll. It was not to be his day and the remaining competitors – Southern Pride and Mighty Red – came together with only a furlong to the line.

Gary was standing behind the running rail between the last fence and the winning post, screaming for Mighty Red to pull out one final effort.

Miles was watching the race speechlessly on a television screen in the bar and could hardly believe what was unfolding before him. Would his extraordinary streak of good fortune continue or was it time for it all to come to an end? If Southern Pride won, he would collect a packet. If he were beaten, at least the £5 Gary had put on Mighty Red for him would provide some compensation.

Over the last hundred yards, riders and mounts engaged in an epic struggle to be first past the post.

Locked together as they crossed the finishing line, the judge could not separate them and the evidence of the photo-finish camera was called for. The cheers of the crowd subsided to a hush as the wait for the announcement of the judge's decision began.

'What an exciting race,' said Ruth to James from their position high in the stands. 'Your Southern Pride was there at the finish.'

'Yes, but which do you think went past the winning post first?' asked James after he had calmed himself following the thrilling experience of the battle for the line.

'I couldn't separate them,' said Ruth, 'and I feel sorry for the connections of whichever is placed second. It would be so disappointing to lose by such a narrow margin.'

They left the stands to go to the winners' enclosure where Charles and Gloria were meeting Jeff and Southern Pride as they returned.

'Apart from that one mistake at the water jump, everything went as planned,' said Jeff. 'It was just a pity that the other horse ran out of his skin on the day.

'Before you ask me, I have no idea which of us was in front at the line. It's down to the camera,' continued Jeff as he removed his saddle and weight cloth.

'It was a great performance and we could have hoped for no more,' said Charles. 'The horse did its best and you gave it every chance, Jeff. He's come back safe and sound and there will be another day.'

A televised replay of each race was shown in the bar and Gary hurried there to watch. As he arrived, he met Miles who was equally keen to watch the finish again.

Uncharacteristically, Gary was almost unable to speak with the excitement of it all and the tantalising wait for the result of the photo-finish.

'Looks like it's you or me, mate,' said Gary. 'What do you reckon – how much did you put on?'

'The size of my bet doesn't matter,' said Miles, 'but, as you'll remember, you put £5 of my money on Mighty Red. I also lent you £20 for your bet on the horse. So, if your horse wins, you need to give me not only the winnings on my fiver but also the £20 I gave you. So whatever the outcome of the race, I will get a payback although it's true that it will be a lot less than if Southern Pride gets it.'

At that point, the public address system crackled to presage an announcement. A tense silence fell over the crowd as the result was awaited.

'Here it comes, mate,' said Gary to Miles with fingers crossed.

'Here is the result of the photograph… Dead heat… Dead heat.'

Gary quickly did the sums. 'This means there are two winners so we'll each be paid out at half the odds we took from the bookies. So we both win which can't be bad, can it? – don't want to be too greedy, do we?'

In the paddock, Charles and the syndicate members were joyous. The prize money for winning the race would be shared but that was not the most important thing. Southern

Pride had come first and it didn't matter that another horse had shared that position. The horse had performed gallantly. He was tired but had returned unscathed. There was much encouragement for the future.

Even at half the odds, Miles had filled his pockets with notes and would be going home a happy man. Everything was rosy and, for the moment, there was nothing further from his mind than his furtive visit to the government offices in the High Street.

'Come on mate,' said Gary, taking Miles by the arm. 'The horsebox won't be leaving for a while so there's time for me to buy you a celebratory drink.' Miles needed no persuasion and the unlikely couple headed for the bar.

At the end of what had been an enjoyable and exciting afternoon, Ruth and James made their way back to the car park. Ruth stopped and turned to face James, at the same time taking his hand.

James pressed her hand lightly as he waited for her to speak.

'Thank you for a lovely day out,' she said. 'It's brought back so many memories of when a day at the races was part of my life. I'm glad you invited me.'

She reached and kissed his cheek gently.

'It is more than enough reward for me to hear that you have enjoyed yourself,' said James. 'I hope there'll be more days like it.'

XXII

James had much to think about as he drove to the office the morning after Wincanton races.

What a memorable day it had been and Southern Pride had come first! It wasn't important that the prize money had to be divided. It was the horse's fine performance which mattered most. Now there were exciting possibilities for the future and hopes for greater things. If progress was maintained, it might even lead to an entry at the Cheltenham Spring Festival, the premier race meeting of the National Hunt season.

It was satisfying that a way had been found to track down Nelson Properties. The process would soon be under way to bring them to book. There would be no escape.

Having found a place in his usual car park, James climbed the High Street contemplating the day's work ahead. From the corner of his eye, he saw the accountant Birch hurrying down the High Street towards him with his folded raincoat flapping over his arm. He was moving much more speedily than his familiar ambling gait and was not carrying his satchel.

'Good morning,' called James as Birch came nearer. The accountant was out of breath and seemed in a panic. James halted and noted his flustered appearance. 'Is everything all right, Mr Birch,' he asked.

'I'm very concerned and can't stop to talk,' he replied.

'After all the trouble over Deepdene Farm it seems that something else is amiss. An acquaintance telephoned me a few minutes ago to ask whether I knew that the emergency services had been there since the early hours of this morning.

'Said something about casualties... I'm going there now,' said Birch as he quickened down the hill.

'What's happened?' called James after him.

'I don't know any more than that,' said Birch as he continued on his way.

James stood rooted as he considered the implications. As far as he knew, there were only two people there – Ruth and Albert – so if there was more than one casualty...

He ran to the government buildings and entered the main reception area. Brushing through the crowd of people waiting to be seen, he asked the counter clerk Alice to telephone his department to say that he had been called away on a personal matter but would be back in time for the meetings arranged for him late that morning.

His heart pumped and his throat dried as he hurried back towards the car park. He heaved the door open against a gust of wind and climbed into the driving seat.

'Not Ruth,' he thought. 'So soon after meeting her.'

It might all be a mistake and perhaps there was just one casualty or even none at all. Rumours could distort and exaggerate the facts.

It was inconceivable that there could have been another fire so soon after the last. The probabilities simply ruled this out. The whole thing might be a misunderstanding and the incident, if there was one, could even have occurred somewhere else altogether.

He calmed a little as he reassured himself that this could well be a false alarm and that, on his arrival at Deepdene, all would be as normal.

But this was not to be the case.

As he entered the lane from the main road to the north of the property, he was confronted by a parked police car. A portly uniformed officer stepped out and signalled for him to stop at a cordon of black and yellow tape.

'May I ask your business here, sir?' enquired the policeman through James's open window. 'Are you a member of the press?'

'No, I am not,' replied James. 'I know the people who live here and need to find out what's happened.'

'My orders are not to allow anyone past this point without official authorisation.'

'But I need to know if there's anything I can do to help.'

'There's nothing I can say about any incident which may or may not have taken place here. I suggest that you turn around and return from where you came. You have the look of someone from the newspapers to me.'

'I've already told you that I am not a reporter. Why should you doubt me? If you don't believe me, let me speak to a more senior officer to explain my position.'

'That won't be possible,' replied the policeman. 'I'm in sole charge at this access point and will be carrying out my instructions to the letter.'

This man was clearly unbending and there was no point in wasting time appealing against his decision. James needed to find another way in. He remembered his first visit to Deepdene when he had approached along the rising narrow lane leading from the coastal south side. It was a fair bet that the police would not be manning the entrance from that direction as it was usual for traffic to enter by the way he had just come.

He went back to the junction with the main road and turned left. Within minutes he had entered the lane leading in from the south side. With his previous knowledge of the route, he was able to make quick progress.

He parked his car near the open gate from where he had first seen the Deepdene farmstead with Brian Day. A couple of cars were parked at the foot of the slope but there was no sign of activity.

Leaving the car behind, he made his way quickly down to the property.

Just as when he first visited with his colleague Brian Day, he passed between the rickety outbuildings until the cobbled farmyard opened up in front of him. There was nobody in sight as he approached the door to the house. On his last visit, it was jammed. Not wishing to attract attention, he resisted the temptation to try to push it open and moved to the side of the house to find a way through to the rear.

He stepped tentatively through the thick shrubbery and bramble which was at least providing him with cover from anyone who might have thought him to be an interloper.

Emerging close to the back door, he looked across the yard leading to the workshop. Standing alongside a police car was an officer exchanging notes with another uniformed person.

Glancing to his left, James saw that the back door was open and slipped quietly towards it. Unseen, he entered the house and walked through the passageway which he knew led to the kitchen.

Sitting silently at the table with her back towards him was Ruth.

His voice trembling, he spoke her name and hurried to place his hands on her shoulders. She rose and spun around, sobbing as he comforted her. After some moments, James stood back and looked into her sorrowful eyes.

'How did you know what had happened?' she asked.

'I met Mr Birch in the High Street on my way to work this morning. He was in a hurry and told me that he was going to Deepdene because he had learned the emergency services were here. He didn't seem to know exactly what had taken place so I came as soon as I could to see that you were all right. It's a relief to find you here.

'Would you like me to make you a cup of tea?' asked James.

'No, let me do it,' replied Ruth. 'I know where everything is.'

Whatever the problem was, it had now become obvious that it must have concerned Albert. He wanted to know more but waited until Ruth returned to the table and appeared sufficiently composed to talk about it.

'It was the early hours of the morning, between one and two o'clock,' said Ruth, her voice quivering. 'I couldn't sleep and turned on my bedside light.

'Then I heard movement downstairs. I assumed it was Albert. That was nothing unusual as he often got up in the night and set about doing things.

'After a while, everything went quiet and I thought he'd probably gone outside.

'I tried to read but a few minutes later there was a loud bang after which my light went out. I got up and tried the light switches on the landing, but nothing worked. Power cuts are not unusual here and I always keep a torch in the drawer of my bedside table. I put on my dressing gown and went downstairs.

'Albert was not in the house and I went out into the yard. There was no sign of any movement and the doors to the workshop were open. All was quiet but I knew he must be in there. I carried on and shone the light inside.'

She paused to restrain a rush of emotion then continued.

'Without thinking, I pointed the torch to where he always stood, alongside the bench at the centre of the space. I saw him lying face down. I stepped closer and saw that he was lifeless.

'I hurried back to the house and telephoned the emergency services. They arrived quite quickly and one of them kept me company while they did their job.

'They said he'd been electrocuted and would have died instantly.'

'I am so sorry, Ruth, this has been an awful experience. You shouldn't be alone at a time like this.'

'It's a comfort that you're here now.'

'Has Mr Birch arrived?' asked James.

'He did come, but the police wouldn't let anybody in until they had completed their work. He telephoned when he got back to his office to tell me he hadn't been allowed in and would be coming back shortly. I gave his name and a description to the police so he can be identified when he returns.'

It was not long before a police officer entered accompanied by Birch.

'Mr Birch,' said Ruth, 'it's good of you to come.'

'Not at all,' said Birch. 'It's terrible news. I'm very sorry.'

'Excuse me interrupting,' said the officer, looking at Ruth, 'but I need to leave shortly and there are a few questions I need to ask you. I am sorry to trouble you at this time but I have to return to the station and file a report. I am afraid the circumstances require that I do so without delay.'

Turning to James and Birch, she thanked them again for coming. 'But please do not wait for me. You are busy and we can always speak by telephone later.'

Ruth led the officer towards the sitting room leaving James and Birch together in the kitchen.

'The officer who brought me here told me what they found,' said Birch after a few moments. 'They say that they will not be seeking to interview anyone in connection with Albert's death. This can only mean one of two things. Either it was a horrible accident or he took his own life.'

It had not occurred to James that this was anything other than an accident, probably caused by some failure of the outmoded and ill-maintained equipment in the workshop.

'I could not speculate as to his state of mind,' said James, 'but we both know he was plagued by ill-health. It's true that people can reach the stage where there seems no point in going on.'

'When he was interviewed by your colleagues, Day and Nicholson,' said Birch, 'Albert left the meeting before it had ended. He could not take any more of the relentless questioning. He's just not used to that kind of thing. Your people must have seen that he was wilting under the pressure.

'I stayed and continued the discussion with the two inspectors. It became obvious that I would need to meet with Albert again to discuss what happened during the remainder of the meeting. Things were becoming more serious and Albert knew by the time he left that the measures being proposed by your colleagues could have disastrous consequences.

'I can tell you that he was made to feel desperate. He may or may not have been guilty of what was being implied but, either way, this was no way to treat a man of his age and condition.

'I believe it's possible that Albert was driven to end it all.'

James knew that Nicholson and Day would have adopted a hard line and been unlikely to have taken into account the vulnerability of the individual before them.

Without being able to say so, he found empathy with the view of Albert's accountant. The man from the Efficiency Unit had pushed for sterner measures to be taken by the investigating inspectors at Hemport. James had feared that it would not come without cost.

'It was I who commenced the investigation into the affairs of your client but I've had no involvement in how it's been taken forward by my colleagues since then,' said James.

'I am aware of that, Mr Stedman, and I can't help thinking your manner of dealing with Mr Mortimer would have been more considerate. You may share my view that there is no point in pushing somebody beyond the limits. In the end nobody benefits.

'I have known Ruth since she first came to stay with Albert,' said Birch, 'and have developed considerable respect for her. You have come to know her only recently but, if I am not mistaken, you hold her in the same high regard. Perhaps you will also share my concern about her future. She has given up so much for Albert and will need to start from scratch.'

'Since I first met Ruth,' said James, 'my admiration for her has grown. I hope that I may be able to give some help and support during the difficult time that lies ahead.'

'Despite her obvious qualities, I don't know how she will cope,' said Birch. 'I am aware that she is not well placed financially.

'My time is short so, on the assumption that you will be remaining here until her return, I would be grateful if you could give Ruth my apologies and say that I'll telephone later.'

Ruth returned to the kitchen following her discussion with the police officer. She looked worn and distraught and was still reeling from the disbelief of what had taken place.

'At least, I shouldn't have to face any more questions,' said Ruth. 'The officer said it was unlikely their enquiries would go any further. I take this to mean that what happened to Albert will be put down to an accident and that there will be no more to be said.'

'That seems increasingly likely to me,' said James.

Ruth sat and sighed deeply. 'I'm sure that the horror of it all will return but for the first time since the early hours of the morning, things seem to have calmed a little.

'Mr Birch has gone?' she asked.

'Yes – he felt he could do no more at the moment and said he would telephone you later. He's very sympathetic and I'm sure he'll do everything he can to help.'

'I expect he'll need to prepare final figures for the Inland Revenue,' said Ruth. 'Oh, I forgot for a moment, that's your department.'

'In unfortunate circumstances like this, and unless large amounts are at stake, it is standard Inland Revenue practice to wind everything up as quickly as possible,' said James. 'I fully expect the investigation into Albert's affairs to be dropped without any further enquiries. Mr Birch just needs to work closely with my colleagues to deal with any loose ends.

'It's been so good of you to come, James, but you'll need to return to your work.

'I'm not sure what to do next,' she continued. 'Albert and I were more than acquaintances. In our different ways, we relied on one another. To the outside world, I suppose that I was just the housekeeper who worked in return for her board and lodge. I imagine that the owner of the property will turn up soon to clear the house. Whoever it is won't want to find me here.

'What about all the things that have to be done? I remember from when I helped with the affairs of his late sister that there will be arrangements to be made and various people to be notified.'

'If you'd like, I could speak to Mr Birch about this,' replied James. 'He'll finalise everything with the Inland Revenue and I'll be glad to help him with procedures if he's in any doubt. He'll also be able to put together a statement of Albert's financial position.

'I'm sure he'll know a local solicitor who can deal with any legal matters. Albert's bank will be helpful in closing everything down.

'It won't be the first time that something like this has happened and it will all work itself out. Don't worry about the formalities. There is no requirement for you to do anything. All you have to do is look after yourself and think about your own future.

'I'm afraid I have no choice but to get back to the office

before too long. Is there anyone else who you would like to come and sit with you?'

'It's sad, isn't it,' replied Ruth, 'but I can't really think of anyone. There are one or two neighbours who will probably want to know more about what's happened. What with that and anything else that comes up, I expect I'll be occupied. I won't be able to stay here for much longer so I'll need to spend some time getting my belongings together.

'That's how life has been for me – tied here with no family and little in the way of social contacts. This day had to come but I'm not afraid. My life has been a succession of challenges and I still have the confidence to believe that I can cope and make my way. We'll see.'

'Yes, Ruth,' said James with a concerned expression, 'I know you'll be brave. If you'd like me to, I could call in over the coming days to keep you company.'

'That's kind of you, James. I would appreciate that.

'I suppose I'll need to think about the box that Albert left for me,' she said, raising her eyes to the shelf on which it had been placed. 'I never thought I would be opening it so soon after he gave it to me.'

'Yes, you mentioned that – where is it?'

'It's up there and the key is on that hook.'

'Stay there,' said James, rising to his feet. 'I'll fetch it.'

He brought the box and key and placed it on the table in front of Ruth.

'I can't imagine what's inside,' said Ruth as she gave it a shake.

She turned the key, lifted the lid and gasped at what she saw.

It was full to the brim with bundles of paper money of

various denominations, each contained tightly within an elastic band.

'I don't understand – where could all of this have come from?'

Ruth started to lift out some of the bundles.

'How much do you think is here?' she asked.

'Hard to say,' said James, 'but it could be over a thousand pounds.'

James noticed that the notes were well used and grubby. They had clearly passed through many hands. Some were stained with black deposits, perhaps soot or oil. It did not need a tax inspector to know that this was the tender of someone engaged in a trade which involved payment by cash and where clean hands were not the norm.

Inevitably, his trained mind turned to whether this money had been properly accounted for. It was more than a possibility that the sum had been kept from the attention of Birch when he was preparing the accounts of the business. If so, the declared turnover for tax purposes would have been understated. Birch would be able to confirm this but it might not be necessary to call upon him to do so.

Should he tell Ruth of his suspicions that the money might represent a concealment of income? He quickly tossed the arguments over in his mind. There had been a bond of trust and affection between Ruth and Albert. If she knew of the possibility that the money may have been gathered covertly, her opinion of her benefactor would be sullied. What is more, Ruth's undoubted openness and honesty would probably result in her not wishing to benefit from what had been left to her if the source was in any way questionable.

James went on considering the way to proceed. Ruth would be disillusioned if there was doubt that Albert had acted with integrity. But he had received no personal benefit from the money and his intentions were laudable and well-meaning. Ruth should be allowed to benefit from this legacy and continue to hold Albert in the regard that she always had.

There was no doubt that the money had been hard earned, like everything else that came Albert's way. The difference was that it may have been kept from the Inland Revenue. But what did that amount to in real terms?

James recalled that the declared trading loss shown in Mortimer's accounts amounted to £1,241. Even if the money kept in the box was added into the accounts, it was likely that a loss would still be in evidence. The view could be taken that no tax would be payable whether or not the amount was included.

Ruth continued to gaze at the cache in front of her. Tucked inside the lid was a piece of paper. She unfolded it and tried to read what was written.

'Albert's writing was never very clear, but let's give it a try.' She went through it slowly:

Ruth. Please take this as a gift for all you have done and I want you to use it to get set up. I'm sorry it's not a cheque but it was easier to do it this way. The bank will probably change the notes for new ones. I want this to be private between us, so best if you don't tell anyone where it came from.

'May I look at the note from Albert?' asked James.

He had noticed alongside Ruth a shopping list and a blue ballpoint pen. The shade of the ink and the thickness of the pen strokes were identical to those on Albert's note. Looking more closely at Albert's writing, there was a freshness to the ink which suggested that the note had not long been written.

Could this have been Albert's last action before he took his own life? Or perhaps he had been so unwell lately that he felt it best to deal with writing down his final wishes without delay. The truth would never be known and it was not something that James would call to Ruth's attention.

'I don't know what to say,' said Ruth.

'Well I do,' said James. 'Albert has his own way of doing things and has made a kind and thoughtful gesture. He's said he would like you to use the gift for your future and I think that should be respected. And so should his wish that it is something to be kept between the two of you. He was a private man and would want it that way.

'I suggest that I take the money and pay it into my account. Then I can give you a nice clean cheque to pay into yours.'

James and his professional colleagues were well known to the bank and he knew that presenting an amount of cash would not give rise to any questions. It wouldn't be the first time that an Inland Revenue officer had handed in a quantity of used notes.

That settled, the couple sat in reflection until Ruth spoke.

'It's curious. Decision making has never come easily to me. I would never have made a good leader, always putting off things with the idea that I would somehow be guided in what I do. Perhaps that explains why I have ended up where I am. If I'd thought more carefully about my life and made positive choices, I might have developed a career and got on better. Who knows what might have happened if I had just stopped and made plans rather than just drifting along?

'Yesterday, I was carrying on in the same way I have since I came here, content enough in the daily routines. That would probably have gone on forever unless something brought it to a halt. What's happened has shocked me, not only because of the awful sadness of Albert's death but also because it has suddenly struck me with the realisation that it's a completely new start and I have to face the future.

'You have already said, James, that there is nothing I can do here, and I understand that. All the necessary things will be dealt with by Mr Birch and the other professional people who will be assisting him.

'I have no entitlement to anything and all I need to take with me are my personal possessions. I won't need a removal van for those!

'But, also, I have no choice but to move out. As from today, my right to be here has ended.

'I have an idea,' said James, smiling.

'I have a house which is too large for one person. There are two spare bedrooms which I keep prepared for the odd occasion when someone visits. They're hardly ever used and you could easily move into one of those for the time being. You can't stay here and be haunted by what's happened. You need somewhere to go.'

'It's so kind of you to offer but I couldn't inconvenience you.

'Over the last few hours, I have reached the conclusion that I must try to do something useful in the next chapter in my life. I mentioned to you that I once worked in the textile industry when I lived in Oxfordshire, and that I have kept in contact with Annabelle, a lady I worked alongside. Flatteringly, she keeps on saying that my old employer would always welcome me back. I'm excited at the thought of being able to brush up my old skills. She also keeps saying that I would able to stay with her, at least to start with.'

James listened with growing disappointment. He had been lifted by a sense of anticipation since he met Ruth. Now, she would no longer be there.

'The pay is not that much, but I would have a regular income and be doing something I enjoy. Together with what Albert kindly left me, I will be independent for the first time since I don't know when!

'It's something I have to do, James, but I wouldn't want it to be the end of our friendship. It's not that far away and we could still meet. Perhaps you might be able to visit and have a look around.

'I intend to speak to Annabelle later to try to make arrangements. From the way she's been putting it, I would be able to turn up at fairly short notice. If all goes to plan, I'll be able to set off by train within the next few days.'

Ruth watched as James rose from his chair and walked slowly away. After a few paces he stopped and looked down while she waited in silence. He turned to face her and it was several seconds before he spoke.

'Ruth, this is very inconsiderate of you. Do you know what it means?'

She continued to gaze at him but gave no reply.

He smiled. 'It means that when I go to Margaret's for coffee in future I might need to sit next to someone I don't know. It could be anyone!'